We hope you enjoy this book. Please return or renew it by the due date.

You can renew it at www.norfolk.gov.uk/libraries or by using our free library app.

Otherwise you can phone 0344 800 8020 - please have your library card and PIN ready.

You can sign up for email reminders too.

D0494179

By the same author

The Good Liar
A Traitor in the Family

A Fatal Game

NICHOLAS SEARLE

PENGUIN BOOKS

PENGUIN BOOKS

UK | USA | Canada | Ireland | Australia
India | New Zealand | South Africa

Penguin Books is part of the Penguin Random House group of companies
whose addresses can be found at global.penguinrandomhouse.com.

First published by Viking 2019
Published in Penguin Books 2021
001

Copyright © Nicholas Searle, 2019

The moral right of the author has been asserted

Typeset by Jouve (UK), Milton Keynes
Printed and bound in Great Britain by Clays Ltd, Elcograf S.p.A.

The authorized representative in the EEA is Penguin Random House Ireland,
Morrison Chambers, 32 Nassau Street, Dublin D02 YH68

A CIP catalogue record for this book is available from the British Library

ISBN: 978-0-241-35439-1

www.greenpenguin.co.uk

Penguin Random House is committed to a
sustainable future for our business, our readers
and our planet. This book is made from Forest
Stewardship Council® certified paper.

For C, always

December

Abu Omar paused as he left the truck by the rear door, looked around, then replaced his baseball cap and continued on his way. The surveillance teams noted his darting eyes and the tenseness of his frame. Jake rushed back to the ops room.

The powder-blue rucksack containing the books was readily visible on Abu Omar's back as, glancing at the neat terraced houses, he strolled down Melwood Avenue, lined with wintry trees, weaved between parked cars, and crossed the road, while invisible cameras panned and tilted and zoomed and handed on to the next relay. The surveillance crews thought his calmness seemed forced, and distances were carefully maintained by using the meticulously rehearsed alternates, ready to pick up the follow if he diverted from his route. They knew Abu Omar's associates would be close by, too, to ensure he wasn't tailed. Each of them had his own covert retinue, whispering to each other, listening intently through earpieces, deconflicting, avoiding the blue-on-blue.

Jake watched him on the screen, his boy now, more heavily invested than he had been. Abu Omar's shoulders swayed with youthful arrogance. As he left one screen he appeared on the next. As he turned into the park opposite the railway station Jake could see his face, indifferent, glassy-eyed as ever. He was chewing gum slowly. An analyst said, 'Message!' and almost at the same moment Abu Omar reached into his pocket for his

3

phone. The fact that Abu Omar wasn't supposed to be carrying a phone registered somewhere in the periphery of Jake's consciousness but remained there as everyone watched. Abu Omar stopped to read the message and everything stopped with him. 'It's on the app,' said the analyst, meaning it could not be decrypted. A hasty consultation took place on the ops room floor between the SIO, George and Jake.

'Any idea?'

'None. He should phone it through.'

But Abu Omar didn't. He paused a moment – it was measured later at 13.2 seconds – seemed to smile and then walked on.

'Call it?' asked George.

'Not just yet,' said the SIO. 'It's contained.'

'Put a stop to it,' said Jake, not loudly, but was ignored.

At this point Abu Omar disappeared from the screen. The camera pulled back at a speed that evoked a nauseous feeling in Jake's stomach. Or possibly, viewed afterwards, it was fearful premonition. But it couldn't have been premonition since he didn't do anything other than gulp down the gobbet of bile that washed on to the back of his tongue. Presentiment of the end of life, perhaps. Presentiment was all. This, however, was the clear vision of hindsight.

The wider picture showed Abu Omar going into the men's lavatory. The surveillance coordinator was shouting, 'Eyes on! Eyes on! Now!' and on other screens Jake could see a flurry of bodies surging forwards. The firearms commander ordered his officers forward, ready. The helicopter was called up.

A shaky image from the body-borne of the lead surveillance officer came up on a different screen. Bill, his name had been, Jake recalled later. He ran towards the entrance to the lavatory and slowed to a casual stroll as he went in. It couldn't have taken him more than ten seconds or so after the command. The camera adjusted quickly to the dark interior and the autofocus closed in on Abu Omar's back as he stood at the urinal. The flow could be heard and the blue rucksack could be seen clearly on his back. As the surveillance operative took his place at a urinal three places down, Abu Omar zipped up his jeans and disappeared from view. Bill whispered, 'Washing his hands,' and the sound of the tap running could be heard, followed quickly by that of the electric hand-dryer. The picture swivelled disconcertingly again and it, too, was making for the exit.

Abu Omar resumed his nonchalant walk and the surveillance re-formed carefully. The other four had not yet appeared but were under control, converging on the railway station from different directions. The distant surveillance cameras picked up the story once more, as it had been written and rehearsed, and something approaching calm returned to the room. He was thirty seconds from the station. It was rush hour. Twenty-five seconds. The 16:58 London train had just come in and those arriving had to contend with the tide of those heading for their trains to the small affluent feeder towns, home to many workers in the financial services firms housed in the glossy glass-sided buildings that provided much of the city's prosperity. In their expensive clothes they must have looked alien to Abu Omar and the other boys, who had scratched an existence in the sullen, crumbling, neglected parts of the east side of the town. Ten seconds.

Almost as an afterthought, the coordinator hollered, 'Someone check out that bloody toilet. Get it sealed off pronto!' Two officers were deputed on this sideshow. They would survive. Abu Omar had entered the concourse by now and the cameras had him, in his nice new white £200 trainers, making his way towards the ticket office, his associates coming through the other entrances. Armed police watched from above and edged out of commandeered offices in the station, their hands on their weapons, held covertly under coats and in bags. This was the provision against the bad eventuality.

Then he thought he could see it as it really was, proceeding to plan. The thing with the toilet had been the usual last-minute scare. Abu Omar had just needed a pee. Jake walked across the room, thinking of later that evening: the debrief, the decompression, the reconfirmation of optimism for the future, the quiet laughter over pizza. He allowed himself the millisecond preparation to smile and to reflect that good old Bill had done a good job. This was when it happened.

March

I

MONDAY

'And your feelings, at that moment and subsequently?'

That moment. The moment when everything fell silent. All those people, up to now busy-busy, talking loudly into telephone handsets, microphones, walkie-talkies, others' ears, getting the business done, transactions here there and everywhere quick as you like, quick as the busiest trading floor, move your team into position four-nine-niner, hold your people back, get the chopper up, pan the view, extend the angle, chop-chop, people moving from here to there and then elsewhere and then back again to take up their stations, all that noise. Outgoing voices with a rich, reassuring calmness; incoming reduced by the electronics to a reedy thinness that went well with the normal, carefully restrained undertone of operational panic. Static. On the air. That self-consciously serious, TV-show-mimicking ops room nonsense he'd never relished, unlike many of the others. All gone quiet. The vibration under the floor and the distant boom had provided the critical information. The screens told him everything he already knew, at that moment.

The moment when he understood his life had ceased. Might as well have, at any rate. The point, though, was that their lives had ceased, with a literal finality. Sixty-three of them. He hadn't known the number, not until later; it'd taken a couple of days or more to do the calculation, to include those who didn't pull through in hospital and the unaccounted-fors, and

9

to count and calculate the limbs, but he knew it was bad. People. Not numbers. Numbers were numbers; they numbed the reality. Real lives. That was the point.

Each of them was reduced now to fatality or casualty, for the media to pick over and harvest for *stories*. Harrowing personal-interest stories, accompanied by cheerful holiday snaps cajoled from relatives or gleaned from Facebook that somehow sucked out the *personal interest* and reclaimed the people as public possessions, owned by all – but mainly the press and TV and social media – complex souls reinvented and remarketed as mawkish one-dimensional symbols of our diverse mortality. As if somehow designed to reassure and unsettle at the same time.

Close call for some surviving victims whether it would have been preferable to have died there, in close vicinity; instantly, more or less. What could the quality of life afterwards be, physically or emotionally?

For him it wasn't a close call by any stretch. He'd much rather have exchanged his meagre self-satisfied existence for any of theirs – all of them, preferably – in a ghoulish trade-off, as he'd watched the screens and become part of the collective shock and awe of the thing. Easy to say. Easy to think.

Staring blankly over the head of the counsel at the white wall beyond him, he placed his right hand in his jacket pocket, reaching for his keys, as if the familiar feel of the cool metal might settle him back to the present.

The covert surveillance cameras nearby had continued to operate for a moment or so before their own fates became evident, like chickens whose lives have ended but they don't know it. Those with a more distant vantage had showed, then, falling dust and debris that, if he were fanciful, might have conferred a certain balletic, grotesque grace on the scene. He was not fanciful; never had been, wasn't now.

Later. The TV images had kicked in, as they always did: the chain reaction of endless, pointlessly bleating burglar alarms triggered across the city; sprinting, stumbling people captured on shaky mobile phone images by those who recognized a media event in motion; emergency service vehicles accelerating across the scene with apparent purpose, sirens blaring, blue lights cutting ice through the evening; then the cordons of police tape in front of which reporters were reduced to repeating, over and over, the banalities that had been uttered in Nice and London and Brussels and Barcelona and Berlin; the scrum of those reporters and their cameramen jostling for the prime vantage points and vying vainly for new things to say. Suddenly everything had been at one remove: fictional. The awful reality had been subjugated to the viewer figures and social media hits that could be squeezed out of the emotion of these events.

The moment when his stomach hadn't so much lurched as vanished, drawing bile into the vacuum before projecting it bitterly into his mouth as he urged involuntarily, emptily. Some in the ops room had actually vomited on to their workstations, souring the calm, subdued-lighting, air-conditioned atmosphere where orders were issued coolly and logs maintained.

The meaning he'd known – all of it, every fragment – had vaporized and he'd known it didn't matter. Nothing mattered. He didn't matter. His life and loves and career and foibles and strengths and weaknesses didn't matter.

Because it was his mistake. Because without knowing it those sixty-three and the countless others condemned to life had relied upon him. They had trusted him. He had betrayed them and failed them.

He withdrew his hand from his pocket. He couldn't see anyone in the room other than his inquisitor, the other legal people and the Chair. He knew they were there, the real people, beyond the carefully installed panels.

It reduced, almost mathematically, to before and after. Before, he'd been cheerful enough, almost relentlessly positive. Mind you, memory might well be as mangled and twisted as everything else inside his head. One comment in an annual appraisal years before stuck in his mind: 'What Jake Winter lacks in charisma he certainly makes up for in enthusiasm and work rate.' He'd thought it hurtful, had no conception that his sour supervisor might be trying to be helpful.

The product of half an upbringing in a fifteen-shack settlement in rural New Zealand and half in this city he now called home, child of a mixed marriage between an Englishwoman and a Maori man, he knew he was a strange person to be among Her Majesty's secret sentinels. But somehow he had found his way here, on the road to his failure.

He knew his mind was wandering and time was passing. His hand went back into his pocket and found once more the familiar profile of his front-door key. He stabbed himself gently in the palm with it, for some perverse comfort, some relief of the deadening. He struggled to deliver himself back to the air-conditioned room in City Hall where the inquiry was taking place.

Disbelief. That's what he'd felt. But with it the acknowledgement that it was always going to end up in a room just like this one, here and now, despite all the inner bravado.

The silence sat for another moment or two.

'In your own time,' said Mr Kerr, counsel for the victims and families, pursing his lips.

'Can you repeat the question please?' said Jake Winter.

Mr Kerr looked at him testily. 'We've established that you were in the operations room when the explosion took place. How did you feel when it happened?'

'Feel?' he said.

'Yes. Feel.'

The members of the panel, the Chair, the inquiry's counsel,

the Service's legal representatives and his own lawyer were, like Mr Kerr, watching him keenly. The other people couldn't see him behind the screen, the families or the survivors. But no one really survived something like this. He wished they could see him. He wanted, at last, to say it all. But he was not an unreliable person. As ever, he would be dutiful.

'I felt terrible,' he said eventually. 'Of course I felt terrible.'

'Of course,' said Mr Kerr. And then, after a moment's consideration, 'Can you elucidate?'

'I'm not sure. How does anyone feel at a moment like that?'

'The inquiry is not interested in how anyone should feel at a moment like that, Mr, erm . . .'

It occurred to Jake that it must be difficult for them, questioning someone with a witness number rather than a name. None of those tiny gaps that the repeating of a name would afford, allowing you to hone the next sentence.

'. . . we are interested in what you felt, no one else.'

'I felt shattered. Numbed. At the same time I felt that my feelings were beside the point.'

'In what way?'

'It didn't matter what you felt. What had happened was more important. It overrode everything else.'

'Did you feel guilt?'

Duncan Blakeley, his own lawyer, stirred. 'I don't know what this line of questioning is seeking to achieve,' he said. 'Undoubtedly the witness experienced a range of emotions at the time. None of which may be relevant to the actual state of affairs.'

The counsel for the inquiry looked at the Chair and raised her eyebrows.

The Chair said, 'Subjective it may be, but we have to remind ourselves that this is not a court of law. We're not here to apportion individual blame. We're here to examine the sequence of events and to diagnose what, if anything, could have been done better. So I think the line of questioning is legitimate. Unless, that is, you would rather your client not respond, in order to avoid the risk of self-incrimination in subsequent proceedings?'

Mr Blakeley shook his head.

'Mr Kerr, please carry on.'

'So,' said Mr Kerr. 'Guilt?'

'I felt . . . responsible.'

'I should imagine so. Responsible. Would you care to explain precisely why?'

'I should have thought it was obvious,' he said dully.

'Well, to my clients little seems to be obvious. They're trying to make sense of this, as are most of the rest of us. Anything you may deign to share with us would no doubt be appreciated.'

'I'm sorry. I feel responsible because Abu Omar was my agent.'

'Abu Omar, the suicide bomber.'

'So far as I know that's not clear. The forensic examinations couldn't establish firmly whether the device was initiated by him, by someone else, whether there was a timing device of which he was unaware or whether it went off by accident. The force of the explosion . . .'

'All right. Let's be punctilious. It's important to be punctilious. But your . . . agent . . . was carrying the rucksack?'

'Yes.'

'Go on.'

'We were trying to prevent the attack that was being planned. Abu Omar was working for us.'

'In what way, "working for you"?'

'As a covert human intelligence source, to use the technical expression. A CHIS.'

14

'And how did you first meet?'

Was it hot in the room? thought Jake Winter. No, the air conditioning was functioning, but he felt hot.

'Abu Omar was a British national. He grew up here and moved to London at the age of eighteen, to study. He dropped out of university at the age of twenty. He married and he and his wife had a son before they came back home to live with his parents. At that stage his views started to become more extreme. They'd always been an observant Muslim family but he began attending private prayer sessions with a group about which the local imam had expressed concern. This group expressed extreme Salafi views and caused trouble at the mosque. Several of them, among them Abu Omar, went overseas to join the fighting against what they considered kafir forces. He returned to the UK about six months ago and that was when I first met him.'

'How would you describe his domestic circumstances?'

'Chaotic. His parents lived on the edge of poverty. Still do, for that matter. He was rebellious as a teenager and was in trouble at school. His parents were determined, though, and scraped together enough money for him to go to university. He was highly intelligent despite what the school described as behavioural problems. His parents were unhappy when he dropped out of university and later came home with a wife and a baby. And then he abandoned them all, to go and fight. His parents understood it to be their duty to keep the family functioning.'

'Did you go out of your way to speak to him, or did he make an approach to you?'

'It didn't quite work like that. An introduction was made –'

'By whom?'

'I'm afraid I'm not at liberty to say. I'm not sure it's relevant.'

'I think that the inquiry will be the judge of that.'

Jake Winter could see the barrister representing the Service whispering to the clerk to the inquiry.

'I'm not at liberty to say,' he said. 'I thought . . . this had been agreed.'

Mr Kerr gave this some thought, glancing sideways at the clerk. 'Very well. We may return to this. I'm sure you would not wish to give this inquiry the impression of being obstructive.'

'Certainly not.'

'But for the moment let us stick with your relationship with Abu Omar. You met him some six months before.'

'That's right. He told me he'd become disillusioned with what he called the cause.'

'Which was?'

'That's part of it. He said he couldn't see what the cause was. What the aims were, apart from inflicting unspeakable suffering on many, many people. He'd been sickened by some of the things he'd witnessed out there.'

'Or so he said.'

'That's right.'

'And you believed him.'

Jake paused. 'My job isn't to believe or dismiss.'

'Oh, really. Isn't it?'

'No. My job is to listen carefully, to report precisely and to analyse where what I've been told fits in with the known facts.'

'But you must form an opinion? As a living, breathing human being?'

'Of course. I have to assess the likely reliability of the people I'm talking to.'

'That can't always be easy.'

'No, not always. People don't always want to tell you the truth.'

'That would seem self-evident. So when you're assessing the reliability, or otherwise, you use common sense.'

'Partly.'

'It sounds more like a finger in the air.'

'Not really. It's not just my sense, though I do have a lot of training and experience. Reports are assessed and examined sceptically. Psychologists can be called in. From that we form a picture of a person's reliability. It's not just a case of my personal opinion. I think some papers on our systems have been lodged.'

'I've read them, thank you. Do you use polygraphs?'

'Not as a rule, no.'

'Not as a rule. I see. And if you think someone's unreliable, you disengage?'

'Not necessarily. But you treat what they say with great caution.'

'And Abu Omar. What was your assessment of him?'

'He was assessed as a CHIS of established reliability.'

'Really? And how did you arrive at that assessment?'

'I'm not at liberty to go into detail.'

Mr Kerr looked at him intently before, it seemed to Jake, deciding not to pursue the point. 'Very well. Let me be clear on this. Abu Omar was assessed by you and your colleagues with all this rigorous thought to be of established reliability.'

Jake thought of the boy, for he'd still been a boy despite having a two-year-old son. His fearful brown eyes and the expression of anxiety on his face that occasionally replaced the proud, challenging look. His thin arms, his down-like scraggy beard. Trying to be a man, but indisputably still a boy. He said, 'Yes.'

'And do you still consider your CHIS to have been reliable?'

'I simply don't know.'

'You don't know? Given all that subsequently happened? If you'll forgive me, that seems to have been a rash judgement in the first place and one that you seem reluctant, in the teeth of all the available evidence, to cease to cling to.'

'We don't know whether –'

'Yes, yes. For the moment you may be able to grasp at that straw. But nonetheless. Your CHIS of established reliability arrives at a mainline railway station at rush hour carrying a rucksack full of high explosive which then explodes, killing sixty-three people. When exactly was the last time you saw him?'

'Thirty-seven minutes before the explosion.'

He heard gasps on the other side of the screen.

'And was he carrying the rucksack then?'

'He was carrying a rucksack.'

'Describe it.'

'It was small, light blue, brand new. A daypack.'

'A daypack. In what way did it differ from the one he was carrying when he entered the station?'

'It didn't contain any explosive. Otherwise it was identical, at least from what we could see on the CCTV. And from the forensic evidence afterwards.'

'What was the purpose of your meeting?'

'Precisely to establish that he was carrying nothing that could pose a threat to public safety. We knew they were planning a reconnaissance of the station and that it was the eventual target. Abu Omar had told us this, and that the attack was not planned imminently. We had to be sure, though.'

'Quite. You checked the rucksack. And?'

'It contained books. Nothing else. It was searched professionally by a police officer and tested for explosive. The bag was new. There were no traces of explosive.'

'What happened next?'

'Abu Omar was to go directly to the station. He was under continuous surveillance. He received a message on his phone. He stopped in the road and read it.'

'What did it say?'

'I don't know. He went into a public toilet. The surveillance followed him. By the time they got into the toilet he was urinating.'

'The rucksack?'

'Still on his back. But . . .'

'Yes?'

'It seems he must have exchanged the rucksack for an identical one containing the explosive. The original one was later found in the waste bin in the toilets.'

'Was he supposed to do this?'

'Of course not.'

'So much for your person of established reliability, then. Was there anyone else in the toilets?'

'Not so far as the surveillance people could see.'

'Surely they checked?'

'They had to continue following Abu Omar. Others came and checked the toilets after a couple of minutes.'

'After a couple of minutes.'

'That's right.'

'And you. What were you doing?'

'I'd made my way back to the operations room.'

'By which time the fates of sixty-three people had effectively been sealed. Could you have stopped him, in theory? If he had been as reliable as you thought?'

'I could have rung him, yes.'

'Surely Abu Omar should have contacted you once he'd exchanged the original bag for the one containing the explosive. If he were so reliable?'

'Yes.'

'How do you account for that?'

'I can't.'

'You could have contacted him, surely?'

'Yes, but it was thought he'd only used the lavatory. The

Executive Liaison Group had given tactical control to the senior investigating officer, and he made a decision.'

'The Executive Liaison Group?'

'Yes. The ELG. It's made up of all the key interested parties and chaired by the police. It makes all the strategic decisions. You must have papers on this.'

'Yes. It's helpful to hear your version, though. Back to the SIO's decision. It was based on your assessment of your informant's reliability?'

'Partly, yes.'

'We seem to have come full circle. Are you aware that the Islamic faith has specific rules regarding personal hygiene and modesty when using the lavatory?'

'Yes,' said Jake, coughing.

'So were you not surprised to learn that Abu Omar used the urinal rather than one of the stalls with locks?'

Jake paused. It might seem a trivial point but the barrister was right. It had been unusual, another thing he'd failed to pick up on. He said, 'I don't think anyone fully registered the fact.'

Mr Kerr raised his eyebrows. 'Too much else going on?'

'You're right. It should have been noted. But in any case I'm not sure Abu Omar would have been that observant in the situation. It is, as I understand it, permissible to use the lavatory with other men provided you do not converse or look at one another.'

'But it is usual, when there is the opportunity, to use the lavatory privately.'

'Yes.'

'And he ignored this when he was about to undertake the most significant act of his existence?'

'We've already agreed he may not have triggered the device. And he showed few signs of strict religious observance when we were together.'

'I bow to your greater technical expertise and knowledge of Abu Omar. Despite all the evidence to the contrary. Despite him being a member of an extremist jihadi gang. You settled yourself in the operations room, then. You heard the blast.'

'We were less than half a mile away, so yes. We heard it. We felt it. We saw it on the screens. It was . . .'

'Quite so,' said Mr Kerr, and from the expression on the Chair of the inquiry's face Jake could see that the day's proceedings, bar the formalities, were complete.

'My apologies for the venue,' said Stuart Calloway. 'I feel a more informal meeting was called for.'

'You people seem to have become rather hooked on informal meetings.'

'I just think we need to reduce the risk of misinterpretation, for both our sakes. Meetings on the record can sometimes muddy the waters rather than clarify matters.'

'Though we must both observe the need for due process.'

'Of course. Never let it be said that I would stand in the way of transparency and due deliberation. Provided always, of course, that security is safeguarded.'

Stuart Calloway's current position could be described as delicate. Director of Operations at an absurdly young age, precocious and extraordinarily gifted (in his own estimation at least), he was faced with a series of what he had learned to describe as challenges – opportunities even – rather than problems: a new administration, sceptical, highly; a new head of Service, chum of the PM, parachuted in allegedly with a specific job of work to do, despite all the denials; and thin, ascetic George, who reported to him as head of the regional source unit. George had been there, done most of it and had the T-shirt and scars to prove it, and was consequently in thrall to the grubby types in the field who were the source of all risk.

This could be the making of Stuart Calloway or the start of his destruction.

'Where is your boss, by the way?' said the Home Secretary.

Stuart Calloway sighed and said, 'I think it's right that a certain distance exists between this conversation and our principals. I need to keep my DG out of the firing line and I imagine that you will not wish to involve the Prime Minister.'

'You mean we can both take the hit?'

Stuart sensed a certain bristling and understood he could have framed his words still more carefully. The essence of it needed to be understood between them, however: the PM and the DG as best mates; and the necessity for the Home Secretary and Stuart to find common cause. 'Not at all. *I* may be expendable . . . but, goodness me, no. I was drawing no equivalence. The Permanent Under-Secretary and I simply felt that this was a conversation best conducted between the two of us. We understand each other, I believe. Home Secretary, I am here to tell you that there is grave concern . . .'

He waited for an interjection, to encourage or discourage him. There was none.

'. . . there is grave concern about the direction this inquiry is taking. You may be aware of the latest session.'

'Yes. Your man seems to be digging himself into a very big hole.'

'Out of which he will have to climb using his own resources. My point, however, is that much wider damage may result. To the reputation of this government and previous ones. To the reputation of the Service. Damage disproportionate to whatever benefits may accrue.'

'The inquiry needs to take its course.'

'Of course it does. I will remind you, however, of our misgivings at the outset, at the selection of the Chair, the appointment of various counsel and the speed at which the inquiry was set up.'

'The PM was clear there had to be quick resolution, that there needed to be assurance of no whitewash, and that the families should be adequately represented as interested parties. And I support that wholeheartedly. There's plenty of precedent for the way we've done this. Albeit that you people haven't been in the spotlight before.'

'Absolutely. But the appointment of a Chair who both as a barrister and a High Court judge was openly hostile to the intelligence and security agencies was bound to create issues.'

'Issues that you and your people need to deal with.'

'Indeed. But it's alarming to see counsel at the inquiry hounding witnesses.'

'I think that's a bit of an exaggeration, Stuart. It's not a court of law. There has to be a degree of latitude in proceedings, especially if we're to be seen allowing the victims' representatives the right to probe and scrutinize. There's a lot of emotion around this, you know.'

'I do,' said Stuart. 'More coffee?'

'No, thank you.'

'There's nothing that can be done, then, to pull the inquiry back on to the rails? As you know, we're more than prepared to implement any genuine improvements. But it can't be good for anyone for our people to be dragged through the mud like this.'

'What do you think? Even if we were perturbed by the inquiry – which we're not, even remotely – it'd be impossible to meddle. The Chair is fiercely independent and wouldn't take kindly to words in his shell-like of the kind that you seem to think might work. We're four-square behind the inquiry, and so should you be.'

'I am. Others, on the other hand, have expressed concerns.'

'Others?'

'Yes. I'm treading a tightrope here.'

'Aren't we all? Your organization issued a statement welcoming the inquiry and vowing to support it one hundred per cent. I can't believe the DG is opposed. Any of your staff caught up in the mincer will have to grit their teeth and take the consequences. I take it that you have provisions to deal with your witnesses if things fall badly?'

Christ. This wasn't the moment to mention in passing that the pot was bubbling on a new operation that the same case officer was managing. No way of finessing that in the interstices.

'Yes. They each have their own legal representation if they require it. Which in one sense poses difficulties but in another would make it easier to part ways if it came to it.'

'I'm glad you set up this meeting this way, Stuart. We can both be frank with one another.'

'Yes.'

'You seem to take for granted that we're on your side. That I'm on your side. Don't imagine that if necessary we won't grind you under our heels. The old orthodoxy no longer applies. It's not beyond imagination that we might decide to rip up the whole thing and start again, with more . . . reliable leadership. You're far from sacrosanct, individually or organizationally. It's nothing personal, and I hope it doesn't come to it. However, this is the new world. When something bad happens there's always someone to blame. Always. It's just a matter of finding out who. May just be your lot's turn for a change.'

2

Adnan

Cities have many secret places. Even when the authorities believe they have all the corners covered. Back there, with the chaos and the heat and the bombs and the gunfire spilling people from their homes, it had been easy to locate a quiet, dark corner – a cellar maybe, an abandoned house, its upper storeys bombed out and open to the skies, a shop whose shutters had been can-opened to allow access. There they had been emperors, with their scimitars and scarves and machine guns and bandoliers, able to strut and command at whim. They had been the authorities. Each had demonstrated his warrior qualities with some captive unbeliever or other. There was a plentiful supply and when done once it became compelling, addictive.

Back here in this grim, grimy northern city of Adnan's birth there were certainly places. It was laughable, trying to cover the brothers. They were invincible and invisible. They would show themselves at the appointed hour and not before. These people were not even in control of the land they professed to be theirs. Back there, his people knew every inch, every shadowy alcove. They'd known the secret places, they alone, and would amuse themselves by finding the opposers and the plotters. They would dance with righteous, joyous fervour after they'd brought the criminals back in the dusty ancient Mercedes, sitting uncomfortably between two brothers as they rocked over the craters and the knives held tight to their throats drew blood. It'd been a blast, a laugh. And into the courtyard and the inevitable. Piece of piss. These people here could not match that, could not hold a candle to it, which was why they would be defeated. It required devotion, the surrendering of a life in an instant, without reservation.

He was heading for the place they considered the most secret of all, more secret still than the private prayer room they'd once used. He alone among them knew that there was still yet one more secret space, where their destiny would be revealed to them. A secret, sacred place. Even he did not know its location.

Still the rain poured from the night sky and he shrugged his collar further up. His hair was soaked and water dripped from his nose. The weather was nothing; the time was close. He had rehearsed this journey in his mind, but hardly needed to, he knew his city so well.

They had all been trained in the art of evading the followers. They'd acquired many other skills too. Bilal and he had known each other as kids, lived in blocks opposite each other, played football, been to the same parties. Never best mates, until they'd both taken the same flight to Turkey, not knowing beforehand but meeting at Istanbul airport. He'd spied him at check-in, of course, but had thought better of talking to him until they arrived. Evidently Bilal had thought the same and they sidled up to each other at the baggage reclaim. Not that they'd travelled with bags: they'd been instructed not to be among the first to walk through the immigration controls but to tag along with a party of four or five. They spoke to each other quietly. That had passed for precautionary discretion back then. Now, since returning, apart from at these meetings they'd not exchanged a single word.

The other two they'd met over there had been unknown. They'd all fought alongside each other and each had been reliant on the others. This was the way that the cause shaped you, to be reliant only on the brothers, and irretrievably so. At the same time you weren't encouraged to become too close. Life expectancy was short – much less than a year for a foreign volunteer – and you had to accept that the brother next to you might fall. The four of them had been the lucky ones. Several boys from the city lay there still, unburied beneath the rubble and dust, their bodies decaying in the heat.

Before they'd come back they'd planned their reunion, in this place. They'd been told where it was. They were not known to associate with each other – to all others even he and Bilal had different social circles – which made it vital that they make their respective ways to the place unseen. The other two were from separate communities in different parts of town. No one asked questions about backgrounds. For some reason he assumed them all, like him, to be college graduates. Something to do with the way they talked, the way they reasoned calmly and maintained the thread of the central argument, the core tenets of faith, rationally and without fuss. They avoided the trappings of their religion. This was acceptable, they knew, in order to fulfil the purpose that had been written for them. Out there, among the burnt-out trucks and the corpses, they had worn their beards proudly. Out there, they had broken bread together. They had killed to protect each other and sometimes simply to show their strength, devotion to their brothers and *taqwa*.

In and out of Debenhams, quickly. A feint and a weave, just like Darius Solomon, City's hulking striker, might execute with a flourish in the opposition's penalty area, and into a side street, then an alley, picking up speed, nimble on his toes. Light, then dark. It was mushy underfoot but there were more important things than trainers. This was far distant from the glass and steel city where the Big Five plied their consultancy trades and where he worked by day.

Stop. In that doorway. He could hear his breath as he looked back. No one. Pick it up again, man. Fast pace now; he might be back there, in what he considered his homeland, despite being born here in this city. He might be back there but for the rain and cold. There were other ways of paying homage. Other ways than killing toe-to-toe. Other ways of being a combatant. Soon it would be his day. Soon it would be all their days.

Through the network of passageways and courtyards over which the concrete buildings loomed, many windows boarded up, others simply dark with no glass. Dodge in here and skip down the steps. And here he was, the first.

Through the long, narrow corridor and into the window-less room, white-walled. It had power and heat and water. Most important, it had internet access, somehow routed to this place as if by sorcery.

He switched on the music and turned it up loud. Just in case, they'd been advised, but shit, he loved it pumped up like this, the music of his home, his heritage, the jihadi rap. No other brother here but him, buried under all this concrete. It made him joyous.

Bilal

Running late. The story of his life at home. Never seemed to happen out there. The urgency of it all cleared what was irrelevant out of the way. His lunch hour today had been shortened as he'd argued with his supervisor, who'd criticized his attitude. Truculent, she'd called him. What's truculent when it's at home? he'd said, though he knew full well. See what I mean? she'd said. No, he'd replied.

He'd dashed home at five, changed out of that bloody suit,

and then his father had insisted on him speaking to his aunt, who was visiting. He'd sat squirming on the sofa, drinking tea, speaking politely for as short a time as possible. Mosul back in the eighties, the olds had talked about wistfully. He'd been tempted to intervene but kept his mouth shut.

He'd known Adnan at school – flash bastard, still was – but he'd earned Bilal's respect out there. Brave as a lion and trustworthy too, stronger than Bilal but respectful at the same time. They were true brothers. But so indeed were the four of them, unbreakable bonds formed on the battlefield.

He needed to focus now, to avoid distraction. To remember the training that he'd received on how to shake off surveillance. A bus to the centre of town. A walk past the pubs where red-faced men guffawed at each other, to the stand near City Hall where he picked up a cab driven by a sullen Kashmiri that took him into the estates, where he walked, shaking off the rain, along the designated route to the designated place. He was safe now, and quickened his pace.

Abdullah

Talk of shelf displays and price points over, he could now revert to real life. Revert also to his true name under Allah. Back from the fight, he'd cropped his hair and shaved the beard, and to the world he'd once again become Dopey Darren, or Ginge, or whatever the blokes at work might toss at him along with all the other crap he had to suck up. Grin sheepishly and bear it, as he'd always done. It didn't matter now, though. Almost touching distance.

He lived on his own so at least he'd been able to turn his bedsit into a shrine. He'd wash himself, change into his modest robes, eat his modest meal and pray. Quietly, so as not to alert his neighbours through the wafer-thin walls. Behind the door he'd fitted with multiple high-security locks, in contravention of his tenancy agreement, he was safe.

Not tonight, however. Tonight they were meeting.

He was convinced he was being followed. But then he always was. He'd already had an altercation with a bloke outside the Multiplex who'd been staring at him. Waiting for his girlfriend, so he'd said. Abdullah had felt his cheeks redden and his fists clench but had walked on.

There definitely was a shadow, though. He ducked into the nearest pub, unnoticed in the hubbub, and went straight to the Gents. He sat in one of the stalls and his brain steamed. He would be late, he would confront whoever was following him and mash his face to a pulp. He must calm himself before continuing.

Rashid

Rashid was second to the meeting. His memories of the battlefront were of constant fear mixed with disgust: at it, at himself. The explosions shattered his peace. The shouts of his commanders, hectoring and spitting in his face, were not the gentle soothing water of Islam he'd expected and for which he had travelled there. He was killing, daily, men and boys whose sin was not to resist but allegedly to have a different opinion of Allah's wishes to theirs. He was not even sure it was a different opinion to his own.

He did his duty, however. Women too, kids. He spilt oceans of these innocents' blood in increasingly barbaric ways according to the wishes of his teachers and leaders. He'd known that he would be called upon in the name of Allah, he had been warned by his religious masters before he left England, but he'd not imagined it would be like this. He'd thought it would be more noble. Perhaps – undoubtedly – he was stupid; he should have known. He discovered new ways to extract pain and fear and to draw out the suffering before the clean strike of the blade, and yes, it was compulsive. It was enjoyable, more than enjoyable, it was as exhilarating as it was horrifying to see life extinguished in such routine, careless fashion. After a while you became ravenous for it. In your hands the power not only to do the deed but to think so little of it. He could not speak of his doubts, there or here, then or now. That would be apostasy, the penalty for which was death. Certainty of right-eousness was everything.

Now his destiny had changed. Sent back to join these other three, he was part of a greater plan, *inshallah*. Each of them would be given a task of utmost importance, to kill the infidels in their beds. They must adopt Western dress, behave like them. Avoid suspicion. Keep their heads down. Attend the mosque occasionally but do not shout down the imam. Do not associate. Pretend, apart from those times when you are together in your secret place.

Yet he had a still separate destiny that he had continually to reconcile, somehow, with his religion. He was a spy, a secret observer for the unbelievers.

Adnan was dancing gently, trance-like, to the music when he arrived. Rashid had paid careful attention, as he'd been trained, to ensuring he was not followed to this place. It had been show, however, just in case Adnan or one of the others was watching him. Jake knew full well where they met. Rashid had told him. As he entered and greeted Adnan he could sense Jake's cameras and microphones in all corners of the room. They must be there, even though Jake and Leila insisted on debriefing him line-by-line after every meeting.

The other boys arrived shortly, Abdullah and Bilal. He did

not know whether these were their real names. It was, in the circumstances, immaterial. Though Jake and Leila would have liked to know, there was no way he could begin to find out.

First, they prayed in silence, kneeling on the mats Adnan had placed on the floor. Once these were rolled away the young boy Abdullah unlocked the cupboard at the back of the room and took out the computer with its 36-inch screen. Abdullah was a white English convert whose eyes darted in all directions. He'd said he had never been overseas until he'd been taken over there to fight. Islam had given his life meaning, he'd said, and the fighting had given him, for the first time, a sense of belonging and achievement.

'No, brother,' said Adnan softly, placing his hand on Abdullah's shoulder and slowly putting the trolley on which the computer stood back into the cupboard. 'Later, perhaps. Before that we must go somewhere else.'

It was the first the others had heard of it.

'It's all right,' said Adnan, smiling. 'Good news. We're taking one more step towards our fates. We will return here later. Anyone got their mobile with them?'

The other three shook their heads. It would have broken all the rules to have brought a mobile phone to a meeting. They'd all received the training.

They ensured everything was locked away securely before quietly leaving the room. As they walked up the ramp they saw a shabby white van parked in the darkness of the parking area below the flats, black scrape marks along one side and bashed-in hubcaps. Adnan opened the rear door but Rashid had no chance to look at the number plate. He could see a stick-on sign next to a heavy-duty lock, black on yellow: NO TOOLS KEPT IN THIS VEHICLE OVERNIGHT. The door slammed shut behind them and Adnan whispered, 'We are to wait.'

There were no seats. They sat on the floor. Rashid looked at his hands, which were about all he could make out in the dark. What was there to tell Jake? He would be impatient for answers, for clues. Rashid felt surreptitiously on the floor for small items he might pocket that might provide evidence of something. There was nothing. He smelt the air: the faint anonymous whiff of diesel was all he could discern. This was just a battered, ancient white van of which there must be thousands in the city.

One of the front doors opened and the van rocked gently as someone climbed in. The driver's seat, it must be. He heard an indistinct cough. The motor fired responsively enough and the van pulled away. It was not badly maintained, he concluded. But what would that tell anyone?

The van went up a slope and slowly turned through the estate. He could visualize where they must be and at what junction they must be arriving. Then they were on the public roads. The crack of light that showed at the edge of the door panels offered no sense of their location. They went left, left again, right and once more left, by which point Rashid was disoriented enough to have no idea where they were heading. He was busy, too, like the other boys trying to prevent himself rolling around the floor of the van like a stray tin can. They were giggling with the effort of it, apart from Adnan who maintained a leaderly seriousness and tried to wedge his long legs between two walls of the van. Unsuccessfully, as it turned out: the van stopped and then suddenly started forward again – Rashid thought it must be traffic lights – and Adnan was pitched forward to join the rest of the jumble.

At one point they accelerated for a distance, giving Rashid the impression they must be on the ring road that had long been superseded by the motorway encircling the city, then swerved left up an exit ramp. But there were exit ramps north, west, east and south.

He didn't think they'd left the city. The next turns and twists, as he held on for grim life to Bilal's coat lapel, could have been on the country lanes to the east of the city, heading towards the national park and the moors he used to visit with his parents when he was a kid, but he thought it was more likely to be city backstreets. The van stopped and the driver got out, leaving the door open and the engine running. Rashid could hear a metallic shutter door being dragged open. The driver got back in and put the van in reverse. They turned into a space and the engine was stilled. The driver climbed out again.

'Wait,' whispered Adnan. 'I was told we should wait.'

Rashid heard the door being closed again. They were inside some building, then. A lock-up, possibly?

A loud rap on the side of the van made them start. Slowly they collected themselves and Abdullah reached for the handle.

They got out and stood, becoming accustomed to the light and to standing once more. Bilal brushed himself down with his hands and Rashid did the same. They were in a large open space of some kind, a disused warehouse or factory unit. Such buildings were commonplace around the city these days. Rashid looked for signs of logos, or any other detail that could later be used to narrow down where they were, but there was nothing that he could see in the gloom.

Nor were there indications of what this place had been used for. Broken pallets could have been used for anything. An old, grimy hoist hung above them. There was a blue-grey oily smell about the place, mixed with the aroma of dusty decay, but nothing specific, so far as Rashid could work out. It was large, that was all he could say. By his reckoning several artics could once have lined up in the loading bay as the hoist was operated and forklifts ferried goods on and off the trucks. He imagined for a moment a world of activity here, a buzz of purpose, sharp-uniformed men checking items off on clipboards, weary drivers opening their flasks and pouring their coffee as they sat on the running-boards of their cabs. The prosperity that once sustained this city and then had died, leaving the weeds that grew up in the gaps between the concrete.

There was another man in the space, they realized, sitting motionless some distance from them. He was smiling, Rashid could just make out. As one, they approached slowly but he raised his hand to stop them. They obeyed immediately.

'As salaam alaikum,' he said.

'Wa alaikum as salaam,' they mumbled in reply.

'Brothers, remain there,' he said pleasantly. 'I must talk to you.'

Light was cast by a small industrial lamp almost equidistant between them. It must be battery-powered. He could not make out the man sufficiently to describe him in any detail. He seemed stout but that could simply be the result of his robes, which made specifics difficult. He had a dark beard and wore a headdress fashioned from a checked scarf. Rashid wondered, for the first time, whether Jake and his people had followed them here and whether they knew this man.

'You have been sent on a holy mission,' said the man. Local accent. No other inflections that Rashid could hear. No Scottish or Welsh or Geordie or London twang or foreign vowels. 'Let's not forget that. When you were overseas, in the heat of the battle, that will have been obvious. But this is as important. This is your fate as warriors. You need to be ready to fight. You need to be prepared to do what is necessary. You need once more to look into your hearts. You have to harden those hearts because you will need to do things that will seem barbaric. You will be asked to kill your fellow citizens and it will be unlike on the battlefields. You must be braver than you ever imagined you could be.'

'We're ready,' said Adnan, and the others nodded. Bilal scuffed his trainers on the floor and looked down.

'I know,' said the man. 'Of course I know. How could I not? You are serious men, scholars. I am here to tell you two things. One, that the moment is soon and you should prepare for jihad. Two, that your brothers and friends are watching from afar and support you with their love. Now, you will listen to the instructions I carry.'

'Yes,' they muttered; it seemed necessary, for there was a pause.

'You are all equals. There are no leaders between you.' He looked at Adnan. 'Adnan was given the initial instruction to prepare for this meeting. It may be another of you next time. It may after all be Adnan. Adnan . . .'

'Yes?'

'I mean no offence by this. You have performed well.'

'I don't take any offence,' said Adnan, but Rashid thought his face showed disappointment and that the man noticed.

'Good,' he said, smiling again, choosing, possibly, to ignore what he had seen. 'This is what you have to learn. You are brothers, not in blood but in a more true sense. You will meet your destiny together. The important thing is now to make your preparations together. Pray together, read the Quran together, listen to the preachers who matter. Make yourselves ready physically. Sleep well. Be in a position to move quickly, within a day or so. You will soon need to obtain the necessary equipment.'

'What will we need?' asked Rashid.

'Simple things, easy to buy,' said the man. 'I will supply the rest. I will contact you again in the next few days. And – this is important. Always be looking out for the enemy. They will know you already. They may be looking at you. Be aware of them and be extra careful when you meet. But never show a sign of it. Go to work as normal. Be cheerful, rude, however you normally are. Blaspheme if you need to. Share the jokes. Socialize with these people. Pity them in your hearts if you must, but extend no sympathy to them. You are reaching the next stage, the final stage. But until the moment when I give the call, lead your lives as normal. Do not communicate with each other. No slips in the security precautions. You've been taught how to behave in this moment. You play a role, you're a part of their world in their eyes. You are permitted to tell lies, be like them for now, because it's for a greater cause. Soon you will be required for your holy mission. Then the pressure will be off. Is that clear?'

They nodded. Rashid saw Bilal and Adnan glance at each other. They knew each other from sometime before, somewhere in the city.

'Do you have any further questions?'

'Who are you?' asked Abdullah.

The man did not lose the serene smile. 'I am no one. That's all you need to know. You do not need to know my name. I am unimportant. I am simply a vessel. I carry your fate. I do not decide it. I'm not so presumptuous. I carry the message from afar. Do you believe me?'

'Yeah. Of course,' said Abdullah, and Rashid saw that he was blushing. 'Sorry.'

'There's no need to apologize. It's understandable. I could give you a name but I would have made it up. I'm not important. Certainly not as important as you fortunate boys at this moment. Now, back in the van.'

3

They travelled back in the same bumpy silence as before, but they knew better how to wedge themselves in the corners to prevent themselves being tipped over. It was a relearning of what had been second nature over there, in the heat of the metal container as they were transported to the next field or street of blood. Then, though, they'd been crammed in, twenty or so brothers in a fetid, dusty space, light and searing heat creeping in through the rusting carcasses of the vans, each grasping his weapon, his salvation, so close they couldn't fall over anyway, so intensely focused that such trivialities as personal comfort wouldn't even have occurred to them. That was life here, trivialities: worrying over what cereal to have for breakfast, what to wear, which music to have in your earphones. Adnan craved simplicity.

He looked at the others in the dark but could make nothing out of their expressions. Bilal, the boy from the next block. He'd always struck Adnan as a kind of whining boy, always moaning. Unlike Adnan he'd not been sporty, though he'd liked to watch the game. They'd been to the match together once or twice, in a bigger group. When Adnan had gone to London to do economics Bilal had studied sociology at some provincial uni Adnan had never heard of. He'd say they'd lost touch, though in reality they'd never been in touch, just members of a loose-knit, wider group into which tighter alliances drifted and from which they emerged. Adnan would never have imagined Bilal to be one of those chosen, of all his associates and acquaintances; he wouldn't have credited him with the strength, physical and mental, to carry it through. You could never tell. To be fair, Bilal, always religiously observant, might find it surprising that Adnan had trodden the path to this miraculous point. Adnan had liked the girls and the drink.

Rashid was looking at him. He was a Pakistani boy. Unlike Adnan, whose parents had fled the First Gulf War, Rashid's family, so he said, had lived here for generations. He was British and yet not British, serious and studious, a business graduate who went out by day suited and booted and by night sat with them as they prayed and watched the sermons and the slick productions on the widescreen in the room. Adnan liked Rashid, though he did not know him. He saw in him a kindred spirit.

Abdullah was the boy to watch. He was the white boy. He'd been easy to spot when he'd appeared first at the mosque, it must have been three years before. He had ginger hair and he'd cultivated a luxuriant red beard. He worked at a local supermarket and Adnan had seen him there, with his little notebook, discussing stock levels or refrigerator temperatures. They'd never acknowledged each other and then, suddenly, they'd been out there together. It was practice to team up boys from the same place, possibly even with this, the return to carry out jihad in the heart of the West, in mind. He'd performed well, with a bloody relish that was almost unnerving. He'd been instructed to shave off the beard and to keep his hair shaved close. He looked more like a rugby league forward than a religious convert. He trusted all of them but Abdullah would be the one not to trust, if it came to it.

The van came to a halt and a hand slapped against the partition between them and the driver's compartment. They climbed out and Abdullah made to turn. 'No,' said Bilal quietly but with intensity. 'He'll not want us eyeballing his driver.' The van pulled away and they stood by the door until the sound of its engine faded into the general hubbub of the city. Adnan opened the door.

They took tea, black and sweet as usual, and sat on the cushions facing each other. It might have been a pause from the hostilities in some basement bunker piled with sandbags, had there not been the chill in the air that required the fan heater to be on full, had the rap music not been playing.

'Put you in your place, didn't he?' said Abdullah, and Adnan had to look to determine that he wasn't being caustic. Abdullah's blue eyes looked back at him with sincerity. 'Sorry, brother,' he said.

'No worries,' said Adnan. 'You're right.' In truth he had been riled when the man had spoken. Someone had to organize this. Someone, surely, had to direct.

'Won't be long now,' said Bilal.

'What did you reckon?'

'What do you mean?'

'Him. The robes, the headdress, the beard, the "keep-your-distance-brother" act.'

'Yeah,' said Rashid. 'Like "I'm the sheikh, man".'

'I like it,' said Adnan. 'The sheikh. I like it.' He leaned backwards and laughed. He noticed Abdullah looking at him. 'Chill out. It's all good.'

'You don't think he's been sent by the tabloids, do you?' said Rashid. 'The Fake Sheikh?'

They all laughed, then stopped.

Bilal switched on the computer and went through the lengthy security protocols. Soon they were watching the latest production, professionally filmed, slickly edited, HD quality, riveting, moving.

There was music, interspersed with the muezzin's dawn call and funeral ululations and a frantic high-pitched commentary. None of them could speak more than rudimentary Arabic so they watched the English subtitles that exhorted them towards their destination. Adnan found it hypnotic in the room, where the lights had been dimmed, the mixture of anger and peace he felt, the sense of revulsion and joy, the visions of horror and beauty. All these things, he understood, must exist in the same space, the same moment, the same action.

Later, back home, Adnan could relax. He crept in; his flatmates, it appeared, were already in bed. The next morning he'd have to allude to an especially amorous encounter. Having gone to his stash under one of the floorboards in his bedroom, he went into the lounge and swept seven beer cans off the coffee table before putting his stockinged feet on it. It was sticky to the touch. Disgusting.

He needed this blow, to take the edge off. As he inhaled deep and long, savouring the astringent rich fullness of it, he switched on the TV with the remote and scanned the channels idly. Fucking need to kick back, know what I mean? he muttered to himself as he slouched there. He looked at the clock. One fifteen in the morning. Sheesh. It was a crock of shit, he thought. All of it, even this crap. Pursed-up Bilal. Fucking Paki Rashid. Fat white wannabe boy Abdullah. It was all shit. But at least soon it would all be over, in a blaze of glory.

It was getting through, now. More mellow. He might just crash on the sofa.

They sat in their living room, Mr Masoud and his wife. They had been to bed but could not sleep. He had been first up, and moved carefully through the dark, thinking that his wife must have taken some of the tablets the doctor had given her. As he sat in his chair looking at the family album he heard her come down. She brought his dressing gown and slippers. What's the point? he thought. I might as well freeze to death.

'I'll turn the heating up,' she said, 'and put the kettle on.'

She was the strong one. She knew how to carry on. He had little notion of where things had stopped, let alone where to pick them up again. It was commonplace, he knew, this grief thing. A nation's grief, they said in the papers, but that didn't magnify it. It stole something from him. My tears for Aisha and Samir are mine and my family's, he thought, these people are sincere and sorrowful and well intentioned, but this is my loss, my pain, not theirs. They did not know my lovely ones. This suffering was not theirs to own.

He realized he was being ungracious, and he was known to be a gracious individual. This did not stop him wishing he could jealously guard his grief and keep it for himself.

What he could disguise no longer, from himself or his wife, was his fury. Externally, Mr Masoud was the same self-deprecating moderate soul who went about his business quietly and prayed devoutly at the mosque on Fridays, demanding no more from the world than that it should afford him the freedom to run his small business, practise his religion and enjoy family life. Now he realized the rage he felt had been there for a long while. Possibly always. Anger at this country of his birth for the disadvantages it had so obviously bestowed on his family. Anger at this city with its squalor and its spiteful people whom he was obliged to treat as esteemed customers. Anger at not feeling anchored here, despite never having lived elsewhere. Anger at his own self-deprecating modesty. Anger at not belonging any more.

The attack that had taken his son and granddaughter had changed everything. He was now consumed by a fury that could find no satisfaction.

The media. Those vultures, those reptiles. It didn't matter whether they represented the outlets he respected, they hadn't taken long to find out where he lived and to bombard him with requests for interviews. 'This is your chance to put your side of the story, Mr Masoud,' one note, torn from a spiral notebook and thrust through the letterbox, had said. My side, he'd thought: what other side is there than the terrorists'? And this scrap: they hadn't even bothered to write neatly on a decent piece of paper. It was the dismissiveness of it, as if his family was merely an accessory to the news. Which, he supposed, was the way they looked at it.

He knew them. Before this, he would sit on his stool behind the till once the morning rush was past and work his way through the papers, his spectacles perched near the end of his nose so that he could look over them to see new customers entering the shop, and the odd potential shoplifter. He worked methodically, the tabloid trash first, so that towards his eleven o'clock tea break he could begin to savour the broadsheets. He'd never been sure whether he was more a *Guardian* or a *Telegraph* man. Now it was simpler: a plague on all your houses, he thought. I can see how it works. Truth dies in the scramble for stories. You all have it all wrong.

He was boiling. 'Calm down,' his wife insisted as she set the tea down carefully on the coaster on the side table next to his chair. She settled in her own chair. 'Nothing will make it better. Simply time. And then it will not become better, only more distant.'

They thought they had arrived when, five years before, they'd bought this detached house on the prosperous west side of the city, looking over green fields. It was a large house, unnecessary for the two of them, but perfect for family get-togethers or when the grandchildren came to stay. For years they'd lived – literally – above the shop, and liked it there, but Mr Masoud had saved assiduously and invested wisely. His nephew, with his young wife, had taken over the flat together with the running of the shop. Now Mr Masoud might as well, for all he cared, be living in the gutter and begging in the town where his grandfather was born, rather than owning a place with two en suites and a private drive.

'These people,' he said.

'Which people?'

'These security people. They disgust me.'

They'd attended the inquiry diligently since its opening, and had formed friendships with several of the other families. Some had distanced themselves from the Masouds, and the reasons – their Muslim faith and the colour of their skin – were clear.

Matters had commenced with the counsel to the inquiry reading, slowly and without emotion, the names of the victims: the dead first and then the injured. It had been strange to hear Aisha and Samir's names called out, as if in a school register. The Chair had made some sombre comments about the gravity of his task and explained who the four other members of the panel were. Mr Masoud made notes in the notebook he'd brought for the purpose. It had then been time for the first recess. It seemed as if the process was to get the emotion and the regrets out of the way first, before moving on to the dissection of events and the inevitable eventual apportioning of blame. He'd been maintaining that notebook diligently ever since and reviewed it regularly. It never told him any truths, or even lies that might help.

They'd listened carefully to the introductory statements of the various counsel and just about established what was going on. Each interested party, including the victims and their families, had been granted representation as it was a full judicial inquiry. There was also a counsel to the inquiry who, with her team, led the questioning of witnesses.

They'd paid attention as the witnesses spoke. The first forensic expert took them through the composition of the explosive, the open question as to how it was initiated, the spread of the blast, the kind of shrapnel that had been packed. A medical expert detailed the broad nature of the injuries, the likely speed of death and its cause in most cases, and the likely recovery rates of survivors. Each of the experts brought photographs which were displayed on the large screen. The families were given the option of being seated without sight of the screen but despite the horror Mr and Mrs Masoud wanted to look, squinting and peering in the hope of finding the meaning of it all in these lurid colour pictures. It all seemed so disconnected from Aisha and Samir.

The police came next, an inspector talking them through the video footage of the station concourse from various vantage points, including the static CCTV at the station and that taken by the surveillance team following the attackers. Mr Masoud learned that fourteen police and intelligence officers from the team were among the dead. The films were timed to run concurrently on different screens and the inspector paused proceedings every so often to point out salient facts. It was a slick production but nowhere did Mr Masoud catch sight of Aisha or Samir.

Eventually, Abu Omar walked on to the scene in his brilliant white trainers as if on to a stage, the blue rucksack on his back. There were gasps in the audience. He looked so young, and at the same time so cocky. Mr Masoud had known the boy, years ago. He could only have been eleven, twelve max. He'd been a bright boy, polite and respectful too, and would come into the shop to buy sweets with his friends. Mr Masoud knew his father, who worked at the garage where he'd serviced his car, and they used to nod at each other at the mosque. Still the same boy, Khalid he was called, still gawky, head down as he gangled towards his fate, and that of Aisha and Samir too.

The inspector froze the frame just before the explosion took place. 'I don't propose to continue,' he said.

No, I want to see, thought Mr Masoud.

The next witness, the police senior investigating officer, began his evidence by explaining the decision-making process, as recorded in detail. He said that the authorities had come to know of a plot to carry out an attack in the city and that the intelligence agencies had provided details of the probable sole attacker, Abu Omar. Counsel for the inquiry asked why no action was taken at the time. The officer explained that no prosecution would have been possible and that the intelligence needed to be *developed*. While there was reporting of his intent, there was nothing that could be adduced as evidence.

'Where, then, did the information come from?'

'From Abu Omar himself,' said the officer with a cough.

'Did you know that yourself at the time?'

'Yes, a very small number of us knew. I needed to know as I was in charge of the investigation.'

'Then why wasn't this conspiracy nipped in the bud?'

'I see your point,' said the officer, 'of course I do. But there were said to be others involved in the plot whom we hadn't identified. We needed to do so in order to prevent future plots. Abu Omar, according to what we knew, was simply to be the carrier of the device.'

'The mule, so to speak. Or the putz.'

'If you like. We didn't just know this from Abu Omar. We had corroboration from technical. Things like microphones and what have you.'

'So you'd found the others.'

'That's right. We worked with other agencies to identify them.'

'So why didn't it stop there?'

'We considered it. We'd have had enough evidence to mount a prosecution with a reasonable chance of success. With lesser charges, probably, than if we arrested these men in possession of weaponry. And we believed there was at least one more person involved, possibly pivotally.'

The counsel asked the officer to describe the day of the explosion. A dry run had, according to the reporting, been planned. The terrorists would prepare a blue rucksack identical to the one actually to be used and Abu Omar would carry it through the station at five fifteen to see what the security reaction might be. A low-risk, for them, run-through.

'You believed the reporting.'

'We had no reason to disbelieve it at the time,' the officer said.

'Well well. You placed your faith in what your shadowy colleagues told you?'

'If you put it like that. I wouldn't. In any case, we had provision with armed officers on the scene to intervene if it was deemed necessary.'

'But, with tragic consequences, it never was deemed necessary.'

'That's right. The bag was checked by one of my officers just before Abu Omar headed to the station. Witness T brought my officer to the meeting and a thorough visual and technical examination took place. It's in the logs.'

'We've read the logs. But then everything went wrong. Did you at least apprehend the other suspects?'

'They died in the explosion too. They were watching Abu Omar's back in the station.'

'And this fifth man, shall we call him? What became of him?'
'No trace.'

'So Abu Omar set the explosion off under your very noses.'

'We're not entirely sure he did. It could have been triggered remotely. Or there may have been some kind of timer device. The fact that the other terrorists died in the same explosion would seem to suggest that, or that there was a technical malfunction.'

'He was also carrying an initiator.'

'He was carrying something in his hand that resembled a switch, yes. It may not have been to trigger the device. Fragments of a smartphone were also recovered. That could have been used as a timer or as a remote initiator.'

'This was supposed to be a dry run, without explosive.'

'That's what the reporting said.'

The counsel for the victims had been more aggressive still. Mr Masoud had not liked the man when he'd met him along with the other families. He was well known, Mr Masoud had found out when he'd googled him after the meeting, a celebrity barrister with dyed blondish hair and a tan that seemed to accentuate his wrinkles and his age. He was vain and rude, and impatient with Mr Masoud's wife in particular. These qualities he brought to bear with the witnesses as well. No doubt it was his stock-in-trade and could be useful, but Mr Masoud couldn't help thinking that a more subtle approach might bring greater rewards. Do not show your rage so blatantly, he longed to say. Or was it fake, theatrical rage, quite unlike Mr Masoud's silent, hidden version? Softly-softly, as Kipling – or someone – had said. There was little softly-softly about Mr Kerr. Mr Masoud had felt sorry for the police officer.

Not, however, for the spy. After lunch that day they'd returned to the inquiry room to find that a system of elaborate screens had been erected, purely in order that the public should be unable to see the witness. The public; he and his wife and the other family members and the survivors were no longer intimately involved in this, they were members of the public now. Mr Kerr, however, could see him.

The man, Witness T, had spoken quietly and the Chair of the inquiry had asked him to speak up. He had given answers as brief and unemotional as he could. He felt terrible, shattered, numbed, but it didn't sound like it. It sounded as if these were words he'd thought of afterwards, to cover his absence of feeling. He didn't feel guilty but he felt responsible. He wasn't at liberty to say certain things. He related what he could say in almost robotic tones. How could this heartless man be given such responsibility, the responsibility to play with Aisha and Samir's lives, to lose the gamble and lose them too?

4

'We're calling him the sheikh, like,' said Rashid. 'Adnan thought it was funny.'

'Can you describe him?' said Jake.

'Like I say, nothing to describe. He wouldn't let us close to him.'

'Was he tall?' asked Leila. 'Fat? Thin?'

'Couldn't tell. He was sitting. And wearing robes.'

'What colour robes?'

'Dark. Probably black. A checked keffiyeh.'

'What colour? Red or black?'

'What difference does it make?'

'I'm just trying to get you to focus. To imagine yourself back there.'

'No thanks,' said Rashid with a darting smile. 'Couldn't tell in the dark.'

She was good, thought Jake, but ever so slightly too pushy. Too definite. He felt like yawning. It'd been a long day and it wasn't over. They'd waited for hours while the meeting took place, blind as bats, reliant on Rashid's eventual reporting. Now he was tired too, irritable, wanting his bed. Join the club, thought Jake, and glanced at the clock behind Rashid's head. One fifteen. Good grief. Time was, he'd have taken everything in his stride. And a second day of deep joy to come at the inquiry in a few hours.

As ever, the mechanics of the meeting had been complicated. They'd had to wait until Rashid had reached his parents' house before signalling the start of the long process. First they'd needed confirmation that the other three were safely tucked up in bed, then they'd set in motion the long sequence of events that ensured Rashid was safe and that they were safe from Rashid, should he be bad. These measures weren't as elaborate as had been required with Abu Omar – none of the technical testing for explosives upon which the Americans insisted – but on one of the first relays Jake had had to frisk him thoroughly. At first Rashid had been amused at this process; latterly he'd become resentful. Haven't we come to trust each other? seemed to be the subtext. Difficult to say to him: that's the point, we never will trust you, not after what we've been through, not after what you've been through, not even if you served up Baghdadi's head on a plate. Especially if you did: we'd be looking for the angle, the pound of TATP inside his skull.

On the other hand, he was a thoroughly likeable young man; trapped, so he said, by his foolishness; remorseful, haunted by his actions in battle and out of it; wanting out and a way to assuage his sense of sin and make amends with Allah and his family. Jake felt an urge to believe him.

'Age?' persisted Leila.

'No idea. His beard was long and thick. Dark. Maybe a bit of grey. Look, I'm having seconds about this.'

'You know you're doing the right thing.'

Jake thought he might be even more tired than he'd thought. He was letting this meeting slip by. Of course Rashid didn't know that he was doing the right thing. He looked terrified.

'We're here to give you security and safety,' Leila continued. 'Certainty.'

Whoa there, thought Jake.

'How you doing, mate?' he said.

Rashid looked at him as if he hadn't been there. 'I'm doing all right, man.'

'Don't be too tough on yourself. Take a nap if you need to. There's a room at the back. We'll get you home for morning.'

'It's all right.'

'Listen, I've got no answers. We've got no answers. Nothing's for sure. We're all just doing our best. What we can say is that we're watching your back. We're on your side.'

Rashid nodded.

'Let's just get through this, eh? Then you can get home and get some sleep.'

'OK.'

Leila picked up where he'd left off, altering her tone. 'Any idea where the van took you, Rashid?'

'No. I was listening out and trying to work out . . .'

'I'm sure you were. Nothing stood out?'

'Nothing. We were on the ring road for a bit. It was difficult, you know. We were being thrown about in there.'

'It must have been,' she said.

'And when we got there it was just an old warehouse with loading bays. I couldn't see any signs or anything.'

'It's all right. Don't worry.'

'And the van. I never got to see the number plate.'

'Doesn't matter,' she said. 'We'll get there in the end.'

'That guy frightened me,' said Rashid. 'It was like being back there. Smiling, friendly, but . . . I don't know what. That evil kind of grin.'

'You could see him grinning in the dark.'

'Kind of. Adnan didn't like him either.'

'Did you get the sense Adnan knew him?' asked Jake.

'No. He told Adnan he wasn't the leader. We were all leaders, or some such.'

'Do you remember his exact words?'

'It was something like, "You're equals. There aren't any leaders among you." Is it important?'

'I don't know. I'm not sure what's important. Anything and everything could be. You know we have to get this right?'

'Yeah.'

'So we have to know as clearly as possible what this sheikh says, and Adnan and the others. You had enough for tonight?'

'I'm all right,' said Rashid.

'We'll get you back home in a minute. Did you have the feeling that this stuff about there being no leaders was genuine?'

'I think so. Adnan was pissed off.'

'He wasn't play-acting?'

'How do I know? I don't think so. He's not that great at pretending. Unless he is, of course.'

It was nearly two thirty by the time they got back to the office, having dropped Rashid off. She knew that Jake had a meet the next morning and then was due at the inquiry again, so suggested they skip the wash-up.

'We can't,' he'd said.

'Why not?' she'd asked.

'Something might get lost between the cracks of our minds. Something that's there and may come out if we talk now. Something that'll vanish if we leave it too long.'

So here they were.

'I'm sorry,' she said.

'It's OK.'

'No. It was stupid. How many times did you say it in training? You may have some idea of right and wrong. Don't expect your clients to.'

'My very words. Rehearsed and regurgitated for every course. It's true, though. Rashid's not looking for moral certainty. He's had a bellyful of that. He's looking for us to save his life.'

Jake had always struck her as imperturbable – until recently, that was. Ever since she'd arrived in the section they'd double-teamed on casework. He was a kind of mentor, had trained her in the first place, though he was the opposite of pushy. She wondered how he'd ever got into this: the orthodoxy was that to be successful you had to be outgoing and forceful. There was with Jake, though, a kind of core of stillness. She felt she hardly knew him. She knew he wasn't married and didn't have children. But whether he had a partner, whether he was straight or gay, where he lived or what he did in his spare time, these were unknown. The odd thing was that despite all this he didn't seem withholding, or unduly jealous of his privacy. He'd always seemed complete in a way she never would be, with her restless ambition.

No longer, however. No one who'd known him before could fail to notice. That unfailing courtesy had gone or only showed itself patchily. He'd become prone to irritated outbursts about the weather, about HR, about the car they were driving. About anything.

And the optimism he normally exuded. Gone, too. There'd always been something vaguely un-English about him. He could rediscover that positivity, enough to put it on for the likes of Rashid, but that too took its toll. After meetings he looked spent, as if it were fatigue as much of the soul as of the body.

Back in the day he'd been the training supervisor for her intake. Back in the day: it wasn't that long ago. She'd ended up in this line of work more as a result of stubbornness and a streak of perversity than by accident. Unlike her peers she'd never wanted a career in medicine or the law, or a marriage to a wealthy businessman. She'd wanted something different. She'd dreamt of becoming a police officer, specifically a detective who unravelled the tightest mysteries to deliver astounding results. This wasn't so far from that, but her chosen career wasn't one she'd contemplated in childhood.

Her parents had had conventional expectations. When

she'd studied politics at Oxford the law seemed most likely. It was a shock to them when – as they'd thought at the time – she'd decided to become a mere functionary in the Home Office, a policy wonk. She'd been told by overzealous recruiters not to tell her parents what she'd signed up for, but after a year or so she thought better of it. Her father, a great fan of the James Bond films he'd half-heartedly forbidden her to watch, was delighted. It isn't like that, she told him. Her mother simply thought that, all those years after fleeing Uganda, this was the true point of arrival in this country.

It wasn't as her father dreamed. Nowhere near. Jake had made that clear from the outset, with his little sermons about ethics and the mission that others on the course found pompous. He was conceited, of course he was, in that curiously self-effacing way. But at the same time she felt she was in the right place.

The bond, he'd kept saying. You can't buy anyone, whatever people say. People don't sell their souls for sixpence or six million quid. If you're lucky you get to lease a tiny part of their souls briefly, like a room in a hotel that rents by the hour. Don't squander it; use that time to build something more real and durable. Something resembling respect. Something resembling trust. Something resembling love. Don't think, either, that you can snow them, other than for a split second. No one in this room is capable of doing that, not with the people we deal with. We're not dealing with idiots who'll fall, hook line and sinker. It's a tougher game. You can force people to cooperate, and they will to a certain point, that crucial point when they suddenly turn on you, probably without you even realizing. You need something more real. The bond.

She could remember the exact words now, hear him saying them.

This the gospel according to St Jake? someone whispered, none too quietly.

He blinked. Yes, if you like. And finally, find something to like in them. There always is.

And if your subject is a paedophile or a racist?

I don't know. I really don't know. Give it a go, I'd say, because it's the only way you'll get what you need. Just trust your instincts.

No wonder he was so strung out. He'd broken all his rules with Abu Omar. Hell, she was shattered too. Her mind was wandering.

'Do you think this sheikh guy is the same as the one with Abu Omar?' she asked. 'The one they called the boss?'

'I don't know. Probably. If so, it's an interesting way of working. Not seen it before. How are we doing on the van?'

'None of the CCTV near the meeting place picked it up.'

'Interesting in its own right.'

'They're going through the traffic cameras all over the city as we speak. But at ten in the evening on a Monday night white vans are ten a penny.'

'We have a time when they returned, though. That should help. They may strike lucky. How did Rashid seem to you?'

'All right,' she said. 'He seems to be coping. Why? Did you see anything amiss?'

'No, not at all. You may have picked up something that I didn't, though.'

Rashid was a strange boy. He wasn't so different from her. Her parents had considered her a peculiar child and obligingly and frequently told her so. She'd known for herself, too.

Jake had known Rashid far longer than she had, nurtured the case from its inception when he'd still been at university and popped up in radical circles only during the vacations. Somehow Jake had eased alongside Rashid without pretending to be anything other than what he was. According to the terse version of events Jake had given her when she first became his oppo, Rashid had accepted it without a word and for a while they'd simply talked, about college, about the weather, about anything but the circles in which Rashid moved. Then it had stopped. Rashid had completed his studies and disappeared from the radar.

Other reporting later had it that he was at the battlefront, then that he'd come back via Turkey. Jake hadn't had to make contact again. Within two weeks Rashid phoned in.

It was possible, of course, that it was a dangle. 'No idea,' said Jake when she'd asked him, but she knew that if he'd harboured true suspicion he'd surely have played the case differently. Rashid, so his story went, had been told to lie low and would later be called upon, with three boys he'd met out there. There were, meanwhile, other jobs in the pipeline.

Motivation? she'd asked when they were preparing for her first introduction.

He'd drawn breath. 'Sorry. Not much good at that. I know that's what they say we should think about but I find it clouds things. There's rarely a single reason why anyone does anything. These aren't method actors, they're vulnerable, imperfect human beings. If you try to unravel all the things that are going on in their heads you can go crazy. For me, I just focus on what seems to be real. Don't overthink it, don't force it, would be my advice. But no doubt I'm wrong. You'll have your own way of doing things.' He'd cast a self-deprecatory smile. She hadn't forced it.

Rashid had surprised her when they'd first met. He was polite and well mannered, for starters, unlike many of the other joes she'd run. He must cultivate a different persona when running with the jihadis. With her and Jake he was docile and showed no signs of resentful chips on the shoulder.

Nor had he been remotely fazed by her presence.

'This is Leila,' Jake had said in that matter-of-fact fashion he'd said he'd employ.

'Hello, Leila,' Rashid had said. 'How you doing?'

'Fine,' she'd said, and it was.

Abu Omar had hoved into view, and she could tell at the time that despite his cheerfulness Jake didn't like it at all. 'I'm no good with the Americans,' was all he'd said to her at the time, laughing. As a consequence she'd had to do various solo meetings with Rashid which at least enabled her to establish a rapport with him. Sometimes Jake deliberately skipped meetings so that she could develop the bond further. The bond, again.

They'd liked each other. He was a nice boy, taciturn but pleasant with it, even if she couldn't fathom how he'd become caught up in this.

'You from round here?' he'd asked once.

'No, I'm a Manc,' she'd said.

He'd shrugged, then nodded. 'Well, you do all right for one of them.'

The thing with Abu Omar had happened, and Jake had been forced to take some time off. Time off, rather than suspended from duty, was the rumour. Then Rashid had said they were all coming together, in this place, and demanded to see Jake. The hierarchy hated it, but she'd heard it first-hand.

'He seemed fine,' she said now, in response to Jake's question. 'Perfectly all right.'

Jake sighed. 'I think it's time to call it a day,' he said. 'I'm making no sense at all, least of all to myself.'

5

TUESDAY

In truth, Zaki was a pain in the arse. Needy. Garrulous. In your face. Nasty piece of work into the bargain. Sup with a very long spoon. But a source, nevertheless, and once he'd been a useful one, if not in Jake's area of business.

Zaki had been a police informant before being introduced to Jake in the scramble to squeeze the juice from every potential lead to extremists in the community. Once a prominent figure at the mosque, he was never ostentatiously religious but an acquaintance of all the leading personalities.

It was heroin that had brought him into contact with the police. They had an informant – a user himself – who claimed that Zaki had established a new line of supply and was muscling in on the market. A rival, so word on the street had it, had disappeared and it was whispered that Zaki was the man.

Zaki was hauled in. He claimed he'd met some Turks who wanted to 'lead him astray', as he put it. Jake had watched the video of the original interview and seen Zaki smirking. No, he didn't want a lawyer present. He'd committed no crime. As soon as he'd realized what these guys were about he'd broken off contact. Anything else was just dirty rumour. Couldn't someone be allowed just one moment of weakness in life?

He'd known he'd insulated himself effectively from evidence. The original police informant also suddenly changed his mind about Zaki. But he feared for his standing in the community, and it was this that Dave Philpott, his eventual handler, discerned. A long relationship, characterized by misgivings on the police side judging from the frequent case reviews, ensued, at first focused on drug dealing in the city and latterly on what Zaki called 'the young hotheads' in the city.

Before all this Zaki had worked for the council, managing the dwindling estate as the authority diligently divested itself of its holdings in line with government policy and budget cuts. Jack of all trades, he'd had to dabble in it all – buildings maintenance, plumbing, electrics, telecoms – as the crumbling fabric crumbled further with zero investment. He said he'd known he would be made redundant and had prepared for his next life, as a businessman. He hoarded his contacts and networked assiduously.

He'd used his redundancy cash to reinvent himself, setting himself up in a one-man import-export business that dealt with any commodity that yielded a profit. Reinvention was Zaki's thing, like survival. He was a creature who adapted quickly and without fuss to the changes in the world. He surfed waves, he followed trends, he reckoned the odds, he spread his bets. He was a man to be reckoned with, at least in his own version of his life.

Mobile phones from China, soft furnishings from the Indian subcontinent, discounted luxury cars to Dubai and Bahrain. Okra, Jake could remember: at one stage Zaki had cornered the market locally for okra from Africa for sale to curry houses. And then to heroin.

Jake hadn't probed Zaki's attitude to Islam deeply. There was hardly any need, it seemed. Zaki would be guided by expediency. The religion into which he had been born had become an opportunity for networking, for respectability. There was rarely a need to look for anything profound in Zaki Ibrahim.

'I know everyone,' Zaki would claim, and it seemed he did. But in fact he seemed to have the opposite of the Midas effect: people he highlighted or about whom he was asked for an opinion often left the city, moved away from the mosque or disappeared altogether. Or they shunned Islam. Jake had long suspected that Zaki's powers of eliciting information were far too crude for his purposes. But he was tolerated, as a kind of freebie.

Dave Philpott brought Zaki to the safe house.

'Sorry about the early start, Zaki,' said Jake.

'You know me, Mr Winter. Twenty-four/seven. Duracell bunny.' As ever, he was immaculately turned out, black hair swept back on a wave of gel, long-lashed eyes sharp and alert, expensive blue suit, crisply ironed white shirt. Pungent aftershave applied much too liberally. A broad smile that showed startling white teeth. Jake felt still more tired looking at him.

'So what's the word, Zaki?'

'A lot going on, Mr Winter. A lot. I was saying to Mr Philpott. This inquiry has stirred everybody up. Everybody's looking round for the informants. Not good for our business, I can tell you.'

Dave raised his eyebrows. 'We're careful, Zaki. We look after you.'

'No, no, don't get me wrong. I wasn't implying nothing. You treat me good. I feel safe. Just saying I got to be careful about going round asking questions. Don't want no trouble. I'm just saying.'

'No one wants you to do anything risky,' said Jake soothingly. 'Business good?'

'Can't complain, like. You know, stuff here and there. Got to be busy-busy, if you want to make your way in the world.'

'But doing all right, are we?'

'Not too bad. Depressed economy, Brexit and all that. I keep my head above water.'

'Not thinking of going back to your old business, are you?'

'What do you mean?'

'The smack, Zaki. Those big bad Turkish boys leading you astray.'

'Why? Who's been spreading lies?'

'No one. Just pulling your plonker.'

'Ha. Well, I'm not going near that stuff again. Learned my lesson.'

'Good to hear.'

'Been away at all recently, Zaki?' asked Dave.

'Why?'

'I only ask because I tried to text you last week. Didn't get a reply.'

'As it happens, I did get away for a few days. Didn't sort out my roaming properly, so didn't get your message until I got back. Sorry. It was only a couple of days before we were supposed to meet, so I –'

'That's all right. Go anywhere nice?'

'Yeah. Croatia, as it happens. Last-minute booking. Spur of the moment.'

'It'll be lovely out there this time of year. Bit of winter sun?'

'That's right.'

'Hot, was it?'

'Compared with here it was. But you know me. I love the sun. Can take any heat. I just lap it up.'

'Who did you book with?' asked Jake. 'I'm thinking of taking a week off soon, so if you've got any tips . . .'

'I forget. It was one of them last-minute websites. The hotel was lovely, four star and all that. Can't remember the name of it for the life of me, though.'

'When you have a moment, look it up,' said Jake. 'I'd be interested.'

'Right you are.' He beamed at both men.

'And you do know that you need to tell us if you plan to go away, don't you? We don't want to worry about you unduly. Always looking out for your welfare. And none of us wants you to have an awkward time at immigration anywhere, do we?'

'No, Mr Winter. Forgot. Sorry.'

'No need to apologize, Zaki. Slipped your mind is all. Lot on your plate. What's the temperature like on the street? Apart from the inquiry, I mean.'

'Things are all right. This thing's got people talking, though. That guy there now giving evidence. He's some kind of bastard, they're saying. Not one of your lot, is he?'

Jake smiled. 'It'll soon blow over. Like the weather. But how are things more generally?'

'Tensions are high, I can tell you. People are expecting the backlash any minute. Muslims are fearful. Some of the young boys are saying we should get our retaliation in first.'

'The police are doing their best to make sure there'll be no backlash,' said Jake. 'Any specific names of people trying to stir up trouble?'

'Nah. It's all hot air. People need to shout. It's the ones who don't shout you need to be careful of.'

'Quite.'

'So, anything bubbling under at the moment, Zaki?' asked Dave. 'Any ones to watch for the future? Any boys who aren't shouting who need looking at?'

'Nothing I can think of. Sorry.'

'You can't help it if there's nothing going on,' said Jake. 'And we wouldn't want you making stuff up, would we?'

Dave left with Zaki to return him for his next meeting while Jake waited for the car that would take him back to the inquiry. Another trying morning. At some point he and Dave would have to square what Zaki had said with the alternative version of reality: that Zaki had been living it up in Turkey the previous week talking heroin with old associates. Or not square, as the case might be. Trouble was, these alternative facts were backed up by immigration records and flight manifests. At least a shot had been fired across his bows. Even Zaki couldn't fail to pick up the messages they'd been broadcasting.

The hoary old chestnut about speculating to accumulate might have some truth. In fact, Jake had always been an advocate of the steady, mundane conduct of the business, believing it would bear eventual fruit, rather than making spectacular attempts to pull rabbits out of hats. But it could be wearing. For every gold nugget there were a million pieces of rubbish and complications galore. Sometimes there were no gold nuggets.

'Take us through your decision-making processes,' said Mr Kerr. 'You have certain protocols for this between yourselves and the police, I understand.'

'That's right. I'm sure the details are in the documents submitted to you.'

'We've read the documents. I'm trying to probe what it's actually like on the ground.'

'It's just as the documents state. The Executive Liaison Group decides the direction. Everyone takes their lead from the ELG. Each meeting is documented for the record.'

'Even if matters are proceeding rapidly?'

'Even then.'

'This seems rather a stately and bureaucratic set of affairs. One would rather anticipate that sometimes the reality on the ground would overwhelm your ability to make decisions. That what happened here?'

'No. The ELG meetings are to set the direction. Specific responsibilities are vested with relevant bodies. And if things move very quickly in the direction of some kind of . . . event, the police officer in charge will take control.'

'Event. Is that what you think of this as? An event?'

'No. That's not what I'm saying. I'm trying to describe for you how the process works. An event doesn't necessarily mean an attack, or an atrocity.'

'What else could it mean in this context?'

'Well, erm . . .' He could not instantly think of an example. 'For instance . . . if some conspirators weren't planning an imminent attack but prepared some kind of device that was assessed by the police to be potentially unstable and unsafe. They would probably decide to intervene at that point.'

'I see. So what informs your decisions? What's the most vital thing to you? Catching the perpetrators in the act? Collecting intelligence about terrorist organizations? Protecting your source?'

'First of all, I don't make the decisions. The strategic decisions are made above me. The police are the only people who are enabled to and have the duty to make arrests. So they make the final decisions. And the underlying principle is that throughout, for everyone concerned, the overwhelming concern is to protect public safety.'

'I see. So it's the police's fault, is it?'

'That's not what I'm saying.' He strove to keep exasperation from his voice. 'Everyone involved has a personal responsibility to protect the public. That's why we exist.'

'And in this situation, no one more than you.'

'I suppose so, yes.' He looked down.

'Public safety,' mulled Mr Kerr. 'Didn't go so well for you, did it?'

Jake looked straight at him. 'No. You're absolutely right. You have to do everything within your power. You have to give it your best judgement.'

'Best judgement wasn't good enough on this occasion, though, was it?'

'I suppose not. But I tried my best.'

'Accidents will happen. That what you're saying?'

'No, not at all.'

'The best-laid plans? Everyone makes mistakes? Is that the best we can offer the survivors and the victims' families? Really?'

'No. Listen to what I'm saying.'

'Please,' said Mr Kerr. 'Let's not get tetchy. That would be most unbecoming. I have been listening carefully and in one sense you're transmitting loud and clear. Process is everything. In another sense, I wish I could work out what on earth you are saying. And I'm sure most of us share that frustration. Bit of a cold fish, aren't we?'

'Sorry?'

'You've laid out your position with crystal-clear evasiveness. You've used your officialese to express anything but contrition. You've not uttered anything that could be construed as an apology. It's arguable that you've been concerned with two things: saving your own skin and obfuscating. Or are the two connected?'

'That's unfair.'

'In what way is it unfair? Is it any less fair than going about your daily business at your local railway station only to meet your death because of the incompetence of our intelligence services?'

Jake did not answer immediately. Then: 'I think you're trying to compare two different things. Of course I'm sorry. My sorrow is such that I can't express it in terms that make any sense. I failed, and I'm trying to work out what I did wrong.'

'It's pretty clear, isn't it?'

'Not really, no.'

'It's not clear to you what your failures were?'

'No. Other than the blindingly obvious. I was hoping this process might give some clarity. Perhaps you're about to enlighten me.'

'The purpose of this process is not to provide you with solace,' hissed Mr Kerr. 'It is to establish the facts and to provide the survivors and families with some assurance that this has been examined thoroughly and openly, that systemic mistakes have been rectified and that those guilty of negligence or misconduct in a public office,' he looked directly at Jake, 'are dealt with under due process.'

'Mr Kerr,' said the Chair mildly. 'That's enough. We will maintain the dignity of these proceedings, please. We will not permit the badgering of witnesses to this inquiry. I think we will break until tomorrow.'

'Yes, sir. My apologies,' said Mr Kerr, but Jake thought he saw a smirk on his face as he turned away.

'I feel sorry for the man,' said Mrs Masoud to her husband later.

He was looking pensive. 'What?' he said.

'I said I feel sorry for him somehow.'

'How can you? This is the man who is responsible for Aisha and Samir's deaths.'

'He isn't, you know.'

'Of course I know. Partially responsible, at least. You have to admit that.'

'I thought he sounded reasonable. He was trying his best. I don't think our lawyer should be pestering witnesses.'

'I try to ignore what that man says. He clouds the issue. But he has his job to do. This is the system. He has to push as hard as he can.'

'I'm uncomfortable with this, Hatem. It seems obsessive.

Whatever we do, we won't bring them back. It just seems like a search for vengeance.'

She always was more balanced than he was. 'But the truth,' he said. 'We want to know the truth.'

She gave this due consideration. 'That's right. I want to know the truth. But we should search for it in a spirit of forgiveness. This lawyer is just trying to cause trouble and to increase his status. This is not what I want. Is it what you're looking for?'

'Of course not. There's nothing we can do about it, though.'

'I suppose not.'

'His voice,' he said.

'Who? The lawyer?'

'No. The man behind the screen.'

'What about it?'

'Sounds just like someone on TV. Can't work out who.'

'No idea.'

They drank their tea.

'I've spoken to the surgery, Hatem,' she said. 'I'm going back to work the week after next.'

'The inquiry won't be finished by then,' he said in confusion.

'I know. It'll drag on for months. I can't wait that long. Do you plan to go back to the shop sometime?'

'I need to see the inquiry out. I can't see beyond that. I'm awake all night and then drop off just before dawn. Then I wake up suddenly and I don't know what's going on. Where I am, who I am. There's always that moment when I think . . . I don't know, not that it's a dream, but somehow that it's all right, that it's unreal. It's not happening. Then reality strikes.'

'Perhaps you should see the doctor again.'

'No,' he said definitively. 'I don't need treatment. I don't need sympathy. I just need to reach a point where I can grasp it somehow. Where I can hold it in my head, and keep it there without it overwhelming me. I know I need to snap out of this, and I will at some point. I just don't know when. I'm going to see Tawfiiq. I'll be back later.'

'What is it that you see in that young man?'

'He has a certain serenity in his heart. He's the only one at the mosque who seems to understand, to really see what I'm going through. He's the only one I can speak to. When I'm with him he gives me a sense of belief that perhaps one day . . . As soon as I leave, that feeling disappears.'

6

WEDNESDAY

They waited for the sheikh to speak. He sat smiling beatific-
ally as they assembled, legs apart, elbows resting on his thighs
and hands clasped. Rashid felt a sense of theatrical anticipation
and wondered whether the sheikh was in fact an imam, with
that sense of drama that attended religious rites, as the man
sat there glowing, basking in their expectation. They were
attentive. Rashid looked at the sheikh as long as he dared, seeing him also looking back, bestowing his attention on them
each in turn, then again, and again, watchful.

It had been five o'clock in the morning when the text came
to convene at the normal venue, via the messaging system
they'd been told was secure. Rashid had been told never to
bring his phone to meetings. They could track it, the *mukhabarat*.
They could do all kinds of things. But they couldn't get into the
messages. WikiLeaks had demonstrated that, together with
the moaning of the British government, which amplified their
weaknesses. So at all other times, when they were leading that
separate life, the mundane decadent English existence, they
should keep their phones beside them.

They had come here via a bewildering series of cut-outs and
changes of vehicle. It was similar to one of his meetings with
Jake and Leila in this respect, the toing and froing, the disori-
entation, but Rashid suspected the sheikh had fewer people at
his disposal. The instructions had been in two halves: one held

70

by Bilal and the other by Abdullah. Bilal had driven them in his mother's ancient Nissan Micra to one of the city-centre car parks. They had entered Mandela Park in the half-dark of dawn, climbing over the wrought-iron fencing and, following the careful directions, left it at its opposite end, where a pre-paid taxi was waiting to take them to a pub, closed with blank shutters, by the canal. There, Abdullah's set of instructions had kicked in, to walk down the towpath and cross to the other side at a set of locks. Here the old white Transit waited for them and they'd climbed in. At least Rashid had been able to make out the registration number. He timed the journey to this place from there at twenty-five minutes.

'Well,' said the sheikh when he decided the moment had come. 'This is a sombre moment for us all. It may be the last time we see each other, brothers. Now is the time, if any of you has reservations about what you will be expected to do, for you to withdraw and wait outside in the van. There will be no recriminations or repercussions. It must be clear to each of us that we need to feel called to take this path. You are all warriors and have nothing to prove. You can return home with pride if that's what you want.'

He paused and looked at them expectantly. No one moved. How, thought Rashid, could any of them do so? Each would have realized that, even if he no longer wanted to do this, to leave now would be an act of suicide.

'Good. That's settled.' He leaned back and crossed his legs. Rashid could see the soles of the sheikh's boots and was mesmerized by the urgent twitching of his feet in the half-light.

The sheikh coughed. 'This is it. This is the cold truth. The action you are required to carry out is designed to kill not tens, but hundreds. Thousands perhaps, *inshallah*. It will shake not just this city but this complacent country to the core. It will be the next step on the path to our caliphate.'

'You have one week before you find your place in paradise. You probably know that on Wednesday evening next week there is a big game at the ThreeD. City are playing Real Madrid. They are impudent enough even to be sponsored by an Arab infidel airline. There'll be seventy thousand people there.'

Rashid could not help looking at Adnan who, even in mid-battle when chasing the enemy down the desert road, had been obsessed with finding a mobile signal to look up the latest transfer gossip. Adnan claimed to have had trials with City but not to have made it purely because of where his parents had been born. Now, he showed no emotion.

'You need to make your preparations. You need to acquire materials, to train and, most importantly, to ensure that you have done everything in this world that Allah could require of you. You need to rest, to pray and to find peace in your souls. Now, the plan. It is simple. Each of you will play an active role. You will each approach the ground at the end of the game from a different direction, as the crowd is leaving. One of you, more perhaps, possibly all of you, will carry an explosive device. It is yet to be decided. You will also be armed with other weapons. I will get hold of all of the weaponry and message each of you with individual instructions how to collect it. This will be at the last moment.'

'Wouldn't it be easier for us to collect the weapons together?' asked Adnan.

'We must be wary. We must guard against the possibility that one of you may be detected. If that happens, the others must be free to carry out their tasks. In the meantime, you will need to acquire various items. You will need to obtain vehicles so that you can approach the area of the ground without using public transport.'

'I can borrow my mum's car again,' said Bilal.

The others laughed quietly, and the sheikh smiled too.

'No. This must be done in a way that shields your identities. Your families and associates will realize you are no longer there, but we must make the authorities work hard. There are others preparing to take part in the next wave of this holy work, and we want the infidels to be as occupied as they can be. Abdullah, I understand you know how to steal cars.'

Abdullah nodded.

'Then you will spend the day before the mission – next Tuesday – finding four cars that you can steal and store. Before that, you need to buy sharp knives, for self-defence. You will need also, all four of you, to acquire materials with which you can make it seem as if the cars, when you abandon them near the ground, are loaded with bombs. That may well divert the police from their tasks at the ground, as well as causing panic that is helpful.'

'What kind of materials?' asked Rashid. He did not want to be the only one who did not speak.

'I'll leave that to you,' said the sheikh. 'You will also need to plan your approaches to the stadium and the timings. This is for you to work out as well. You have the skills. In the meantime you continue to live your lives as normal. Until the very last moment. Except . . .' he left a pause for dramatic effect. 'Except this coming Sunday. You will need to test your plan. City have a home game that day against Liverpool. The crowd will be as large, as will the police presence. You won't have vehicles, so you will have to walk or take public transport. The next part is important. You must carry rucksacks but no offensive weapons on this rehearsal. This is critical. You cannot under any circumstances carry anything incriminating. This is to test the enemy's security awareness. That is all.'

'It won't be like the station?' asked Abdullah.

'Does any of us really know about the station? Who were the brothers, what were the instructions? Do not believe the

73

Western media or their so-called inquiries. No, this is clear. This is *your* holy mission. It is not a copy of any other. Is that clear?'

'Yes.'

'This is purely to practise the elements of a very complex operation. If any of you is apprehended, we'll have to think again. You must each have a cover story for your presence in the area. Think about what you will say. If challenged by the police, you must not give them any reason to take action against you. Is that clear?'

'Yes,' they all said again.

Jake Winter was in a hurry. He'd overslept and it was already seven forty. He might just make the seven fifty-seven bus but he'd have to be quick. He'd need to buy something to eat at the supermarket on the corner.

He felt dishevelled, though he'd shaved carefully before showering. He only rushed these things if it were a matter of great urgency. To perform well, he needed to feel that he looked and felt as good as he could. Not, he thought, that that meant much, given how little sleep he was getting. He wasn't required at the inquiry today, he'd been told by text message, owing to some obscure in-chambers legal debate. That meant no suit was necessary but he took as much care when dressing in jeans. He needed that careful calibration of casualness and professionalism, that curious alchemy of friendliness yet distance, informality and efficiency that put his interlocutor at ease. He was dishevelled less in his appearance than in his psychological state.

Rashid had asked for a meeting. The call had come at seven fifteen. He'd have been worried if Rashid hadn't phoned in because, as he'd confirmed in a quick call to the ops room afterwards, the boys had met unexpectedly early that morning. A quick dash to their venue, triggered it was thought by the end-to-end encrypted messaging service that they still hadn't managed to get into. Rashid had texted in quickly to report but by then he was running against time.

The surveillance teams saw the other boys going there too. Bilal was driving his mother's car. When they all got into the car the surveillance must have thought this was going to be easy. The boys' first mistake, perhaps. But whoever was pulling their strings knew the city well. Jake could imagine it. The leisurely follow to the northern gate of Mandela Park, closed at that time of the morning. The boys scaling the five-foot railings nimbly, dropping down on the other side and disappearing into the bushes in the darkness of an overcast dawn. The on-the-hoof health and safety assessment that prevented the team from following directly, for fear of an ambush. Cars dispatched to drive frantically around the perimeter to chase time, knowing they could never hope to cover the other three exits. What was a three-minute stroll across the park would, what with the one-way system, be a seven-minute dash in a car to the furthest exit, even through deserted streets. By the time the cars had done the circuit a couple of times and teams were combing the interior they'd have realized they'd lost them. The audio and video at the boys' normal venue were worthless; quick scans of the CCTV coverage around the city revealed only the normal morning traffic of early workers, night buses and taxi drivers going off shift.

It was reassuring, therefore, that Rashid had called in. Reassuring too that he'd said, somewhat breathlessly, that there was no change of plan that brought things forward but that they needed to meet today. Leila and Jake had made Rashid memorize a series of fallback RV arrangements in case the wheel threatened to come off in the form of an unanticipated impromptu attack, but each of them risked blowing the whole covert operation. Surveillance had confirmed that Rashid had gone home, changed into his suit and was on his way to work. The others had also resumed their normal routines.

He looked around. In the refrigerated section there were some of those dreadful-looking ready-made cereal concoctions in plastic boxes, placed there for people just like him. In the end he decided on a banana and a cappuccino from the machine and took them to the till.

'Mr Masoud not back yet, then?' he said.

The young man, Mr Masoud's nephew, so he said, looked up from his newspaper. 'The inquiry, innit?' Jake looked at him as if he had not the slightest idea what he was talking about. 'He goes to the inquiry every day. Doesn't miss a minute, him and Mrs M.'

'Of course.'

'It's hit him hard, this has.'

'Understandable. How long is it now since it happened?'

'Three and a half months. Three and a half bloody months.'

'It's not long,' said Jake. 'Give it time.'

'True, true. Take a lot longer to get over something like that.'

'You expecting him back anytime soon, then?'

'No idea, man. Doubt it. Maybe six months, maybe longer. Maybe never.'

'Well, pass on my regards if you see him, won't you?'

'You always say that, man. I always do.'

A day off. He'd taken the phone call from the lawyer's office before they set off. It'd been the clerk; the man himself obviously had better things to do. There was some procedural stuff being sorted today between the counsel and the Chair. 'Give yourself a day off,' the clerk had said.

What did he know? A day off? There'd never be a day off

from this. He'd only been trying to make conversation, the boy, but still. Mr Masoud's silence had made the end of the conversation awkward, he'd known that, and he'd felt the urge to call back and make amends. But no, he realized he hadn't the heart or the will.

So Tawfiiq had come around. He'd expressed his gratitude and they'd sat in the dining room with the door closed. His wife had raised her eyebrows in that way and continued with the housework.

He could talk to Tawfiiq, the young man whose expression was always watchful but never displayed even the smallest impatience with Mr Masoud's rambling commentary on life and its evils. His hands remained still and he simply watched. He never betrayed emotion which, Mr Masoud guessed, would make him a good spiritual leader.

'You'll be a fine imam one day, Tawfiiq,' he once said.

'Thank you, Abu Samir. If it be Allah's will.' He smiled non-committally.

They'd been there half an hour or more when the doorbell rang. The door-stepping journalists had become less frequent. But there was still the occasional one prepared to chance his or her arm. He looked at the display from the security camera hidden near the front door.

Zaki Ibrahim. No, please, no. He'd avoided Zaki since it had happened. The worst kind of prurient, prying gossip. The man purported to be of the faith but showed the worst of Western excess. And that sports car. Zaki Ibrahim was a businessman of sorts, known to have mixed with the wrong people and rumoured to have been involved in the drugs trade at one point. Word at the mosque had it that he'd cleaned up his act, but you never knew.

These were, Mr Masoud realized, uncharitable thoughts and unworthy of him, even in his present condition. Zaki

Ibrahim was, after all, just another human being with human frailties.

Mr Masoud had parked the car on the drive this morning in preparation for going to the inquiry. He couldn't pretend he wasn't at home. If he failed to open the door, Zaki would know he'd been shunned. Both would lose face.

'Will you be opening the door, then?' asked his wife, who had just come into the room.

'It's Zaki Ibrahim,' he replied, a plea in his voice. He looked at Tawfiiq and saw reflected: nothing.

'I must go,' said Tawfiiq, and stood.

'I'll put the kettle on,' said Mrs Masoud.

Tawfiiq and Zaki exchanged greetings, Zaki effusive, Tawfiiq blank as ever; and then Tawfiiq was gone.

Zaki Ibrahim sat on the edge of the sofa, leaning forward, one large hand in the other, as if in supplication. He looked up as he spoke. 'Abu Samir, I've not had the chance to speak to you properly since the funeral. I'm sorry, I should have made the time.'

'It's all right, Zaki. We've been rather . . . preoccupied.'

'Of course. But I wanted to come and pay my respects.'

'It's kind of you to do so.'

'I'm sorry about what happened. Your son and granddaughter. Beautiful people.'

Mr Masoud was not aware that Zaki had ever met Aisha in her five years of bountiful life. The thought of her again made his eyes prick. Who was this man, with his silly sleek hairstyle, his shiny suit and black shirt and those ridiculous boots, to comment on Samir and Aisha?

He said nothing, but continued to hold a banal half-smile on his face. It was that or burst into tears once more.

'If there's anything I can do,' said Zaki.

'That's kind,' said Mr Masoud.

'These terrible, terrible people.'

'Yes.'

'And they call themselves good Muslims.'

'I know.'

'These boys. Who knows how many more there are in this city, and elsewhere? The community is anxious, Abu Samir. The city is in turmoil.'

'I'm afraid I've not kept up with . . .'

'No. Of course not. But who knows what will happen next? No right-minded Muslim condones what happened. Your family and other Muslims are direct victims of this. Yet the community feels under threat.'

'Is there something you wish me to do, Zaki?'

'No, not at all.'

'Because I wouldn't feel capable of making a statement or doing an interview or anything like that, I'm afraid. I'm sorry.'

'No. I wasn't suggesting that. I was only expressing my feelings.'

'I see.'

'It's a sense of frustration we all feel. What can we do, as a community, as individuals? Your friends at the mosque, this Tawfiiq, what use are they? I fear for us.'

'It's natural. I'm no wise man, Zaki. I have extreme diffi-culty getting through each day. I don't think we'll ever understand what these people are thinking. If they believe they can find justification in the Quran for their actions, by taking its words out of context and distorting them, why are they seeking such justification in the first place? What has caused their hearts to be so full of hate? What are their aims? They cannot truly believe that this worldwide caliphate can ever be created. But I'm simply repeating what so many others have said. I think all we can do is to wait. All things must pass. We need to have hope and to be as kind to others as we can be.'

'These are sage words, Abu Samir. You are wiser than you give yourself credit for.'

'Thank you. It wasn't false modesty.'

'In fact we do know what these people wish to achieve,' continued Zaki Ibrahim, 'better than the Westerners, at least.'

'We do?'

'The Westerners think they get it but they don't understand the seriousness of it. Its literalness. These people simply want to annihilate everything this civilization is made of. Every scrap of it. They don't need to create anything, they simply want to destroy everything and everyone. This is what Westerners don't see. They can't believe these people really do want to kill everyone and to destroy everything. They think there must be some deal to be done, somewhere down the road. I know how to do deals and even I can see there's nothing to trade. Who can blame these people in a way, when you look at society here, its hopelessness, its lack of respect, its decadence?'

'Are you saying that you believe in some of what they're doing?'

'Of course not. I'm simply saying that there are huge injustices and immoralities inflicted on Muslims both here and in the lands from which our forebears came.'

'I'm sorry,' said Mr Masoud, 'but I feel a little fatigued. I'm nearly always tired at the moment. I hardly get any sleep at night.'

'I apologize if I've been insensitive,' said Zaki, looking abashed. 'When you have so much to contend with. My mouth runs away with me occasionally.'

'No, it's perfectly all right. I'm just tired.'

'Of course. I'll go. But if there is anything, just let me know. If you need anyone to help in the shops, I know some very good boys.'

It took some effort for Mr Masoud to hesitate. 'That's extraordinarily kind of you. I know how busy you are, so it must have taken something to make the offer. It's all right, though. The family have all rallied round wonderfully.'

When Zaki had left Mr Masoud felt the rage bubbling still, bringing on his heartburn. 'Why has this man come here?' he said. 'With his stupid comments about this society and these people. These Westerners, he calls people here. But we're all Westerners. This is where we are, this is who we are. Does he just want to show how fortunate he is at my expense? I hardly know him.'

'He was only paying his respects,' replied his wife. 'It's normal. I don't like the man either. He's vain and he shows off. He has no modesty. But it was decent of him to pay a visit. It's what you would expect from an honourable man.'

'He is a man without honour or belief. But he is someone with an angle. Zaki Ibrahim always has an angle.'

7

'I don't know why you've dragged me down to London, Stuart,' said Jake's boss.

'George, you have to pull Jake Winter from the case. I'm taking heat from the Home Sec and from the police.'

'From the police? First I've heard.'

'Perhaps you're not speaking to the people who matter.'

'Possibly not. Do we really have to go through this again? The agent won't deal with anyone else, it's that simple. I've tested this extensively, believe me.'

'He'll have to deal with whoever we field, I'm afraid. I thought the first rule of this business was that until an asset had been handed on to another case officer they hadn't been fully recruited.'

'So did I. But we live in exceptional times.'

'I've no patience for the cult of the individual.'

'Nor have I. But Jake leaves the case and our boy walks away.'

'Walks straight into prison, you mean. Does not pass Go.'

'It's a risk he'd be prepared to take, I'm sure of it. He knows well enough.'

'How do you know?'

George looked wearily at Stuart Calloway. 'Because we conduct bloody due diligence. We watch the recordings of the meetings. We cross-question the case officers. We get the psychiatrist on the case. We read the tea leaves, we sacrifice goats to the god of true sources and we examine the entrails of especially prescient lizards for signs. Jake and Leila have been through this with the source several times, assiduously. The management team has looked at options. We're certain that we can't withdraw Jake. We can't afford to freak the guy out.'

'Couldn't Jake Winter fall ill? Break a leg, die even? These things happen.'

'If we told the source that, he'd probably still walk. That's what the psychologists say. He has a dependency that may not be healthy but is what it is. It's a fine balance. It's a tightrope we're walking anyway. After the station attack he's very twitchy.'

'Aren't we all? And if I insist?'

'You're not in a position to insist, Stuart. You can push it and you can have Jake's resignation and mine. I can't speak for the rest of the team.'

'There's no need to be melodramatic. This is a reasoned conversation between friends.'

'I'm not being melodramatic. I'm trying to give you a sense of the reality. We're in the middle of something quite dramatic in itself and none of us can afford to be drama queens. There's a lot at stake. What we need to do is to move forward slowly and carefully without distractions. If we lose this case now we lose sight of what this group is doing. If you want my view, which you probably don't, it's more than tenuous as things stand. It looks so much like the prelude to the station attack, and I sense the police are hanging on in there simply because we're so bullish and upbeat. And I'm not broadcasting the fact that Jake's involved.'

'All the more reason to get him out of there.'

George sighed. 'We've been through this, Stuart. I would if I could. My professional judgement is that we can't.'

'We need to bring this home. We're scrabbling for cred as we are. We need a success.'

'It needs to be brought home safely, though.'

'Of course safely. Of bloody course. Bloody hell, George, what do you think I am? We have the technical. And the data feeds are spectacular, from what I'm being told.'

'They'll only take us so far. There's nothing incriminating on the technical. Maybe minor offences, nothing that would attract custodial sentences. If we were to arrest at this moment all it'd do would be to alert them to our interest and stop them for a few months.'

'We need to do better than that.'

'Agreed. But we need more if we want to keep this running. The data sets tell us everything about the boys' normal lives but nothing at all about their secret plans and intentions. We can only be grateful that everything the source has told us that could be corroborated has been. I can't pretend that the police aren't nervous as hell about the bits that can't be verified. The really hairy stuff. As we stand, though, there'd be nothing on which to charge these boys apart from these trivial offences. Unless another of them apart from the source decides to turn, which is unlikely. As it is, his evidence on its own would be torn apart without corroboration. Especially after Abu Omar. The CPS think there's the faint possibility of conspiracy charges but they're not optimistic. They see everything, day by day. Everything depends on the agent.'

'Disruption? Not in favour at all at present, but how'd it look?'

'They'd be back, I'm sure. And sooner or later it'd all come out when they carried out their next outrage. We'd have endangered a source, we'd have screwed up a live terrorist investigation, and the conspirators would live to kill another day. You know how it would play. The spooks had a handle on these people and dropped the ball.'

'So we're agreed? Full speed ahead. Don't frighten the horses. Or the cops. Don't give them extra stuff to fret about.

And think again about bloody Jake. It's a complete hostage to fortune.'

'No, it isn't.'

'Do you trust him? After he bolloxed everything with Abu Omar?'

'Did he actually, Stuart? You're leaping to conclusions from circumstantial evidence. You're hearing the media reports and not the facts. Jake's playing the faithful soldier at the moment, at the inquiry, not telling any porkies but not volunteering any of the embarrassing detail.'

'For how long, though? I ask again. Do you trust him?'

'I do. And to answer your first question: for as long as nothing comes along to disrupt that highly attuned moral compass of his.'

'Is that supposed to be a warning to me?'

George sighed. 'Come on, Stuart. You're a big boy. You can deal with it. We've more substantial things to deal with than our egos.'

'The inquiry has been adjourned for a day. Legal wrangles, apparently.'

'That's the reason you called me down?'

'We've no idea what this is about. Our counsel and those for the survivors and the victims' families have been excluded. We're hearing that the Chair is in discussion with the counsel for the inquiry, but nothing more.'

'So?'

'So there's peril here. God knows what tomorrow will herald. They may bring out some dirt about Jake Winter. That's where the smart money is.'

'Should I warn him to be careful?'

'God, no. It was an inspired moment when the lawyers told us that anyone appearing at this thing should get their own personal legal advice.'

'You know how I felt about that.'

'Water under the bridge, George. It was correct, though, wasn't it, in hindsight? None of us could actually visualize a situation where the legal interests of the organization might diverge from those of the individual. This could be the moment.'

'We owe it to him to protect him.'

'Not if he's done something naughty that he hasn't told anyone about.'

'What makes you imagine he has?'

'Nothing at all. But there has to be some reason why they need this confab right in the middle of his evidence. Just be clear on this, George. If something appalling emerges tomorrow regarding Jake Winter, you will bring me his head on a platter by close of play. And we will deal with the consequences.'

'I'll make it easy for you. If that's what you want, you can have both our heads and I'll DHL them to you. Special delivery. But it won't come to that.'

'Won't it?'

The safe house was cold. Jake fiddled with the gas fire.

'So it's on,' said Leila.

'Home game against Real Madrid next Wednesday,' said Rashid.

He went through the details of the meeting.

'He said it was the last time you'd see him?'

'It may be.'

'How will you receive your final instructions? And the stuff he says he'll provide?'

Rashid shrugged. 'No idea. We'll find out next week, I suppose. He said he'd find some way of giving us things individually. He was hot on the security thing.'

'How would he do that? Use the messaging app?'

'How would I know?'

'The explosive devices. Any idea what they'll be? Belts, rucksacks?'

'Not a clue. I've told you everything he told us.'

'We're just trying to think this through. What about the things you have to obtain?'

'We're going to start on that straight away. Abdullah will be doing most of that. White face. We'll collect everything together at the room.'

'And what about Sunday?'

'He was clear we shouldn't have anything incriminating on us. No weapons, no documents, nothing. It's just a rehearsal.'

'Right. But we can't ignore what happened with Abu Omar.'

'I know. I was just thinking that.' He breathed deeply. 'Bloody hell. But from what he said I think he meant it.'

'This is where we need to be really careful,' said Jake.

'You're telling me.'

'I am,' said Jake.

'I'm not sure I'm up for this,' said Rashid.

'That's only to be expected,' said Leila. 'We've been through this.'

'Think about it, though,' said Jake. 'What options do we have?'

'I'm just saying, man,' said Rashid. 'I know where we are. I should have walked when the sheikh said.'

'Not sure that would have done any good,' said Jake. 'I don't think they'd have let you just walk.'

'I know. I'm just saying.'

'If it comes to the point, just speak to us. We need to work together. You can trust us on this. You can trust us on everything.'

Rashid simply looked at him.

'But will it work?'

'I think so,' she said. 'But no one can make any guarantees. If we're professional and work together, that increases the chances. Thing is, we don't have much time. We need to work out how the three of us get through the next few days, in practical terms. You want out, just say. At least we'd have clarity on one thing.'

'I'm so scared. I'm afraid I'll show it.'

'It's normal,' said Leila calmly. 'Think about it. You're on a suicide mission and everyone's blasé?'

'Adnan seems to be.'

'You're not Adnan. It's natural for you to be on edge. To put it mildly. And also to try to hide it from each other with varying degrees of success. They won't think anything of that. They'll be too busy thinking the same things about themselves.'

Rashid sighed. 'Yeah, I know. I guess.'

'We need to talk about contingencies,' said Jake. 'I don't mean to be harsh but we need to get this sorted. If it starts to go pear-shaped and we have no contingencies then we really are in trouble.'

'Contingencies?'

'Yes. If A happens, we do B. If on the other hand X happens, we do Y. We need to be clear and precise, and what we decide needs to be easy to remember and to do. Right?'

'Yeah. I guess so.'

'This is boring,' said Leila, 'but important. We need to agree some basics.'

'All right.'

'First point. If at any stage for any reason you need to step out of this, that needs to happen in the right way, so that you don't cause yourself any harm.'

'What reasons?'

'You tell me. If you genuinely think you've come under real

88

suspicion from the others, for starters,' said Jake. 'If you've been asked to do something you know you can't, legally or for other reasons. Or if it all gets on top of you and you genuinely can't cope. But you need to realize that this is a difficult thing to do, so you have to be certain you have no alternative. There's no way back afterwards. We can't predict every circumstance, and you'd have to be moving quickly. We can't design the perfect response for every situation. Much of it would be done on the hoof, in emergency mode.'

'So what do I do?'

'Make yourself safe first. Most of this is basic common sense but it bears saying. Don't say anything to the others, don't make it obvious you're getting out. Be as normal as you can in your demeanour. Disappear between meetings. Take yourself to somewhere they can't find you. Not home, not somewhere you usually go. Ditch your mobile.'

'Where should I go?' At times like these he seemed helpless, a child.

'I don't know. Think of somewhere. Go and have a look. Check it out. Then if you need to use it, give yourself ten minutes or so to clear your head. Make sure you're not followed. Then make your way to one of the safe places we've talked about. But only afterwards. You remember them?'

'The list. Yeah.'

'Remind yourself of them. Make sure they're engraved on your heart. Get yourself to the nearest one. There's a phone at each one. All you need to do is to switch it on and press the green button. We'll be there in a few minutes. If you really feel you're in imminent danger then make your way to the nearest police station. Report there and give them my number to call.'

'And they'll let me in?'

'They won't know who the hell you are. So you'll probably need to convince them that your life is in danger. Once they call the number we'll get things moving as quickly as possible. And as smoothly as possible.'

'What happens then?'

Jake looked at Leila before replying. 'Then you're safe. It's over. It's time to think of the rest of your life. It'll be messy, but it'll be all right.'

'It's going to come to that one day, though, isn't it? I'll have to leave my family behind. This place.'

'I think so,' said Jake. 'This is where we are. There's no going back and starting again.'

'We need to be ready for other things, too,' said Leila. 'Like if you're stopped by the police.'

'That's not going to happen, is it?' he said.

'I hope not. But we can't rule it out. For obvious reasons, we can't tell every single police officer in the country that you're working for us.'

'So what do I do?'

'You need to be completely compliant. You need to be polite and you need to do everything you're asked, instantly. This applies especially if the officer is armed. Don't resist and above all keep your hands away from your body and wide open.'

'This is getting serious, isn't it, man?'

'This is well past serious,' said Jake. 'But it'll be all right. Trust us.'

Rashid understood now, with the full force of a jolt in the stomach, what his future, in this next week, held. He'd known, in a way, before, but now it became real. The hours of planning with the other boys. The walk to the stadium, rucksack on back. The inchoate sense of being followed, with the concrete knowledge that somewhere behind him they were indeed following him. The shouted challenge. The gun pointed at his head. The panicked expression of the officer in his plain clothes and baseball cap or beanie with POLICE in big letters – he'd seen all the TV series and the films. After that, what?

Rashid had been delivered home and they were back in the office.

George had returned from London and dropped by, leaning on the door jamb and looking distracted.

'So it's all go for next week.'

'Looks like it,' said Jake. 'We'll see. That's our aiming point.'

'The police know?'

'I've done a verbal briefing of the SIO. We're writing up the report.'

'Action stations, then. They'll call an immediate ELG.'

'Yeah. Everything'll ratchet up.'

'The ELG will need to consider the risks again.'

'Losing the faith, George? Or is Stuart?'

'No. Stuart's as keen as ever. Sees the possibility of redemption.'

'But?'

'It's easy for him to say.'

'He deals with the consequences too.'

'I know. But at one remove. I'm not sure about this at all.'

'None of us is. Is this about me again?'

'It's the whole thing, Jake.'

'How many bloody times do we have to go through this, George? I made my mistake. I'm not going to mess up again.'

'Jake,' said Leila.

'I know, I know. I'm not normally like this, blah-di-blah. Sorry.'

'It's understandable,' said George.

'Bloody unlike me, though. That what you were going to say?'

'Something like that.'

'Well, thanks. Perhaps this is the new me. Yes, in answer to the question you can't bring yourself to ask: yes, I feel the pressure. Yes, I can hack it. Could do without you on my back, though. Or the inquiry. At least I should get shot of that tomorrow, my brief says. Was supposed to be there today but I was stood down. No idea what that's all about.'

'I heard.'

'Just as well, given where we are. How was London?'

'Still there. Trains were murder.'

'Good meetings?'

'You know. All right, I suppose. It's a pain having to go down there.'

'Yeah.'

'Hope it is all done and dusted tomorrow,' said George. 'I need to get ready for the ELG. Be careful, won't you?' He was gone, pulling the door to as he took to the corridor.

Jake raised his eyebrows and Leila did the same in reply. 'Pillock,' he said.

'Where were we?' she said.

'The coverage.'

'Right. The technical corroborates what he said. Or at least it doesn't contradict it. They returned to their venue for a quick chat and then went about their normal daily business. Nothing out of the ordinary according to the surveillance.'

'I guess they'll want to up the surveillance now. Double shifts, no time off. Anything from their computer?'

'No. Just stuff from the sites they've been visiting. Beheadings, haranguings, masked guys waving guns; haranguings followed by masked guys waving guns followed by beheadings. Highly professional, highly compelling, can't take your eyes off it.'

'These people know what they're doing,' said Jake. 'Terrifying.'

'Yeah. Anyway, there's nothing specific to these boys.'

'Messaging?'

'Still can't get in. Rashid's still letting us know the messages he's receiving – so far as we know – but no clue about the others. We can track the volume, and there haven't been any blips. Just the two or three each month, not sure of where exactly they're emanating from, but it seems to be overseas. Nothing to suggest any of the others is receiving more or fewer than Rashid. The van . . .'

'Yes?'

'The registration number Rashid gave us leads nowhere.'

'Did he get it wrong?'

'I don't think so. We've tried all the permutations and variations. I think your man must be alive to the risks and have stuck on false plates just before the boys got in.'

'Nothing on number plate recognition?'

'Nothing. Except, that is, six hundred and thirty-seven white vans circulating in the city between five in the morning and nine thirty. They're still looking but it's needle-in-the-haystack type stuff.'

'Six hundred and thirty-seven.'

'This is a city of three million. What can I say?'

'Anything else?'

'Not that I can think of. Do we trust him?'

'Don't you have to get off?'

'What?'

'Pick Anoushka up from the childminder?'

'God, yes. Thanks. I'd forgotten what day it was. I thought it was Robbie today.'

'It's Wednesday. Isn't he Monday, Thursday and Friday?'

'Cheers. Thanks for reminding me.'

That was the more normal Jake: considerate yet distant. She pushed the chair back and made to go. As she did so she asked again, 'Do we trust Rashid?'

'That's the question, isn't it? And the answer is, of course not. We listen to what he says and correlate, triangulate. We take what he says seriously and test it. If there's a pattern of reliability, it gives us a presumption of confidence. A working hypothesis. But that has to be tested continuously, and we need to have things in place in case he's lying. Source handling 101, if you like.'

'But what do you think?'

'What I think doesn't matter. We behave as if we don't think anything. We're completely neutral. We respond to facts and events.'

'Yes, but what *do* you think?'

'What do you think?'

'I believe him, I think.'

'Yes, well, he is very convincing, isn't he?'

8

THURSDAY

This time, the meeting was formal, like all the weekly counterterrorist briefings that Stuart Calloway was required to attend as Director Ops, in the Home Secretary's office and recorded on a steno pad by a civil servant who would convert his shorthand into a minute of the meeting, crafted of gilded prose, to be circulated by midday.

Stuart waited in the outer office until it was time to enter the presence. The Commissioner was not yet here. Must be running late. This was bad form indeed and privately he hoped that the Home Sec would derive a subliminal message from it. It was all very well the boss and Stuart's underlings chanting the mantra that they and the police were joined at the hip on all matters. He, on the contrary, was alive to the realpolitik of the situation. He had perhaps to be more sly than if it were a matter of open warfare, but there were many ways of skinning the particular cat of sharp elbows with the Met, he thought, furiously mixing the mental metaphors. Faint praise and feigned puzzlement were always useful tools to have in the armoury. However cheery relations were at present, it would always do to be operating at a slight advantage, to be pressed home as necessary should things become more strained. So sod the boss, with his messages of unalloyed sweetness and light. Stuart took it upon himself to paint in the contextual shadows.

95

When the young bespectacled Private Secretary opened the door from the office, he had his opening gambit prepared for the few minutes before the Commissioner arrived. The police, he'd say, were extraordinarily adept at their particular business of catching criminals and prosecuting them, as well, of course, as protecting the public. Extraordinarily, that is, notwithstanding recent events. Yet were they quite so highly attuned to political risk and, more to the point, opportunity? Small 'p', naturally: those risks that threatened the futures of the agencies involved in these joint enterprises and the careers of their principals. Including Chief Constables, the Commissioner and, of course, himself. Not, in the main, ministers. Should, indeed, the police's lives be cluttered by such considerations? Nevertheless, someone, somehow, had to take a wider view. It sounded hollow in his head, for ministers would hardly be concerned at the best of times for the welfare of functionaries, and there was clear benefit now to be derived from the spooks taking the sins of all-comers on to their shoulders. The Home Secretary would need to be braced up by something different: existential personal peril.

He gave his best, most winning smile as he entered, only to find the Commissioner already sitting at the conference table.

'We had other business, Stuart,' said the Home Secretary, not looking up from the pieces of paper on the table, by way of welcome, introduction and explanation.

'Of course,' he said, the smile intact, and sat down in the seat the Commissioner slid back for him. They murmured hellos.

'Now,' said the Home Secretary, 'I understand you wish to update me on this operation.'

'Thank you, Home Secretary. Though the Commissioner will undoubtedly also be able to add value. After all, when it comes to it, it will be a police matter. In the best possible way, we hope.' He smiled, and bowed slightly at the Commissioner as if to signal deference.

'Fire away.'

'The intelligence indicates that an attack is imminent. It's due to take place in six days' time, next Wednesday.'

'It's the big Champions League game against Real Madrid that evening,' explained the Commissioner.

'The plan is to mount the attack at the end of the game, outside the ground, as the crowd is leaving,' said Stuart.

'I see,' said the Home Secretary. 'So you're making plans to deal with it.'

'That's right. We have continuing good access to intelligence on the attack planning, and the police should be well placed as things stand to time their interventions.'

'But?'

'Pardon?'

'I sense a but, Stuart.'

'No. No buts. You will wish to be aware, however, that this operation does not come without risks.'

'Do they ever?'

The Commissioner and Stuart both smiled.

'Well then?' said the Home Secretary.

'You know the basic story?'

'I believe I can retain these things in my mind, yes. And Angus keeps comprehensive notes.'

'You will understand, then, that this scenario has more than a passing resemblance to the events of last December. Not merely that these events are being enacted in the same city.'

'Carry on.'

The Commissioner said, 'Down to the fact that a rehearsal is planned before the attack proper.'

'That sounds fairly uncomfortable for you. And you have an asset in the centre of this, Stuart?'

'Indeed. But this situation is rather different.'

'Your business entirely. But out of curiosity . . . ?'

'We have developed several strands of reporting, all of which are being fed direct to the police. And I have to say that our pivotal source is very firmly established and stable.'

'Where have I heard that before? Your judgement, of course. Go on.'

'There are, as ever, risks and benefits to be weighed and fine judgement calls to be made. There are the obvious concerns about the previous incident and not least the optics should things not go well this time round.'

'The *optics*?'

'And the reality of course,' said the Commissioner. 'The Chief Constable up there is very conscious of the need to protect public safety.'

'I bet he is. How long's he been in post now?'

'Two months. Bob's sound. I've talked it through with him and for the moment he's content.'

'For the moment.'

'For the moment he's prepared to let this run. All we have at present are the alleged conspirators' reported words. We have little that would constitute compelling evidence. It's even possible that it's all empty aspirational rhetoric.'

'But unlikely,' Stuart said.

'As things develop we'll be looking to intervene as soon as public safety becomes an issue.'

Stuart said, 'I agree with everything the Commissioner has said. The converse is, of course, that if intervention were precipitate and premature we'd have wasted an opportunity and there could be media blowback. The bottom line is that we have the potential for a real success that would place the station incident, with all its tragic consequences, in its correct perspective.'

The Commissioner looked at him.

'So it's all under control? Is that what I'm hearing?' asked the Home Secretary, looking from Stuart to the Commissioner and back again.

'Yes,' said the Commissioner.

'More or less,' said Stuart and beamed.

'So? Are you looking to me for a pat on the head? A gold star?'

'No,' said Stuart.

'Or, more to the point, some endorsement? Are you reinsuring, Stuart? A little bit of an each-way bet, is it?'

'Certainly not.'

'But a problem shared, eh? Let's be clear. The decisions are for you to make based on your knowledge, expert skills and experience. I don't know enough of the detail. And anyway, it'd be inappropriate for me to interfere with your operational judgements.'

Stuart smiled. 'We felt it prudent to alert you to the political risks.'

'How considerate. There's no need to be so concerned about me, Stuart. I can look after myself. Things will fall as they fall. As I may have said to you on more than one occasion in the past. Focus on the operational judgements you have to reach, and what will be will be. The division of responsibilities between the three of us is perfectly clear. I have every confidence in you. Well, you evidently both have a lot to think about. You'd better get on with it. By the way – not for the notes, Angus, so you can put your pen down, please – I'm reliably informed that the counsel for the inquiry plans to drop a little hand grenade today.'

'Really?' said Stuart, with apparent insouciance.

'Something to do with the American dimension.'

Stuart looked alarmed and glanced at his watch before standing. 'How on earth do they know about that?'

'I really can't imagine,' said the Home Secretary. 'Still, it might help clear the air a bit, mightn't it? And I shouldn't bother rushing, Stuart. I'd imagine the inquiry's in session by now.'

'Did you really have to, Stuart?' said the Commissioner as they left the building.

'What do you mean?'

'The *optics*. The *correct perspective*. Give me strength.'

'Mr Kerr yesterday was pressing you over whether you felt contrition and remorse,' said Ms Jarvis, the counsel for the inquiry. 'Did you feel that to be unfair?'

'Not at all,' said Jake dully. 'I may have been unable to describe my feelings adequately.'

'These proceedings are not conducted for your benefit, a fact of which I'm sure you're aware.'

'Yes, I am. Anything I can do to help I will try to do.'

'Good. There were, however, areas you were reluctant to go into.'

'There were things that I'd been advised I wasn't at liberty to discuss. That was all, not reluctance.'

'Then to whom should this inquiry go to probe these matters?'

'I don't know.'

'You'll see our difficulty. The government has promised this inquiry free rein to investigate what it needs to; to go where it needs to.'

'Was there not a reference to aspects that could cause damage to national security?'

'Indeed. Well spotted.'

'Presumably there are agreed methods of pursuing those aspects?'

'There are. Yes,' the counsel agreed. 'Where there are matters of genuine security concern . . .'

She paused, before looking at Jake again.

'It won't surprise you to learn that we spent some of yesterday considering this.'

'I had no idea what you were considering.'

'We were considering what might constitute damage to national security. We thought we might consult the counsel for your employers.'

Jake looked blankly at her.

'But in the end we decided we shouldn't.'

'I don't really see –'

'I'm simply trying to explain our thinking processes to you, the interested parties and their representatives.'

The counsel for the Service stood.

'Now, would you like to tell us all about the Americans?' asked Ms Jarvis with a smile.

The Service's counsel sat down.

'The Americans,' said Jake. He recalled the conversations in the office.

Under no circumstances mention the Americans.

And if I'm asked?

You won't be.

But if I am, I'm not going to lie. I'll tell it as it was.

Feel free. But it's a hypothetical question.

'That's right. Take your time.'

'I'm not sure I –'

'We've taken external legal advice,' said Ms Jarvis, 'and reached the judgement that these are legitimate questions.'

The counsel for the Service stood and said, 'I wouldn't wish to interrupt proceedings, but if it would please the Chair . . .'

Ms Jarvis sat.

'. . . I would at this point like to question relevance.'

The Chair looked at him. 'Relevance? It's not a question of damage for you?'

'Not at this stage. We would not wish to convey the impression of being obstructive or to use the concept of national security as a catch-all to prevent areas being explored. Nevertheless, we would wish to pose the question whether this is germane to this inquiry's remits. Whether this will actually assist the process of discovering the reasons for this tragedy and what needs to be put right. Perhaps a brief discussion of the issues between counsel?'

'Thank you,' said the Chair. 'I'm grateful for your desire to expedite matters. As the counsel for the inquiry indicates, we've considered this question at length. We'd thought it possible you might raise objections for reasons of national security. We had reached the preliminary conclusion that such objections would be valid only if there was the potential for sensitive techniques, sources or relationships to become public in a manner that damaged security. We'd have wished to test your representations, of course. We'd already concluded, for instance, that the intelligence relationship with the United States is so widely known that its mere mention could hardly fall into this category. So your statement clarifies and confirms this helpfully.'

The counsel nodded. His assistant scrabbled through his papers.

The Chair continued. 'So far as relevance is concerned, I rather think the point is that the relevance of this line of questioning will be determined once it is exhausted. I remind you that this is not a court of law and that our primary concern must be for the positions of the families and survivors and the future assurance of public safety. I'm content to allow a certain latitude. It may reassure you that we will not be inviting questions to this witness on this matter from the other interested parties, so as to minimize the risks to national security.'

Ms Jarvis stood again. 'The Americans, then.'

'Yes,' said Jake. 'The Americans. May I say one thing?'

'Yes.' She looked at him suspiciously.

'I'm glad that this has come up. It's right. I wasn't expecting it to, however, so I may not have the full detail in my mind. That's not being evasive, I simply may not remember.'

'We'll see about that. Was it the Americans who introduced you to Abu Omar?'

'Yes.'

'This was when?'

'About ten months ago now. About six months before the attack. I can't recall the precise date.'

'In what circumstances?'

'Sometime before that, the London representatives of our US counterparts came to see my superiors. I wasn't present at the meeting. It was written up at the time, though.'

'I don't think we have any papers relating to this in our packs.'

The Service's counsel stood up. 'We'll put that right. An error of omission.'

'Now then,' said Ms Jarvis. 'You're saying that about ten months ago your American counterparts introduced the notion of bringing Abu Omar to the UK.'

'That's right.'

'And how had they come across him?'

'I gathered that they came across him on the battlefield. He was captured as a prisoner while fighting for IS.'

'What happened then?'

'He was in detention in the field for some time and when he was interrogated he apparently agreed to assist them.'

'I see. And what did he offer?'

'He was an English boy. He said he was about to be tasked to come to England as part of a terrorist team.'

'And what did they do to elicit this "offer"?'

'What do you mean?'

103

'Did they mistreat him?'

'No. They said not. They provided written assurances that they'd treated him kindly and well within the bounds of the Geneva Convention, and that he'd volunteered his services. When I first met him I asked him directly about this and he confirmed that.'

'With his handlers present?'

'Yes, the first time. But later, when I saw him on his own, I probed some more.'

'You asked him directly?'

'The circumstances weren't like that. We were building up to the event itself, and there was no way I could conduct a formal interview.'

'But you were happy with the Americans' assurances.'

'They were what they were. What with speaking to Abu Omar I felt I'd done all I could. I felt as satisfied as I could be that he'd suffered no maltreatment.'

'But not one hundred per cent convinced, by the sound of it.'

'One hundred per cent assurance is never entirely possible if you haven't been there every step of the way.'

'That doesn't sound at all definitive. Or reassuring. We'll leave that to one side, however. We will return to it later. Abu Omar comes over to the UK. Was he handed over to you?'

'Yes. I took control of his handling while in the UK. I met him with my American colleagues for some time and then it was decided that I should meet him solo.'

'Decided on what basis, and by whom?'

'I'm not quite sure on either score. I was told the Americans would no longer be attending meetings. I took it to be because we were nearing the moment of executive action.'

'When would this have been?'

'About a month or two before the attack.'

'So they were involved at least part of the way through Abu Omar's presence in the UK?'

'That's right. Though they kept clear of our operational planning and the policies.'

'They would do. When exactly did the specific notion of the attack come up?'

'When he first came back to the UK. It was the reason he was sent to the UK.'

'According to the Americans?'

'According to them, and according to him too.'

'Did you ever wonder why he was speaking to you?'

'Yes, all the time. As one does.'

'And what were your conclusions?'

'People have all kinds of reasons for doing things. Often contradictory, often a close call between a number of things. I wouldn't like to single anything out.'

'Well, can you itemize one or two things for us?'

'I can. But it's essentially speculation.'

'Or the professional judgement of the person handling him?'

'There was a maelstrom of things affecting Abu Omar. One of the factors was that he felt battered by all these things coming from all directions. The Americans had offered him a way out. They'd also probably saved his life. He would have been fearful of a long prison term. He may have liked them. He may have understood that what he was doing out there wasn't what he'd imagined, or what he wanted to do. He may have wanted to come back to the UK. He had a little son here, in the city. There are undoubtedly other things that I haven't remembered or that didn't even occur to me at the time.'

'You said that he may have liked the Americans. Was that the impression you had?'

'Not especially. I tried to build a rapport with him. I don't think they made a particular effort. It was rather more transactional.'

'Transactional.'

'Yes. It's not a critical comment. My approach is to try to build some kind of rapport, a personal trust of some kind. I find it helpful. But we all use the same techniques of validation and verification.'

'Did you feel that what Abu Omar said was sufficiently validated and verified?'

'It's easy to conclude in hindsight that it wasn't. But remember that we still don't know, and may never know, the precise circumstances of those final minutes. Abu Omar may have been a victim like the others.'

'Not quite like the others. The others weren't carrying a rucksack full of high explosive.'

'True. You're right. But he may have been placed in an impossible position.'

'What's your gut feeling on that?'

'I don't have one. I'm not sure gut feelings help. Some things point to him having acted in bad faith. Once he'd been given the other rucksack, for instance, he could simply have stopped there and then and contacted me. But I don't know the duress he was under at the time.'

'How were your relations with the Americans?'

'Professional.'

'Professional. Not warm, or amicable, or friendly?'

'Professional is surely best. It's immaterial whether we're best buddies or not.'

'Unless you want someone to go the extra mile.'

'That's a matter of opinion. I've always found that pride in one's work is a better driver than friendship.'

'Who, then, was running this operation? Was it you, or the Americans?'

'It was definitely under our control. We are accountable for its outcomes, not them. If the implication of the question is that the Americans were pulling our strings, that's not accurate.'

'It wasn't. I think we will return to this in the next session. May I remind you that in the interim you should not confer with others on the evidence you have given or will be giving later.'

'I can give you my assurance on that,' said Jake.

'We shall adjourn until Monday,' said the Chair.

9

As soon as Jake Winter left the inquiry room and was changing into his jeans in the small room set aside for those anonymized, alphabetized witnesses, his mind turned to the unseasonably warm spring day almost a year before when he'd been called down to London. Bloody London, as it was known in the office. Not to Jake Winter. Though he was glad to be working in his unprepossessing northern hometown, with its familiar grey terraces and grey skies, he was always happy to go down to bloody London. Besides, he'd been rather chuffed to be selected for this 'special task'. Before, that is, he found out what it entailed.

The air conditioning had been down in the knackered old train that dragged itself the length of the country into King's Cross and he'd sat primly in the tut-tutting, whingeing hubbub and the can-strewn detritus of those who'd thought that knocking back a few lagers on the ten o'clock train was the remedy to it all. But he'd been happy enough, with a juicy bit of casework in the offing.

He'd been placed in a holding pattern in the anteroom to Stuart Calloway's office before being wheeled in, the bashful young operative come blinking from the sticks. Stuart was all affability and mid-Atlantic tonality, with the uplift at the end of the sentence and the insistence on naming the person towards whom he was directing his remarks at the end of each utterance. Frank and Jimmy, Jake's two new oppos, had deferred to the big beasts, Stuart and his US counterpart, as they shared gossip of London and Washington and insincere smiles over the rack of lamb and the Gigondas in the executive dining room. Jake had followed suit.

'This is gonna be so big,' Stuart had said, with considerable if unintended foresight. 'You'll wanna see the whites of this guy's eyes,' he drawled alarmingly at the end of the meal. 'Run along now, do your worst.'

Abu Omar was waiting in a safe house with a babysitter.

It was a done deal already, George had made clear. 'Bought sight unseen, "no sale" an impossibility, caveat emptor, no return to sender. Pig in a poke for all I know. Stuart tells me we're in desperate need of brownie points at Langley.'

Abu Omar proved not quite as disappointing as Jake feared. The sullenness was to be anticipated but the spark of connection – meeting a countryman, a native of the same town, and not another bull-necked, bullying American – seemed to fire momentarily. They chatted over a cup of tea about nothing in particular, each sizing the other up, while Frank and Jimmy chafed to, as they put it, 'get down to business'. This *is* business, Jake wanted to say, but didn't waste his breath.

Over dinner that evening, Frank and Jimmy set out their prospectus for the future. They began with a stock preamble. Notionally based at HQ in DC, they'd done their stints in Gitmo, Abu Ghraib and Afghanistan, but were now essentially roving reporters on the international terrorist threat. Jake muttered the obligatory polite words of awed respect. Frank and Jimmy said they were on TDY in the UK for as long as this little thing took. Alphabetti spaghetti: the curse of the spooks.

They'd cavilled at everything. This, too, was normal. It didn't matter especially, at that point. Jake was used to it; there were always – almost – ways to iron things out along the way without having a fight. Abu Omar had sorted out his own accommodation, it turned out, before returning to the UK. There was no possibility of establishing the parameters of where he might live. Special security procedures had to be instituted at the safe house on which they finally agreed in the rural outreaches of the city to make it impossible for him to blow up his US case officers. Frank and Jimmy were unhappy at living in what they'd been led to believe was a war zone so were chauffeured up the M1 twice a week for meetings and straight back to London afterwards.

The arrangements and conditions for crash meetings took days of negotiation. They arm-wrestled over the presence of a second British case officer, especially after they learned that George had selected Leila.

'No issue with a woman or a Muslim per se,' Frank had said. 'But we gotta consider the impact on our friend. No way is he gonna accept this.'

This was remitted to Stuart, who overruled George. 'I bow to no one in my insistence on inclusion,' he said, 'but I don't believe in tokenism.'

The legal niceties were a bore.

Niceties! thought Jake: those things that Frank and Jimmy considered indicative of British prissiness. He had spent a wearisome afternoon, together with George and a legal adviser, with them plus their two attorneys in a stiflingly warm, windowless conference room in Head Office.

What had been Abu Omar's role in the battlefield?
Enemy combatant.
What did that entail?
Why, fighting.
Yes, but in what capacity?
Soldier.

OK, but a soldier in line with the Geneva Convention or a soldier committing acts that might be construed as war crimes?

The former.

You've established that beyond reasonable doubt?

Check.

How?

We asked the guy.

No further corroboration?

You try collecting evidence out there. No, we polygraphed the guy and he came through.

With flying colours?

He passed.

'Anyway,' the Americans had asked, 'you seen any evidence to the contrary? Far as we knew, the burden of proof is to establish guilt beyond reasonable doubt, not the other way round. You seen anything in all those thousands of beheading videos, for instance, to suggest our boy took part?'

The legal adviser had shaken his head.

'This is crucial,' George had said. 'We're going to have to talk to the boy himself about this. It's a minimum requirement.'

'We'd advise against that,' they'd replied. 'Disruptive. What's he gonna say?'

They'd gone ahead anyway, Frank and Jimmy sitting in the corner of the room just about keeping the smirks from their faces as Abu Omar gave the anodyne denials he'd clearly rehearsed.

The dry issue of control and governance was left to ripen and rot after the Americans' opening shot: a fourteen-page memorandum of understanding giving them decision rights in the case. Jake was told that Stuart didn't want to have an open disagreement with them at such a delicate point in relations and that Legal would work on this quietly behind the scenes. It seemed they never did; the MoU was never signed. When Jake asked Frank and Jimmy, they were amused. 'Hell, never figured you for a bureaucrat,' said Frank, and he and Jimmy laughed. That had been an end to it.

After four weeks Abu Omar moved into the flat he shared with his four associates. Abu Omar said they claimed to be asylum seekers from North Africa but nowhere could they be located in official records. The flat was in a block where surveillance could not easily deploy. The four, who Abu Omar said called themselves Salman, Jamal, Abid and Hassan, were to be his co-conspirators in whatever was planned. Equally evident was that Jake, Frank and Jimmy were entirely dependent on Abu Omar for all their information regarding the as yet unspecified plot.

For the first three months there was little reporting other than that the five of them prayed together and slept long hours in the flat as a long, hot, somnolent summer stretched towards September. Abu Omar had still not been able to provide sufficient descriptions of the others for surveillance to identify and follow them. He claimed that they lived off benefits, just as he did, but was unable to identify how, when or where they received them. Jake suggested he might generate an opportunity to go through the belongings of the others.

'If they're out, then,' he said, 'you could risk a discreet look. Have a cover story ready. We can talk through possibilities. They must have something. Bank cards, social security papers, travel documents, phone contracts, something. Anything.'

'They're never all out at the same time,' said Abu Omar, blinking slowly and turning his hooded eyes to Jake.

'Are you not trusted by them?'

'I'm trusted,' he said indignantly. 'We fought together.'

'But you know nothing about them?'

'You don't need to know anything when you're in the battlefield, fighting for each other.'

Jimmy nodded in sage confirmation.

Thirteen weeks in, Abu Omar volunteered, 'There's this guy who'll provide the necessary when it comes to it, says Jamal. Jamal's gofer, he calls him.'

'Who is he?'

'Never met him.'

They'd always been playing catch-up, that's just how it was with Abu Omar. The tantalizing lead, without the possibility of corroboration, then the race to see what it meant. Jamal's gofer, whoever the hell he was. The numerous meetings in places that sounded wholly convincing yet could never be found. The cars for which Abu Omar could provide no colour, marque or other identifying detail. 'It was dark, man, how the hell do I know what make it was? It was, like, normal size and the dashboard lights were blue. Or maybe white. I'm not interested in cars, man.'

Were there echoes now, thin and faint or booming and ominous, with Rashid? No, thought Jake, but he wasn't certain. He placed little stock on certainty generally, but a little of it wouldn't have gone amiss just at the moment.

Frank and Jimmy's immediate boss, Tom, a tall, straight-backed linebacker of a Texan with the blue-eyed certainty of the true believer, came to visit. Whether it was to rally the troops and raise morale, an exercise in intelligence tourism, or the chance for a spot of light Christmas shopping in Bond Street wasn't clear. Certainly it was to take his measure of Jake and George. He described himself as a great friend of Stuart's; whether this was a warning or he thought it would serve as a character reference was equally opaque.

'How's our boy doing?' he asked.

'He's OK,' said George.

'OK? That the best we can do, guys?' He directed his question at Frank and Jimmy. They looked at each other. 'Or maybe this is your great British understatement.'

George smiled.

'It'll be fine,' said Jake. 'He's great. We need to get things moving. That's maybe all.'

'This guy's a one-off,' said Tom. 'He doesn't show it but he has cojones. Like all you English. You need to get to the beat of his heart is all. Frank'll tell you that.' Frank nodded. 'Once you do, it all comes together.'

'They're all one-offs, of course. By definition,' said George.

'Hell, you're right, George.'

Jake said, 'The current reporting about IS identifying informants among foreign fighters with unexplained absences from the battlefield. Do we need to worry about that?'

'I saw that,' said Tom. 'Good point, Jake. Kind of thing circulates all the time. They push this stuff out. We took good care of this boy. And he's got a head on his shoulders. Anyway, unexplained absences. It's chaos out there. On their side everything is unexplained. He was out of the field maybe a week. Frank?'

'This was how we worked it,' said Frank. 'He was captured in battle. No one else saw it, no one else saw him in captivity. We're certain. He was taken in for assessment and singled out as of potential use. He begged to work for us. He'd had enough. Jimmy and I looked him over, liked the goods. Decided we'd give it a roll of the dice. Some work, some don't. This guy did. We gave him a wound to take back, and a cover story. And we hit pay dirt. They'd have executed him there and then if they didn't trust him. We know what we're doing. You got an issue with that?'

'Not really,' said Jake mildly. 'It's useful to know.'

A table was booked at Two Rivers, the two-Michelin-starred restaurant in the five-star hotel where Tom was staying, and they arranged to meet for drinks at seven.

'This is how it'll play. Frank and Jimmy won't be there,' said George beforehand, once they'd got back to the office. 'They'll turn up later. He'll want twenty-five minutes to size you up on his own. I'll cry off too, so he can get his money's worth. You be OK with the big white shark?'

'I think I can cope.'

Over vodka and tonics Jake said, 'We could have done the tour of the local curry houses, lovely though this is. Still could, if you like.'

'Great idea,' said Tom. 'But I don't think my friends would agree.' He arched an eyebrow towards the minders posted near the door, as close to a public announcement as could be imagined that their principal was of interest. 'They tell me I'm a marked man,' he chuckled. 'Something to do with being antsy with a bunch of terrorist hoodlums. Now, let's get to talking before Frank and Jimmy arrive.'

Jake looked at him.

'You Brits know this espionage business. Didn't you invent it? Frank and Jimmy, great guys but they're kinda . . . linear. They don't have that rat cunning you guys have. That guile.'

'I'm utterly without guile myself,' said Jake seriously.

Tom grinned. 'You bet. You have to say that with a straight face. I love it. These guys, though, are straight up and down. They're my guys, which is the most important thing, and I look after them good.'

'OK.'

'We want this to succeed. We want it real bad. We've worked hard on this asset and it's great to see us working together on it. Sends the right message up the chain. A lot at stake. Both sides of the Atlantic. Know what I mean? How do you see it working through?'

'Depends. We're working on the assumption that sooner or later he's going to be asked to be involved in an attack, right?'

'Hell yes.'

'And our aim is to prevent the attack and prosecute the others involved. As many of them as we can get evidence against.'

'Prosecute the shit out of them, yeah.'

'Then gather up as much intelligence as we can to lead back to the people that are directing this stuff, so that we can do something about them.'

'Check.'

'Then you need to think carefully about evidence. Unless you want Frank and Jimmy testifying?'

'Hell no.'

'Here, if a piece of information exists, and is relevant, it's evidence. The days when we could put the fix in and make ourselves disappear are long gone. Long before my time. I doubt they ever existed. It comes down to relevance, and you don't need to hire an expensive lawyer to realize that you guys may well already have relevant things to say. They could be central. I'm certainly expecting to be called myself.'

'I see,' said Tom and became momentarily quiet, before grinning. 'You know, that's the exact same thing George said. You just trying to talk our guys out of the case, Jake?' Tom laughed.

'I told you I was utterly guileless, Tom. Why would I want that?'

'Nice work. I like it. You guys are a class act.'

Jake shrugged. 'I did at least try. Apart from that, I'm just worried about our friend. This bearded man, for instance. I'm not sure he exists. He may be inventing him for some purpose.'

'What purpose?'

'I don't know. I'm paid to be sceptical and suspicious. I doubt everything I'm told until I can verify it.'

'Good policy.'

'It means I worry about getting things right.'

Tom sipped from his drink and leaned back into the black leather. 'I like you, Jake,' he said. 'What's your background?'

Tom and his people would have gone through his bio with a fine-tooth comb. 'I was born in New Zealand. English mother, Kiwi father.'

'Wow. Ain't that great? All Blacks? Rugby? I love that game.'

'I like rugby, yeah.'

'The haka. Those Maori guys.'

'That's right.'

'And you grew up there?'

'Came to England when I was six.'

'Why's that? Family break-up?'

'No. We all came over. Two reasons: money and family. My mum and dad could earn more here, and my mum's parents were ill.'

'What did your pa do?'

'Does. He's still working. He's a bus driver.'

'OK.' Tom had done his due diligence, checking Jake's answers for veracity against his database. The American version of guile. 'Hey, here come the guys now.'

The case began to rumble a little. Mysteriously, the famous five began to be gingered up in preparation for the deed. The gofer perhaps wasn't a gofer but someone more significant. 'Beard. Guy wears traditional gear. Salwar kameez,' said Abu

Omar. He was taken through books of photographs but could not place any of the men as this gofer.

It was at this point that, abruptly, Frank and Jimmy excused themselves from future meetings. Though they didn't say so, and Jake didn't ask, the fear of British courts must have percolated through the system and done for them.

'Hey, we got, like, total confidence in you, man,' said Jimmy laconically. 'We're just figuring four's a crowd as we approach the finish line. We'll compare notes after meetings.'

Was this the beginning of Jake's disillusionment? Not by a long chalk, but beginning, middle or end: what did it matter? He was becoming a different person, and one he didn't like.

The meetings, already captured by the four cameras in the safe-house room, had been beamed down, encrypted, to a secure room in the US Embassy where Frank and Jimmy could share a bucket of popcorn and a gallon of Coke while they watched. After each meeting the handlers would discuss what had gone on and any next steps.

There was talk of the boys travelling to London to attack the transport system. For reasons that were difficult to grasp, the idea died a death over a period of two weeks. Abu Omar made vague references to the difficulties of the logistics, and observed that there were plenty of jihadis down there already.

The analysts tried to stitch together an overall picture of what was going on. Was there some kind of strategic purpose to the stateliness with which Abu Omar and the others seemed to approach their life's calling? Or was it simply that there was no brain behind this: these men had just been sent to do whatever they could, whenever they felt like it? Against this was the presence of the other man, the bearded robe-wearer who might be a gofer or a director.

The debate, in meetings and in papers, which attempted to extract all the meaning and more from the paltry pieces of information available, and sew together the rudimentary fabric of a narrative, came to no conclusions. Some of the meetings involved the Americans, some didn't. Their message was that this would take time and everyone should just chill until the time comes.

'All good things come to those who wait,' said Frank to a frosty reception at one meeting.

'It's not you Americans who are at risk,' said one of the less house-trained police analysts. 'We should pull the plug.'

Cue a little frenzy, kept invisible to the transatlantic partners, between Stuart and the police. A conference took place in London at the end of October, during which the American view prevailed. 'We've got an opportunity to deliver a real blow, to undermine their confidence, to stop a huge thing in the making in your country, to strike at the heart of these people and tell them they can't operate with impunity in our free democracies,' said Tom, who'd travelled over, as Jake suppressed a yawn. 'The President would be upset if we missed this chance. Your call, guys, though. Of course.'

Eventually, the plot started to thicken, to a consistency that resembled something that might actually take place. The idea of mounting an attack in London was refined to an explosion at a transport hub in the city. This meant, effectively, the mainline railway station, the bus station or the tram and bus interchange.

Salman was spotted one day leaving the tower block on his own and identified as an Algerian who'd been living in the city for four years, not a veteran of the conflict. Frank and Jimmy's view that Abu Omar shouldn't be challenged about this prevailed over Jake's, for the moment. They argued that Abu Omar shouldn't be unduly perturbed by trip-hazard trivial questioning of his motives. He might walk. From the identification of

Salman it was a short step to finding the others too: children of immigrants who'd been born in the UK. Abid's parents had moved to the city when he was four, Jamal had moved there from Glasgow in 2014, and Hassan had been born in the city's maternity hospital nineteen years earlier. Each was estranged from his parents, each was a benefit claimant, and according to the discreet enquiries Jake set in motion none attended any of the city's mosques any more. It wasn't conclusive, but there was no record of any of them ever having left the UK.

There was the sense of an unravelling, an unusual thing as a case sped to its fruition, an odd feeling of lassitude rather than energy as issues came close to the surface yet were not articulated, so disenchanted with each other were the various parties. Yet this particular hamster wheel was not one from which Jake could disembark. Frank and Jimmy had become fractious, apparently believing that perfidious Albion had by sleight of hand designed the law so that they could no longer have direct contact with their asset. Abu Omar was deprived of the presence of his comforters and whinged about the refreshments at the safe house, the personal hygiene of his co-conspirators and what he described as the amateur-hour quality of the venture. The notion became embedded in Jake that he was steering this enterprise ineluctably on to the rocks, with no means of stopping it.

It was all running through his fingers: time, control, purpose, optimism. At his next meeting with Abu Omar, in mid-November, he said, 'I thought it'd be useful to run through a few things that still aren't completely clear to me.'

'Yeah?'

'Before things get too busy.'

Abu Omar was bored and regarded him with dull eyes.

'When you first got to know Frank and Jimmy . . .'

'Yeah?'

'How did you come to get seized by the Americans in the first place?'

'We were doing an assault. Not normal, for us foreign fighters at that time. Mainly there for display. Other stuff.'

'What other stuff?'

'Not much. Anyway, I just got caught.'

'How?'

'Like I say, me and this other guy, we were heading around the back of this garage or workshop or whatever, and there they were.'

'Who?'

'Troop of GIs. Waiting for us. Anyway, I'm nabbed.'

'What about the other guy? He get back?'

'No. That's what I'm saying, man. They shot him. He was dead and I knew I wasn't getting nowhere. Put my hands up.'

'What happened next?'

'They cuffed me. Put me in the back of some armoured vehicle. Bit of a blur. Took me back to their base. And the rest is history, man.'

'Not quite. Was it Frank or Jimmy you saw next?'

'Both of them. Didn't they tell you the story?'

'They may have done. But I want to hear it from you.' Jake thought of Frank and Jimmy watching this. He hardly cared any more.

'Don't you trust me or something? Or don't you trust them?'

'It's not a matter of trust. I'm trying to fill in the gaps. How long were you held before they appeared?'

'Couple of days or so.'

'Were you in a compound with other prisoners?'

'No, I was in this cell.'

'Aware of any other prisoners nearby?'

'No.'

'How were you treated?'

'You know, not bad, like.'

'What does that mean?'

'It means it weren't that bad. Pushed around a bit.'

'But no one interrogated you until Frank and Jimmy appeared?'

'Something like that.'

'That, or something like that? Which?'

'Yeah, that was it.'

'And did you agree to help them straight away? Or did you suggest it?'

'More or less. Bit of both. I weren't liking it anyway. Seen too many lads dying. I wanted out.'

'And this was your way out. So what happens next?'

'They got all the information out of me there is, then we talked about the future.'

'Which is?'

'Get back in there.'

'Weren't you frightened?'

'Course I was. Shitting me pants. But I didn't have no option. They tell me this is my exit plan. Otherwise it's formal detention as an enemy combatant – and who knows what'll happen?'

'How long was it before you went back?'

'Three or four weeks. They called it the getting-to-know-you period. I suppose I had to prove meself. And there was all this training to do. Communications, drills, meetings.'

'So you went back after three or four weeks?'

'May have been five.'

'What was your story?'

'Wounded in battle. The Yanks shot me through the top of my arm to make it real. Bloody painful, but they said it was the only way. Insistent, like.'

'Must have been tough.'

'You haven't lived it, mate. Least of me worries. The Yanks made sure it wasn't infected and then I went back. Made up some story about trying to get back across the lines but not making it. Said I holed up for a couple of days, then found a village where some family looked after me.'

'And this was agreed with Frank and Jimmy?'

'Kind of.'

'Were you checked up on?'

'Wouldn't know, would I? I said the family was in a village that the Americans took. Everybody moves around there anyway, it's almost impossible to find anyone. Territory changing hands all the time. The brothers seemed to accept it.'

'And they just sent you over here?'

'More or less. Once I'd been given the get-go, I contacted Frank and Jimmy. And here we are.'

'These other boys.'

'Yeah?' said Abu Omar.

'You said they're from North Africa.'

'Right.'

'What if I told you that three of them grew up here, in this city, and the other one has been here four years?'

Abu Omar shrugged.

'One even went to the same mosque as you for two years.'

'So what? Hundreds of people go to the mosque. I can't know everybody. Why don't you get off my case?'

'I just want us to sharpen up our act. We need to be completely on it.'

'I am.'

'So you were in battle with these boys?'

'Did I say that?' said Abu Omar warily.

'I think so.'

He waited. Abu Omar didn't respond.

Jake continued. 'As far as we can tell, none of them has ever left this country.'

'I think I said they wanted to fight out there.'

It was Jake's turn to wait.

'You got the wrong end of the stick, man.'

Jake smiled. 'Tell me about the man with the beard again.'

'What can I say, man? You've heard it all.'

'Then I'll hear it all again.'

'The first time, we met in this flat on the ninth floor.'

'Does he live there?'

'Like I said, man, I dunno. I don't think so.'

'Have you seen him anywhere else? With anyone else?'

'Would have told you, man, wouldn't I?'

'How does he arrange the meetings?'

'Just calls us on a mobile that's left in the flat.'

'What's the number?'

'Dunno.'

'Have you tried finding out? On the phone itself, like I told you?'

'Too tricky with them others around. Not risking that.'

'Describe him.'

'He sits in the corner. On the floor, cross-legged. Won't let us near him.'

'Accent?'

'From here, like.'

'Height?'

'Like I say, he's sitting. Never gets up.'

'Age?'

'Not a Scooby. He has this light switched on between us. Can hardly make him out. Obviously he wants to make out he's like the big men over there.'

'And he's giving instructions?'

'Yeah. Calling the shots. Knows what's what. Knows the

city. Look, I've had enough. Got to get back. How many times we been through this?'

Jake sighed. 'We'll call it a day, then.' Head. Brick wall. Hardly any point any more.

Was this the point where in hindsight the accumulation of doubt should have become overwhelming? When Abu Omar had shown himself to be wrong about all of his co-conspirators or, worse, actively misleading? It seemed now, as he waited for the corridors to empty so that he could make his unobtrusive exit, so obvious. Yet it hadn't been at the time, as he recalled. No one else showed a lack of faith in Abu Omar apart, perhaps, from George, but then George displayed a fierce, defensive scepticism about every source that walked the earth and crossed the path of his team. Sure, Abu Omar was sometimes flaky, evasive, off the pace. Which agent wasn't?

But doubt isn't like that. It isn't the gradual tipping of a balance. It's either there or it isn't. And Jake knew he'd boiled like a frog.

Then, quite suddenly, it had been upon them. It was often like this, Jake reflected, that startling shift from inaction to it all happening, it all being *on*. The feeling of being unprepared, too – of knowing only half the story and getting that part wrong as well – was familiar, though it was magnified in this case. He replayed each of the dialogues with Abu Omar in his head, didn't respond to the increasingly poisonous missives from Frank and Jimmy in text messages or voicemails – it seemed they didn't actually want to speak to him, just to pass venom under the cloak of sickly sweet, encouraging dispatches embroidered liberally with 'How're you doing, buddy' and 'We're right there with you, pal' – and got down to running this as best he could, against time, against the odds.

Jake could recall now with clarity the day of the final rehearsal. The final RV with Abu Omar, in a specially kitted-out truck. Abu Omar seeming keyed up but confident. He handed over the rucksack to the technician in latex gloves, who did his tests while Jake exchanged a few last-minute words of encouragement with the boy.

'All good?' he'd asked.

'Yeah, man,' Abu Omar had replied, for once looking into his eyes. 'No one's gonna do nothing crazy, are they?'

'Like what?' Jake took the trouble to smile.

'Like fucking nail me by accident.' Abu Omar smiled too.

'No. This is just a rehearsal, remember.'

The technician handed the rucksack to Jake. 'Heavy,' said Jake.

'Books,' said the technician. 'All clear.'

'Take care,' said Jake to Abu Omar. 'No silly moves. Just as we agreed. I'll be with you every step of the way.'

'Except you bloody won't,' said Abu Omar, laughing.

'Well, in spirit maybe. Today's easy. Next week it gets difficult.'

'You will look after me, won't you?'

Jake looked up at him, wanted to reassure him in some way. Instead, he said, 'Course.'

'Right. Better be off.'

Abu Omar opened the rear door of the truck.

IO

The Americans left immediately. Of course they did. Magicked on to the late flight that day to DC and no one had even thought to stop them. On what grounds, given their diplomatic passports? someone would have asked. The last thing we need on top of everything else is a bloody incident, it would have been pointed out. Quite so, someone – probably Stuart – would have said. But the discussion never took place because no one thought of it. Otherwise preoccupied. Within half an hour of the explosion Jake had tried to raise Frank and Jimmy on their mobile phones, just to share the horror of it, but the accounts had been closed down.

He'd been placed on immediate suspension, without prejudice, and told to go home. It was put out internally that he'd taken a few weeks off with no mention of a return date. George had rung him and asked him to report to a police station where he was interviewed under caution. A different SIO had been appointed to look into the circumstances of the incident. George was waiting outside in a car.

'Bet your bottom dollar there'll be a public inquiry this time. I've spoken to Stuart and he's pooh-poohed the notion. "Of course not, George; what are you thinking?" But he would say that, wouldn't he? It's been coming for years. Every bloody thing gets publicly inquired into, these days. The brass will try to prevent it but the shit's got to land somewhere. Government hates us, and someone's got to take the hit. It sure as hell won't be the police. No one likes us, we don't care. I should

cocoa. Brace yourself. It'll get nasty. And it'll happen quickly.'
A week later the inquiry was announced.

The next Tuesday Jake was called down to London. One of the legal advisers spoke to him with Stuart.

'This inquiry will be headed by a former High Court judge and will be judicial in nature. That means it may have the power to compel witnesses to appear, evidence will be given under oath, and the laws of contempt of court and perjury will apply. You'll be given appropriate protection of identity.'

'I'll be called?' said Jake.

The legal adviser looked at him as if he were a fool. 'Well of course you will. You'll be obliged to answer each question truthfully. There are certain areas where a national security exemption will apply. Things like meeting places, techniques, names of sources and so forth. We're working through those items with the counsel for the inquiry. Don't worry about them. You won't be asked. And if you are, the counsel for the inquiry will intervene. It'll be fine.'

'The Americans,' said Stuart.

'Yes?' said Jake.

'We've discussed this at length with the government and together we've reached the conclusion that the Americans' involvement isn't relevant to the proceedings. Therefore, the inquiry will be unaware of our dealings with them. Is that clear?'

'But the Americans served up Abu Omar and the whole deal. Are you suggesting we should be economical with the truth?'

Stuart sighed. 'Earth to Jake. Join us back in the real world. This is about striking the right balance between justice being seen to be done and –'

'The reality? What if I'm asked about them?'

'You won't be.'

'Because if I am, I won't tell lies.'

'Of course not. But the subject won't come up. Trust me. Nothing to worry about.'

'There's one more thing,' said the legal adviser.

'Yes?'

'I'm afraid that as the legal representative of the Service I'm unable to represent your interests at the same time.'

'I'm an employee.'

'This is just a nicety, Jake,' said Stuart. 'One of those bloody legal things.'

'The issue is,' said the legal adviser, 'that one could imagine circumstances where our interests could be different. For example, if the Service chose to assert that you'd failed to obey the rules of your appointment or meet minimum professional standards . . .'

'See what I mean?' said Stuart with a wry smile. 'Never going to happen, but this is what the legal beagles tell us.'

'. . . or, for instance, you were to claim you were under some kind of undue pressure from the Service, or it hadn't looked after your personal welfare sufficiently. You see, it's possible our interests could diverge. To that end, we suggest that you engage independent legal advice for yourself. We'll give you a list of expert counsel in this area who have the right clearances.'

Christmas shopping. Samir was an absolute sucker for Christmas. Had been: Mr Masoud still hadn't adjusted his language. Always overdid it, spent money he didn't have, loved the lights and the trees. Decorated the house to within an inch of its life. Aisha loved it too. It was only Mr Masoud who gibbed. The waste. The commercialism. The godlessness, too. His wife tut-tutted at his sourness. 'You grumpy old man,' she said.

Worse still, Samir had taken Aisha out of school for the day, so that they could buy something nice for Mummy and see the displays in Hamleys and the lights along Regent Street. Samir had told the school that Aisha was unwell. Samir's wife had asked Mr Masoud to take on the job of phoning the school a few days after the attack to tell them what had actually happened. It was just one of the several horrible tasks that death necessitates.

Mr Masoud was occasionally asked, usually by white people, whether he had ever been back to Pakistan. Back. He was always polite in his response. No, never, he'd say. Only rarely, and with careful tentativeness for fear of being regarded as a pedant, would he say: I couldn't go *back*, I've never been there in the first place.

His parents had come to England in the mid-sixties, a year or so before he was born. So he had not even been conceived on the subcontinent, he liked to joke privately with his wife. They'd built a life in the city, with the corner shop in a predominantly working-class white part of town that during the seventies and eighties became something of an Asian enclave, its Edwardian terraces neglected physically and exploited financially by unscrupulous white landlords. Now it was inhabited largely by young professionals who, Mr Masoud observed with approval, were far more at ease with each other and themselves than his generation, and had little regard for matters of colour or creed. The business had had to adapt to the times and Mr Masoud had made a success of it, now owning two more shops in close proximity. Each had been converted into a bright, clean little supermarket, open from early morning to late at night, selling frozen ready meals, cigarettes, fresh veg, toothpaste, newspapers and magazines, whisky and wine. He was proud of their modern, slick appearance, and the range of products they sold. This was no longer a Paki shop enterprise.

His parents had gone back, in the early eighties, when he

was in his petulant adolescence. He refused to go with them. He was the hothead then, more interested in rock music than his roots. He regretted it now but would find it difficult today to travel to Balochistan. He had no connection there, other than the tenuous threads of family, most of whom he'd never met. And those he had, had come here, to England. What would it mean to visit, other than an exercise in superiority and selfish gratification that he and his had dragged themselves out of such primitive and unpromising circumstances? Or, alternatively, the provoking of awkward questions about his decadent, godless life in the West (questions that were persistent enough as it was)? How could he view the lives of his cousins in their terms?

His wife had been to Pakistan several times, all before they were married in 1986. It wasn't an arranged marriage but their parents had been acquainted. She'd been a good catch: attractive, university education, family of good standing. So must he have been, he allowed: a resourceful young businessman on the up. She'd given up her career ambitions to marry, only much later becoming the office manager at the local GP surgery.

Several times before Samir was born she'd suggested they visit relatives in Pakistan. No, he'd always insisted, too busy. To be fair, to visit her family near Islamabad would have been an easier prospect than his in Quetta.

So. The Americans. Involved in everything. Why did our powers that be always stand so close to them, as if in a perpetual schoolyard infatuation? The inquiry would resume on Monday and they would find out more. That is, if the government didn't somehow try to stifle this over the weekend. The Chair had promised real independence, but they would see.

They filed out quietly with the other families.

Mr Masoud fastened the buttons of his overcoat as they

came out of the gloom of the building into the gloom outside. It didn't look promising but it wasn't quite raining yet. He linked arms with his wife as they walked down the steps of the City Hall, turning right down Napier Street towards the multi-storey car park. They walked quickly; there was some kind of disturbance outside the hall, a demonstration of some kind held back beyond metal barriers by police in high-vis jackets. There was shouting and waving of fists and enraged expressions. They hurried as the noise became louder.

Drinking water from a plastic bottle, Jake sat in the room that had been set aside.

'Weekend off?' said Chris, one of the drivers.

'Chance'd be a fine thing,' said Jake with a rueful grin. 'We going, then?'

'Take your time.'

'It's all right. I need to get moving. Onwards and upwards.' He picked up the suit carrier in which he had carefully packed his clothes and they made their way down into the sub-basement, with Phil, the other driver, going ahead and giving the all-clear along the route. Phil took the wheel of the mini-bus while Chris sat in the passenger seat. Jake climbed into the back, behind the darkened glass.

'Bit of a demo on,' said Phil. 'Britain First thugs, apparently. We'll go round the other way.' He navigated the minibus smoothly around the pillars and up the ramp. The security guard operated the switch to open the garage door, which rat-tled sedately to allow a view of the street and then the grey sky. Phil nudged forward and the door wound down slowly, with a steely finality. He eased out on to the street, looked each way and was about to turn right towards the inner ring road when he said, 'Uh-oh.'

To the left Jake could see five young men running down the

side street. They were in pursuit of someone who at first was behind a lamp post and not visible. Then he saw them: two smartly dressed figures with linked arms making their way awkwardly towards the minibus, turning in fear at their pursuers.

'Bollocks,' said Chris. 'Last thing we need. Better back up.'

Phil drove quickly on to the street and then engaged reverse gear. The gearbox shrieked as Phil sped backwards, one hand on the wheel, head turned to see where they were going.

'That'll do,' said Chris, and they braked abruptly to a halt.

'You stay in the van,' said Jake to Phil.

'We're supposed to keep you –' said Phil.

'Stay in the driver's seat,' insisted Jake as he slid open the side door.

They had already knocked them to the floor by the time Chris and Jake were there, and were kicking them. One of the men, maybe in his late twenties, double-chinned, crew-cut, with lazy, hard eyes, looked up. 'Aye-aye. What the fuck's up here? Who are you? International fucking rescue?'

Chris offered no reply but the man was shortly on his back, rolling and bleeding profusely from the centre of his face. Jake grabbed the next man and took his legs from beneath him with a sharp, well-placed kick. He took the man's right arm and wrested it behind his back, pushing upwards until the man groaned loudly, while pressing his face into the gritty surface of the pavement. The only judgement now was whether to dislocate the man's shoulder. He decided it wasn't necessary. It was difficult, however, to suppress the urge to push until he felt the give and heard the crack, to pummel, to let the blood and the adrenaline flow, to feel the exhilaration of letting it all go and taking everything out on this unfortunate individual. The other men – boys, really, these – were already backing away as Chris advanced, half an eye on their prone, out-of-action comrade who was trying to blink back his senses.

The boys began to run, but coming towards them were their own friends, who had just noticed the commotion.

Chris gathered up the elderly couple and ushered them quickly into the back of the minibus. Before releasing his own grip, Jake told his man quietly, 'Lie there until we're gone. I can get rougher. Be aware.' He stood and, while Chris watched for further threats, climbed into the back of the minibus.

Chris jumped into the passenger seat and Phil pulled away smoothly. 'Left a bit of a mess back there,' he said. 'Which first? Cop shop or hospital?'

Jake found himself facing Mr and Mrs Masoud. The husband was shaking uncontrollably and his face was bruised. He brought a crisply ironed handkerchief to his face to wipe away the sweat, the dirt and the tears. At length he raised his eyes to Jake and blinked in shock. Jake nodded. Mrs Masoud said, with surprising calm, to Phil, 'Neither. We don't want to cause any trouble.'

II

They sat in the Masouds' comfortable lounge. The minibus was parked at the rear of the house and Chris was on his mobile phone in the hall explaining, in tones that were quiet but unmistakably those of the supplicant, what had happened.

'Please. We don't want the police to be involved,' Mrs Masoud had repeated when they reached the house.

'I'll try to get this straightened out discreetly,' said Chris.

Mrs Masoud made sweet tea and disappeared upstairs with her husband to change from their creased and dirty clothes.

When they returned, Jake asked, 'Are you all right?'

'We'll have to be,' said Mr Masoud. 'We have to be at the inquiry when it reconvenes,' he added almost plaintively.

'I know,' said Jake. 'But these people . . .'

'What?'

'It's all so unfortunate.'

There was a pause.

'It was you, then,' said Mr Masoud quietly.

'Yes,' he replied.

'The man behind the screen.'

'I'm sorry.'

'What for?' He looked genuinely perplexed.

'For everything.'

'Ah yes.' Mr Masoud appraised him for a long while. 'Why do you do what you do?'

'I, I . . .'

'I don't mean to be aggressive. I'm curious. It's a strange profession.'

'Over time you forget how strange. You think it's normal. You lose your perspective. It makes sense when you're inside.' He looked at his cup. 'I liked the idea of doing something worthwhile. Something purposeful. I liked the idea of the thrill, I suppose. And the notion of secrets. The real answer is more prosaic. I applied for a lot of things when I came back from travelling after university. It was the best option at the time. But . . .'

'Yes?'

'We shouldn't be talking about this. Not with what just happened to you.'

'No, I'm interested. Has it given you what you were looking for?'

'No. The excitement is just terror, in small segments, surrounded by a lot of routine. You feel elated when you do something well. Secrets can be depressing, too. You learn things about the world, people you previously respected, that disillusion you. Half the time you're being lied to and the other half you're unable to use what you've learned. I wanted to do something with meaning . . .' He became silent. 'What about your family? How are you coping?'

'We're not,' said Mrs Masoud firmly. 'But that's to be expected.'

'I'm so sorry.'

'Thank you.'

'The inquiry. Is it . . . ?'

'Helping? Not really.'

'It's not what we expected,' said Mr Masoud. 'We thought we'd get closer to the truth. We thought we'd find the answer.'

'Perhaps there is no answer,' said Mrs Masoud. 'Perhaps that is the answer.'

'You must feel anger.'

'We do,' she replied. 'Not as much anger as sorrow, but we do.'

136

'Then you must want those responsible for it all identified.'

'Those responsible blew themselves up along with the others in the railway station. Do you feel responsible?'

'I do.'

'It's right that you should. You people aren't supposed to let this kind of thing happen, especially when you know all about it.'

'If we had known all about it . . .' Jake pointed out.

Mr Masoud stared at him with an intensity Jake could not divine. He imagined it must be loathing. Mr Masoud said, 'We're looking for a resolution. An explanation.'

There isn't an explanation, Jake thought. However hard you search for it, in an inquiry or elsewhere. There is no solution. 'I wish I could help.'

Mr Masoud sighed. 'But you can't.'

'No.'

'I apologize,' said Mr Masoud. 'I'm very tired. I must take some rest.'

'Of course.'

Mr Masoud left the room. Jake heard the sound of a distant upstairs door slamming before the house resumed its deathly silence.

'My husband is a very angry man,' said Mrs Masoud.

'He doesn't seem so,' said Jake.

'He wouldn't. Despite his mild exterior he's always been a man with strong moral views and a tendency to judge. Once it was buried deep. Now, he would kill you if he could. There are only two things that stop him trying. His physical inability to complete the task and his civility. Perhaps only the second of those.'

'He's every right to feel like that.'

'He may have the right, but he's wrong. He probably knows it too. But the correctness or otherwise of a feeling does not

137

make it disappear. And it is only my opinion that he is wrong to hate you. I understand it's also the opinion of his spiritual adviser at the mosque.'

'You don't feel similarly?'

'No. I find it difficult to know what I feel. It's not hate or rage. I'm unable to name it.'

'I should go,' said Jake, but continued. 'You can't exactly show your emotions when you're giving evidence at the inquiry. It's impossible to say how sorry I am for what happened.'

'You made mistakes?'

'Yes, indubitably. I've been told by my legal representatives not to say so, but yes.'

'Do you know what they were?'

'Not precisely. In a general sense, yes. I took too much for granted. I worked from assumptions about people and events. The very things I'm trained not to do. I wasn't ruthless enough. But that's the argument of the person in denial, the weak. "My mistake was that I didn't trust myself enough," that's how the self-justification goes. It could simply be that I'm weak.'

'Is that such a bad thing?'

'What?'

'To be weak, to be afraid, to have flaws. To make mistakes.'

'Does that mean you think I deserve some absolution or forgiveness?'

Her features were thoughtful and stern. 'Not at all. Would my forgiveness offer you any comfort? I don't think so. You are so busy blaming yourself as it is that my blame or my husband's is irrelevant. We are all weak, every single one of us; the difference is that your weakness has been discovered and exposed. It's simply something that you need to contend with, or fail to contend with. It simply *is*. Does that sound unduly harsh?'

'No more than it should.'

'That's what I thought. I was listening carefully at the inquiry. It wasn't clear to me whether anyone knew how the device was passed to the young man or detonated.'

'It's assumed it was passed to him by someone in the public toilets.'

'There's been no trace of such a person?'

'No. Whoever it was must know the city well. None of the cameras that we had in the park to follow our man picked up this other person, before or afterwards. There was no DNA on the bag that was left in the toilets. The person seems to have appeared and disappeared with no trace.'

'Unless it was placed in the toilets beforehand.'

'Yes. We've been through all the permutations. We just can't arrive at one that's more likely than the others.'

'And the detonation?'

'Similarly, did Abu Omar set it off? Was it remotely triggered by a mobile phone or a timer, or did it go off by accident?'

'I would have thought your scientific people would know.'

'So would I. But you heard what was said at the inquiry. The impact of the blast. There are no likely, logical explanations. The other conspirators, for instance. Why were they there if this thing was supposed to explode? In your place I don't think I'd be as rational and enquiring about this as you are.'

'I am emotional, believe me.'

'I didn't mean to imply –'

'But I am a logical person as well. I look for explanations. I know I'm not about to find one in religion: mine, yours, any-one's. I seek it among the facts, knowing all the while that if one was to be found there, it would have been discovered already. We are in an age of unreason. Perhaps it has always been this way. Perhaps rationality is the way we paper over the cracks of the world's irrationality and close our eyes to the hate that flows from it. This age of hate. Those thugs who attacked us, are they any different in their way from the boys who killed Samir and Aisha? The same dark anger. Will this inquiry tell us why they did these things?'

She paused, seeking no answer.

'No,' she said. 'It's just something to cling to. To fool us into thinking justice is being done. None of this will bring Aisha or Samir back.'

'I'm sorry,' he said again.

'Yes, well,' she said. 'That doesn't do much good either. You have to be very careful, you know.'

'Yes.'

'Pardon me, but I think you may not fully understand what is going on. We live in rage, all of us. It envelops everything we do. Epitomized by those young idiots who wanted to do harm to me and my husband. They didn't know our son and our granddaughter had died in the explosion; and if they had, they probably wouldn't have cared. We were simply something they could blame and hate and take revenge on. I've been at this inquiry from day one. I started out thinking it was about justice. About me finding out exactly what went wrong, discovering true culpability and putting things right for the future. About being objective.'

'But?'

'If you believe that then you are rather more foolish that I'd thought. It's about anything but those things. It's about politics. It's about those in charge insulating themselves by having an investigation and then finding fall guys among the little people. You'll do. Not that I believe necessarily that those in charge should be held responsible. It's possible that it was all terrible but unavoidable. I'm reserving my judgement for the moment, but I see little prospect of clarity one way or the other. That's not what's at stake in this inquiry. It's partly about fame and celebrity and being in the media spotlight. Our strutting counsel is in it for the showbiz, though I'm sure he can persuade himself that that's emphatically not the case, and the Chair isn't immune either. Above all it's about vengeance. Believe me, I've seen these people, the other families. They're full of hate. It's to be understood, I suppose. They look askance at my husband and me, a little like those stupid boys. What they see as justice seems to me to be just vindictiveness.'

'You can't blame them. Not everyone is as strong as you.'

'Strong,' she laughed bitterly. 'I suppose you can't blame them. What has been wrought upon them is not right or fair by any measure. There's nothing that you can do about it, that anger, it's like a tsunami, which is why I say you must be careful. Whether in reality your judgement was flawed, whether you behaved improperly, whether you had a moment of uncharacteristic inattention, whether you did everything right but someone else made the bad decisions, whether the systems are somehow wrong, or whether it was simply a tragic coincidence of mistakes and circumstances, all these possibilities are beside the point of this inquiry despite its sober face. A blood sacrifice, or so-called civilized society's version of it, is required. Unless you can somehow paint yourself as a victim in the general opinion, I fear for you.'

'I'm not about to do that.'

'I didn't think you would. I have no words of comfort for you. It seems your errors led in part to what happened. But you aren't primarily responsible, and you were probably doing your best. It is right that you suffer. You are a victim, though you shouldn't compound your errors by trying to take on the whole responsibility and by telling yourself these people are right. They're not. It's a hateful situation for all of us and none of us should afford ourselves the luxury of wallowing.'

He looked at his hands, clasped in his lap. 'I must be going.'

She ignored him. 'You are still looking for these people?'

'Yes.'

'There will be people here manipulating these youngsters,' she said with certainty.

'It's incredible how much can be done online.'

'Yes,' she said impatiently, 'but there must be some human link at some point. The inquiry's shown that much, surely. Are you looking in this city, here and now?'

'I think I can hardly –'

'Possibly not.' She looked at him sternly. 'I wonder whether you are actually doing anything worthwhile. Whether they have won because you are frozen in inaction.'

'I can assure you –'

'I'm sure you can assure me. Whether I can take anything from those assurances is a different matter. The point I'm trying to make is that these people, they will be living normal lives in this city. Those who are encouraging this behaviour will seem harmless. They will not be radical imams shouting loudly at the mosque and on street corners. They will be more insidious than that. You will need to be very sensitive to this.'

'I'd hope we already are.'

'Not judging by the evidence. Are you any closer to identifying this other individual?'

'I can't comment on that.'

'No. Let me think. Can I contact you if my thoughts take me anywhere?'

'You too need to be careful. You're well known in the community. Even more so after what happened. You can't afford to be seen as reporting to the authorities.'

'I will be careful. I am accustomed to being careful. Every Muslim woman of my age with academic achievements, a career and an independent life knows what it is to be careful. I am assuming we can play your James Bond 007 games if I think of something and we need to meet?'

'I suppose so,' he said.

'Well, then. May I have your number?'

It was becoming darker and the rain lashed down, brought off the moors by the east wind, when they left.

'It's a bit of a mare's nest but I think we've contained it,' said Chris. 'Apparently the kids are saying nothing. They're claiming to the police that a ruckus developed between them. It's thin, and there's CCTV that says different, but the police aren't minded to pursue it. It'll all go pear-shaped if this lot here decide to file a complaint.'

Jake was thinking of Mrs Masoud's resolve when he said, 'I don't think they'll do that.'

He felt suddenly exhausted. It was their quietness, despite whatever hatred Mr Masoud might be concealing, that he found merciless.

12

FRIDAY

It appeared it was on. If you were perceptive enough – and Jon Brough was – you could smell it in the atmosphere in the days and sometimes weeks leading up. Something in the senior officers' demeanour with their juniors, the tension, the finicky attention to detail, the drive to have every piece of equipment cleaned, operational, charged and in its designated place. These things were normal in routine circumstances; perfection was all that would do. There was no eighty per cent solution when you were drilling hostiles. But at times such as these the demand was for more than perfection, if that were not an oxymoron; unease and twitchiness pervaded as kit was checked, rechecked and checked once more, medical records were queried and attended to if jots and tittles were out of place, and vehicles were vacuumed and polished twice a day in the compound. Not so's a civvy would know the difference. But if you were trained so that your senses were on high alert, you knew.

He'd well understood that something was in the offing, that somewhere somehow intel had become available. The bods had been identified and somewhere in this city were planning their worst. The powers that be had some kind of handle on what was going on and when it would all kick off. That sooner rather than later the team would be on the street making the calls. This was how it was supposed to work, at least. Then the station attack had happened.

His feeling was confirmed that morning when he had a text politely wondering whether he could come on shift early, in the next hour in fact, instead of at 13:00. For Jon and his colleagues such polite queries were calls to action and everything else – plans, family crises, dentists' appointments, leaking roofs, holidays – had to be dropped instantly and, more than that, forgotten for the duration. This was why Jon Brough eschewed the complications of dependencies, whether him relying on others or the other way round. One day he'd like to have a dog, a big one that he could take with him on his fourteen-mile hikes; one day he'd like to have love in his life, a simple, conventional love (he knew he thought along straight lines); one day he'd like to have children. There'd be plenty of time: before long his reactions would slow and his eyesight deteriorate marginally, and he'd be out. He would call it before the medicos did and he was called in for a friendly chat with the gaffer. That much was a matter of pride. For now, his one abiding connection was with his mother, in her bungalow just out of town, but she knew she came second by some distance, and accepted it.

He shaved carefully and put his gear in his bag. He might need it if events began to overtake everyone. He packed three clean pairs of underpants. He knew he had spares of both shaving kit and underwear in his locker at work, but he found a back-up to the back-up reassuring. That was it – no, some anti-perspirant too – and he was out, in the car, the flat all safely locked up and double-checked.

At least this wasn't Helmand. Always the advance force of some other advance force. You didn't need shaving kit or deodorant there – and as for spare grollies, you'd need a pantechnicon full, the number of times each day you thought you were going to shit yourself. The work there was more uncomfortable, dangerous and elemental, but simpler. No judgement calls. In, do the job, and with a bit of luck out again. Maybe the odd task took three or four weeks but you could put up with it: the heat of the day, the cold of the night, the dust, the fear, the vacu-packed rations, crapping into cling film to carry home so as to avoid leaving ground trace. You were on mission and, as some would say, this was what it was all about.

Jon had never thought of himself as a macho man. Had left uni with a second-class degree in English and aspirations somehow to do good. Wandered into the army, as much as anyone can wander in that direction. Specifically hadn't wanted a commission, wanted to be at the coal face of it. Thought it'd mainly be development work in Africa, that kind of stuff. No problems with that. No airs and graces. Craved the discipline in a way. Discovered he was good at it; very good at it if the scores from the various tests were anything to go by. And apparently they were. He found himself one day being interviewed by a gimlet-eyed blond-haired officer with a gob-shite Scouse NCO in tow. They'd liked him; he'd liked them. Rest was history.

Killing is easy for those without a conscience. Those were the ones 22 weeded out early on and rejected. A certain cold-ness was required for sure and no, you couldn't afford to get too far up your fundament about the rights and wrongs of it. The ethics were for others to fret about: your job was to exe-cute with precision and dispassion. Execute being, of course, the operative word, almost all the time. When 22 were called in, the possibilities of nicey-nicey, less extreme solutions were usually long exhausted. Which was why you had to have faith that the moral issues had already been worked through. You had to obey orders and you could not afford hesitation or prevarication. Conscience was something different. Killing someone should be hard; it should fill you with questions and doubt, before and after. Bloodthirsty bastards, of whom there were more than a handful in the army, were not fitted for the Regiment.

Civilian life was different. He'd wanted out because he was a moral person. Not that he thought that the life was immoral, but because he liked to think, to make his choices for himself. Or so he'd believed at the time. But choice made life more complicated. Doing this job – now, here – there were a thousand choices that had to be made, most of which were distant from the strictly professional. It was strange to be doing this on the streets of the city in which he'd grown up, among the people he knew. He was infused with the place, it *was* him and he was it: that northern tang, the hard-nosed expression concealing emotion, mawkish at times. The humour, the nuance of expression. The city, glowering, towering over him. The ghosts of industry in the form of street names like Foundry Square and warehouses converted into nouveau-chic retail outlets. The pubs, raucous and rowdy and bright while he supped quietly in the corner. It was more vivid, fully immersed, than in the Regiment in some far-flung shithole. He couldn't go in, do a job, get out. He was already in when he did a job and there was no getting out.

All those choices inevitably boiled down to one, at that moment. Challenge or no challenge? Would shouting 'Armed police!' cause the suspect to do exactly what he was trying to prevent? Was the suspect carrying? If so, what? Left-handed or right-handed? Is there a trigger device in the hand? Danger of collateral damage to innocents? And the central question: what is this person's intent? What is in the eyes that speaks of what resides in the heart and will, in a fraction of a second, be translated into a decision and then action: to submit or to detonate. If the latter, it has to be pre-empted; with the classic double-tap to the head, which was as cold and brutal as it sounded.

He was admitted to the compound, parked up carefully and went to the locker room. He changed without haste. Pacing was important, he knew from experience. There would be sufficient adrenaline spilt later in the party. Or it might be a no-show non-event. Either way, it didn't make much sense to raise the pulse rate unnecessarily.

He would never have reckoned on his acquiring an addiction to the action. He'd always believed himself to be a calm person, easy-going but not to the point of passivity. Maybe this life had changed him, or it had been latent in him the whole time. When he'd left the military he'd joined the police and within three years become a detective. A change of air, he'd thought, one that played to his intellectual tendencies and gave him the scope to think and make those deductive, elective choices he'd missed. It had been a mistake. The head-banging routine of catching no-hope no-marks trapped in their own tiny, vacuous, vicious circles of offence, addiction, capture and reoffending – victims in their own right, of circumstance, of society, who had not the first idea of how to market their drugs, complete their burglaries, abuse their partners or carry out their sordid sex crimes without being detected – was tedious. There was, naturally, little relation between detection and successful prosecution. But that, too, had never seemed a matter of intellect, of matching his mind against the criminal's. It was much more a case of fortune, good or bad, and resources, invested wisely or badly, as well as a high dependence on overworked, often incompetent or uncommitted colleagues. And the CPS. Don't get me started on the CPS, he thought.

This was different. Back in his comfort zone in one way, with a reliance on equipment, the oily smell of firearms, the sleek black uniform, with its boots and belts and its various receptacles where everything knew its place, and a code of silent, efficient accomplishment. A world where all the working parts meshed perfectly because they had to. A place where periodic fixes of desperate activity near the bounds of perceptual acuity and physical capability were assured, but one where he could say, with justification, that he was doing good. There was little moral equivocation here, no space for it.

Uniformed up in their trousers and boots and fatigue T-shirts, they assembled in the briefing room. The inspector came in, together with one of the young analysts from the Counter Terrorism Unit, the chief superintendent who headed the CTU and one of his chief inspectors.

'OK, people,' said the inspector. 'Here we go. Operation Palmerston.'

For operational names, they were currently working their way through a list of British Prime Ministers. He presumed they skipped the inappropriate, such as Petty, the confusing, like North, and the repetitive, including the various Pitts. He wondered when they would move on to a different system. Perhaps after Churchill. Certainly before Thatcher or Blair.

'This is an evidential briefing which will be recorded. No informal notes should be taken. You'll each receive a summary of the relevant details after the briefing, which you will need to memorize for operational purposes. There is an intelligence background that Jodie here from the CTU will summarize for you in terms of what you need to know. The lead information we have is delicately sourced and it may not be possible to answer comprehensively some of the questions you have. This will be for source protection reasons. Questions should be directed to me once Jodie's finished her piece. Jodie.'

The pale, bespectacled young woman took her place at the lectern and read directly from her notes in a nasal monotone.

'Intelligence from a variety of sources indicates that a group of individuals in the Hanby area of the city are conspiring to carry out a terrorist attack within the next week. The sourcing, as I have mentioned, is various. That regarding the intent of the group is assessed as B1. The reporting indicates that the group intends to carry out a terrorist attack at the ThreeD football stadium this coming Wednesday evening, at the end of the game taking place there. There are four co-conspirators whose biographical details will be in your packs. We have no precise intelligence on the nature of the attack, other than that the attackers will approach the stadium singly at the end of the match towards four points of which we are currently not aware, in close proximity to the stadium itself. A reminder that this intelligence is classed as B1 and is not verified or corroborated by other sources. It is assessed that the attack may well be a suicide attack of some kind though this is not yet firm. We have no current information on the weapons that the group holds, though the same intelligence indicates that weapons and materiel will be sourced early next week, along with vehicles, which will be stolen by the participants. We have reasonable confidence that we will know when that happens. The vehicles, according to the intelligence, will be abandoned a walk away from the stadium with the intention of providing a distraction for the authorities as they deal with the possibility that they may contain IEDs. According to the intelligence, while efforts may be made to create the impression that the vehicles contain IEDs, they will not. One final thing: the group plans to conduct a recce and rehearsal this Sunday at the stadium towards the end of the Liverpool game.'

There were groans in the room. Jodie raised her head, alarmed.

'The intelligence indicates that the members of the group have been specifically instructed not to carry weapons or other incriminating material on this occasion. Vehicles will not be involved either.'

She folded her paper and looked at the audience.

'Thanks, Jodie,' said the inspector, and waited until she had left the room. 'Now, Chief Inspector Mackrell, who is SIO for this case.'

'You've heard the intelligence background. Our task, as ever, is first and foremost to protect public safety and, second, to detect and prevent any crime and to secure prosecutions against those who are guilty.'

'Scuse me, boss,' came a shout from the other side of the room. Jon couldn't see but it'd be John Pearce, the appointed troublemaker in the group.

'Yes,' said the DCI, and everyone braced themselves for what they knew was coming.

'Scuse my French, but is this going to be a crock of shite like the last job? Will it be us blown to the four winds like our mates?'

The DCI paused for a moment. 'You'll not be wanting the politician's answer to that, I'm taking it. Truthful answer is we don't know. If we did know, you wouldn't be asked to be out there.'

'Yeah, but what I mean is we get this stuff from these spooks, or whoever it is, and it's us on the front line, not them. We're just the mushrooms in this, kept in the dark and the rest of it.'

'What can I say? I've seen all the reporting. I can't share it with you but I believe in it. I suppose you either trust me on that or you don't. I need to remind you, though, that you're all members of a disciplined force. I'm quite happy to entertain debate and to hear your concerns. But I'm satisfied this is on the level and we have a job to do. OK?'

'No, boss I was only saying –'

'Right. You've said it now. As you know Five's people will be on the ground too. And you won't need reminding they lost seven people in the railway blast. Any further points before we move on?'

There were none. Now they would get down to the business of planning. Once the SIO had finished his obligatory rabble-rousing speech, they would be on to interoperability, radio frequencies, call signs, code words, then the topography and timings would be flashed up on to the huge screen before a focus on the biodata of the four suspects. They would practise their drills in the out-of-town training facility, protected from inquisitive onlookers by its razor wire and the woods, in improvised mock-ups of the territory itself. They would go on the firing range for final testing. They would do their drug and medical tests and each undertake the short psychological refresh check. Then they would go out on the ground for real.

He wondered what it was that inspired them. Genuinely wondered. He still felt moved by the watching of the moving pictures, the ranting monologues and the earnest discussions in the room. The rage still stirred in him the desire to right the injustices against his people. The fact that he was an unflinching traitor to this cause didn't alter his anger, greater since he couldn't quantify or define it with any precision.

His people. Who were his people? Certainly not those on behalf of whom he had fought. Or rather, committed atrocities that shamed him viscerally, the atrocities he could not mention to Jake and Leila. Shame was certainly part of what he was doing now with them – with the government, in effect, though he didn't quite see it that way. Shame towards his parents for his savagery out there. Even though they didn't know the details, he could often see the disappointment in his mother's eyes. He'd failed her, his father too – though he was beyond knowing – and that made him feel bad. Shame, absurdly, towards the home city that had given him not that bad a life. If he felt a grudging affection for it, why should he be conspiring to deliver such a shattering blow by murdering all those misguided but innocent people? Somehow, however inadequately, he wanted to put things right, which was why he was talking to Jake and Leila.

They were good people, whatever they represented. They were bound to be hiding stuff from him but he trusted them regardless, especially Jake. Jake had found him, seen something in him, looked after him. He'd repaid him with the necessary betrayal, in response to those relentless questions about the battlefield. Who had he met? Where had he fought? What had he done? On which dates? He'd known that honesty would have fractured the relationship, and he needed Jake. He'd looked him straight in the eye and lied. He found he was good at dissembling. It was a vital necessity at the moment.

He liked Leila too, he and she were kind of similar, not that many years apart. Each understood instinctively the life the other had led, felt it, sensed the traumas and the tensions. She was a Manc but it didn't matter. She'd told him in a way that said: come on then, what d'you have to say about it? He'd liked that look, now occasionally ribbed her about coming from the dark side of the Pennines.

They'd missed Friday morning prayers to meet. In the greater scheme of things this was not such a sin, to skip the lukewarm, neutered form of their religion to engage with the reality of it, red and bloody, and to continue to make their preparations. After the log-out procedures had been completed and the screen neatly packed away, they turned to their prosaic horrors.

'I've eyed up possible cars,' said Abdullah. 'I've got nine, so we have some play if some of them aren't there on Tuesday. You're all going to have to help come the day, though.' He read from a piece of paper that listed makes of vehicle and parts of the city where they could be found parked overnight, and together on a fresh sheet of paper they mapped out what amounted to a plan of action.

'You've been busy,' said Adnan with a grin.

'Yeah, well, important, isn't it?' said Abdullah bashfully.

'I've been thinking,' said Bilal. 'Why don't we hire a van for Wednesday? With all those people . . .'

'That's not such a bad idea,' said Adnan. 'But we don't know what the sheikh wants.'

Rashid said nothing, aware of the strictures that Jake placed on him not to lead the planning or encourage any particular action.

'The sheikh won't mind,' said Adnan. 'You still got your driving licence in your English name?'

'Yes,' said Abdullah.

'There you are, then. What do you think, brother?' He directed his question to Rashid.

'Maybe we should just see what the sheikh thinks. We'll still have time. He is speaking to us again sometime, isn't he?'

Abdullah had been to the DIY superstore in the new sprawling shopping complex on the eastern edge of the city. He showed the others the list of tools, boxes and other materials he had purchased, along with sketches of how he would construct the fake devices that would sit on the back seats of the cars they stole. The others murmured with approval.

'What about the real stuff, though? When do we start?' said Abdullah. 'When will we get what we need to do this?'

'I guess the sheikh would say, be patient,' said Rashid. 'Everything will come to pass in its own time. Only four more days after this until the day itself, so we need to keep calm. Sunday's a big day, too.'

13

There was time to cram in another meeting over lunchtime before his commitment in the afternoon. He rang Dave Philpott to set it up.

Zaki was breathless when he entered the room.

'You're in a rush, Zaki,' said Jake.

'Always on the go. You know me. I got no guaranteed salary, no cushy pension. I have to make my own way in life. Not like you lot,' said Zaki, beaming. 'Only kidding. I'll make time for you, Mr Winter, whenever you need me. Just call, and I'll make time.'

'That's good of you. I'm sorry to disturb you. Shouldn't take long. Been to morning prayers?'

'Of course.'

'And how are things, on the street? In the community?'

'They're fine, Mr Winter, fine. Considering.'

'Considering what?'

'All this upset, everything that's going on. It isn't a cakewalk being a Muslim in Britain today, I can tell you that for nothing.'

Cakewalk, thought Jake. Wherever did Zaki pick that up? 'I'm sure,' he said. 'It must be very worrying.'

'We're not all like these animals.'

'I know. Most people do. Most people, I'm sure, just want everyone to get on with each other. There's just a small minority that wants to cause unrest.'

'The newspapers. I mean, have you read them?'

'I try not to, Zaki. They seem to be a distraction from the realities of life.'

155

'Quite right. But most people do. The internet too. Social media. People in our community are worried.'

'We're doing a lot of work on community cohesion,' said Dave.

'I know.'

'So what else can we be doing? Tell us and I'll try to feed it into the machine.'

'Careful. I don't want my name coming out.'

'It won't,' insisted Dave. 'I know how to do this.'

'Presumably part of it is people seeing what's going on in this inquiry?' asked Jake.

'Yeah,' said Zaki. 'People are thinking, this just makes it look bad for us Muslims. There was that demo the other day. Then people are thinking, your people must be all over the place, spying on us. People are getting suspicious. I'm getting to think . . .'

'You've no need to be concerned, Zaki. We look after you, and you're perfectly capable of taking care of yourself,' said Jake. 'Is that not right?'

'Of course it is. We're a team. Work close together.'

'Exactly. We can both see that tensions are running high, inside the community and outside. Which is why we need to know everything, one hundred per cent, about anything that's happening. However absurd it seems to you. It might just be relevant in some context. What's going on, Zaki?'

'What you mean?'

'It's a simple enough question,' said Jake calmly.

'I've not been doing nothing wrong,' said Zaki. 'Whatever people been saying, I've not been up to no good.'

'And who might be saying that, Zaki?'

'I don't know. Malicious people.'

'And what might they be saying about you?'

'You know.' He looked at Jake and Dave, for confirmation.

Their faces were expressionless. 'What I used to get up to. I learned me lesson. Don't go nowhere near it.'

'So you said,' soothed Jake. 'I was thinking more of what you may have heard on the street. At times of tension hotheads begin having ideas. Anything occur to you?'

'Why? Have you got wind of something? Is there something up?'

'Not that I'm aware of. I'm just conscious that we need to keep turning over every stone. All the time. So.'

'Yes?'

'Just think, Zaki. Is there anything or anyone you've seen that gives you pause for thought?'

Zaki looked thoughtful for a moment. 'Can't say as –'

'Think carefully, Zaki. Now is the time we need your help.'

'No, nothing out of the ordinary.'

'OK. It's all right. As you say, feelings can run high. Just let me know if you hear anything. I'll meet you anytime.'

'Sure.'

'And Zaki?'

'Yeah?'

'Don't take any risks. If I need to contact you at short notice, to try some names on you?'

'I'll be around. You know me. Up all hours. Call me anytime.'

'Thanks.'

Zaki was gone and Dave Philpott returned to the room. 'Coming on a bit strong, Jake? Don't really think he knows anything about anything real, do you?' Dave was realistic about the business, his place in it, and Zaki's too.

'You never know. Not really. Zaki's just a bag of wind. I wanted him to feel the heat, though, about the other stuff.'

'The heroin.'

'He has to know we're on his case. He has to desist. He has to know that neither of us has any options if he doesn't.'

'So there isn't anything on the boil at the moment?'

'Not that I know of,' said Jake, looking into Dave's eyes. Dave had no need to know.

He was unsure of his judgement. Was Zaki really just an irritating, harmless albeit repulsive creature? Or with his finger in so many pies was he something entirely different, backing all the horses? Would this be Zaki's downfall in the end? Would one of his criminal associates finally lose patience? Not Jake's problem.

They sipped tea in the living room and she offered him a shortbread biscuit, which he refused.

'I don't work on Fridays,' she said, 'and my husband will be away until at least three. He meets friends after Friday prayers. Since it happened, he's spent longer with them. He tries to find the reason for it, in religion. I can't help him in that regard. I'm much too straightforward. He has this young preacher he talks to.'

'Really?'

'A young man. Tawfiiq. A sweet boy, from Somalia. My husband doesn't trust the older men. He says they're corrupt. Whereas this young man has an aura of innocence, so he says.'

'And you?'

'I don't trust any of them.'

'I see.'

'I wouldn't want him to know I'm talking to you, you understand.'

'I am discreet. It's the least you can expect from someone in my job.'

'Yes. Thank you. I see you haven't arrived in a big car parked outside the house. For that I'm grateful.'

He'd parked a quarter of a mile away, in the car park by the launderette. 'Mrs Masoud, are you sure you feel comfortable talking to me alone?'

'Young man. My unease at speaking to you has nothing to do with my religion. What would concern me more is if you considered me as an informant.'

'I hardly think that's likely,' he said. 'Do you?'

'Is that what you call the people who talk to you? Informants?'

'It depends. Not usually. It's a word more normally associated with the police.'

'Well then, what? I don't generally find your world interesting. When I can be bothered, I imagine you people getting up to all kinds of dangerous things, recruiting heads of state, other spies, things like that. Intrigue, glamour. Staying in six-star hotels, playing roulette.'

He looked at her patiently. 'No. My life's nothing like that. There's a little intrigue, I grant you.'

'It's a grubby lifestyle, then. Dredging up all the gossip from low-lifes like this Abu Omar.'

'I wouldn't put it like that,' he said mildly.

'Then what?'

'Why is it you wanted to see me, Mrs Masoud?'

'You seem to me a perfectly reasonable young man, you see. Perfectly ordinary. There's nothing exceptional about you.'

'Many people have said the same thing.'

'And they're wrong?'

'No, they're right. It's what I want to be, an ordinary person.'

'In a bizarre job.'

'I don't want to disappoint you, Mrs Masoud, but it's not such a strange profession.'

'I'm curious, you see. I've hardly thought about it until now but you must operate constantly in a kind of moral maze.'

'I wouldn't put it quite so dramatically as that,' he said. 'Plenty of people are faced with ethical choices in their jobs. The medical profession, for instance.'

'Your job, though, is to deceive. Your whole professional existence is based on your ability to dissemble.'

He smiled. 'At times, yes.'

'Are you deceiving me now?'

He pondered the question. 'No, I'm not. Very little of what I do involves deception. And that is necessary deception, I should add.'

'Necessary deception. What an interesting concept.'

'Quite workaday, in fact. Lots of people engage in much more of it in their professional or personal lives than me, with less reason.'

'You deceive for a reason, then. Patriotism? Your country?'

'I see it in simpler terms. Maybe less emotive. If I or someone like me doesn't do this job, the risk of bad things happening increases. Very bad things, like the attack in which your son died.'

She looked at him, steely-eyed.

'Sorry,' he said.

'No, it's all right,' she replied. 'I've always thought of myself as someone with unimpeded vision.'

'I simply mean that I don't connect my work with grand philosophies or the national anthem. I'm not sure many do.'

'So it's not morally ambiguous. Or politically?'

'Perhaps it is. Perhaps I'm just a simple soul. I realize that my work does have its ambiguities, moral and otherwise. But they tend to be on an individual level. I have to decide for myself whether it's appropriate to ask a person to do certain things, or not. If I'm ever asked to do something myself that I believe to be inappropriate, I'll refuse.'

'Until now that's not happened?'

'No.'

'But you may not be aware of the bigger picture. You may be contributing to horrendous things without being aware of it. In fact, you probably are.'

'That's true. It's a big and complex world out there. I find value in my work and I can't solve the world's problems, even conceptually. I just get by, day by day. Frankly, I don't buy these larger analyses about morality. They're very trite and claim to be authoritative with, I think, little basis for such authority or firm judgement. Or perhaps it's fairer to say I can't cope with them. The whole world is a series of very close calls, and fine judgements.'

'So you become amoral.'

'No, I like to think I am moral, but within terms I can grasp and affect. I have some sense of the wider issues – we all do – but I don't have enough knowledge to make definitive judgements. From my position I'd find it very difficult to say with certainty this or that government decision is wrong, or it's right. In security or any other area of policy.'

'Surely as citizens we have a right to comment? We have a duty to take an interest in the rights and wrongs of what our government is doing.'

'Of course. It's just that it's almost impossible for you or me to make informed and final judgements on these things.'

'Because of secrecy.'

'No. Simply because there are too many intertwined complexities of detail and nuance that it's not possible for us to take in and process. I can never know and assimilate the whole story, even on issues related to what I do for a living. And when you don't actually have to make the decisions, it's relatively easy to stand on the sidelines and comment caustically. We don't have to weigh the fine balances and make the calls. We can fall back on prejudice. So I revert to what I do know and what I can influence. If I felt that made me a mug, a pawn in some great game played for others' hilarity, I'd be sad. But that's not how I see things.'

'Or maybe you're deceiving me at the moment.'

'To what end?'

'I don't know. It could just be in your genes, to lie. You may have done it for so long that you don't know when you're doing it. You could be the extraordinarily clever one, the one who plays the innocent so well that no one is inclined even to entertain the possibility of deception.'

'And how do I prove that's not the case?'

'Do you feel the need to? I'm such a pliant customer, after all. I'm the unsophisticated wife of a Muslim businessman. I too have a role to play.'

'You're anything but unsophisticated, Mrs Masoud.'

'True. I'm better educated and more intelligent than my husband. I can see through the absurdities of the zealots, violent and non-violent. I have a position in life. I was a mother, bringing up three children. My husband has standing in the community. Certain things are expected of me, and most of the time I'm not too unhappy to conform to the conventions. I run a busy GP surgery. I have to order the doctors around constantly, otherwise they'd never get a single thing done. It's my choice outside work to play the docile wife at times. I don't feel the need to challenge tedious assumptions. My husband knows well enough the order of things. Now I'm a grieving mother and grandmother, I owe it to no one to be polite and respectful. But I will continue to be so until I decide not to be. You seem so very defensive of your career.'

'Do I? I suppose I may be. I don't feel especially defensive about it. You're right, it is a mucky business in so many ways, and we don't always get it right. It's just so easy to be critical of what I do, from a position of high moral certitude. I'm afraid

I don't hold with certainty. It seems so . . . lazy in so many ways.'

'I can see that.'

'Mrs Masoud, why did you ask me here?'

She chose not to hear him. 'I think you are like me, Mr Winter. You lay considerable value on rational thought.'

'That's true. It's what our society is built on, isn't it?'

'Perhaps.' She looked at him. 'I wanted to talk to you about your work. In much more specific terms.'

'Yes?'

'I am not an informer.'

'No.'

'I won't pass you dirty gossip under the table.'

'I wouldn't expect you to.'

'I won't pass you details of names and places. If I were certain of my facts, I might. I don't know. But I don't even have half a suspicion of anyone. So I'm of no use to you in that way.' She paused to look at him. 'Am I keeping you from something?'

'Not at all,' he said.

'I must be. You have, no doubt, a weekend to look forward to. You'll want to tidy up your desk before you finish for the day and forget about work. I know the feeling.'

He smiled thinly. 'Busted.'

'I'll be quick. These people have little to do with Islam.'

'That's not true from my experience.'

'I don't mean that in the literal sense,' she said with a note of frustration. 'Of course they pray, of course they can quote the Quran, of course they have read Abu Sayyaf. Of course they think they're carrying out Allah's will. They're religiously obedient. To them, Islam is everything. Yet Islam is not the root.'

'I'd be accused of condescension if I said that. And it's not true. Islam isn't absent from this.'

'Oh no. Islam is very much present, in every thought and every gesture. It's much more than a pretext or a context. But if Islam didn't exist, these boys – or boys very much like them – would still be doing these things. This time of – what do they call it? global individual consciousness – feels like the beginning of the end of the world.'

'The alternative is to repress individual aspirations. I'm not sure about that.'

'Nor am I. But aspiration leads to despair for most people, and then for some to rage. For everyone who fulfils their ambitions there will be a thousand thwarted. This doesn't help you with the here and now, however. The thing that worries you most, I take it, is this individual with the beard. That at least is what I sense from the evidence from the police and yourselves at the inquiry.'

He said nothing.

'You know very little about this person. He – let us assume it is a man for the moment – materializes suddenly and just as mysteriously disappears. He seems to have directed the activities of these boys. You must fear he's doing the same in this city at the moment. Of course he may be elsewhere in the country, or he may have travelled – returned, shall we say – overseas.'

Still he did not speak. It did not seem to perturb her; certainly it didn't deter her.

'The presumption is that he must have a connection with this area?'

He gave no sign to indicate she was right.

'If that's true, he may well still be around, doing the same thing right now with another credulous set of individuals. He could well be a link man with those people in the Middle East, living here and carrying out their instructions in this country. That would imply communication of some kind. Your people must be scouring your sources of information and databases for confirmation. But I don't need to tell you your business in that regard, do I? Now . . .'

She paused once more; he was not sure whether it was to marshal her argument or to give him space to speak. If the latter, again he did not take up the opportunity.

'. . . these people are different from those you've confronted before. These aren't the Russian intelligence officers with whom you have played your idle games.'

'I don't think any victims of the Russians these days would see it that way. We left that world years ago,' he said pleasantly.

'I would no more wish Putin to be determining our future than those who dream of the caliphate. But I take your point. What I wonder about, though, is the methodology that you are applying. We cannot escape our own ways of thinking, can we? So I'm not about to suggest you do. Here, though, is your problem as I see it. These people believe in destruction, fear and random actions that will cause our society to fall apart in panic and fury. They don't build towards anything, but away from what we have. These boys who offer themselves up are nothing to them. They can die in their attacks or they can rot in our prisons: it makes little difference to their so-called leaders. There's a plentiful supply of outraged young people. That's a counsel of despair, though. You may not fully appreciate what is going on.'

He drew breath, tempted fleetingly to ask her to tell him something he didn't already know, and allowed her to continue.

'To some extent you have to abandon logic and reason. This mysterious figure, he may seem so important to you but I wonder whether he is. You may think he has a function in the structures, but what if there are no structures? It's more likely this person's acting independently. Less a lone wolf than a self-appointed leader who preys on groups of impressionable young men. Perhaps motivated by personal hatred and less by ideology than it may seem. He's possibly a religious person, possibly not. It's possible that religion is unimportant to him. He may be charismatic and intelligent, he may be venal or modest. He may wear robes and flaunt his beard, or maybe not. Of course he must have links with those who say they aspire to the caliphate, but they may not be close. He could simply be someone useful to whom new sacrificial warriors may be directed. Make no assumptions, not even that this is necessarily a man, though from the accounts I've heard and read it would seem difficult to imagine that it isn't so. I'd reckon this person is closer than you think. In fact, I'd say: think less and feel more.'

'So you're saying: look for the least likely person?'

'Not necessarily. When – *if* – you find this person, it will seem as obvious as it could be.'

'Any ideas?' She must know, or have an inkling of, something that he couldn't see or imagine.

'I've already told you I'm not one of your informants. If I had a vague idea, I wouldn't pass on gossip.'

'Well, thank you for that. But unless you have any concrete suggestions . . .'

'These are concrete suggestions. I'm not sure I appreciate your dismissiveness. I'm sure it's much simpler than you seem to believe. You know evil when you see it. We both do. You look at a group of people and you say: that person is not right. These boys weren't evil, they were stupid and immature. You know evil.'

'I wasn't being dismissive. I agree with you, but it doesn't help me discover what I need to know. I'm just . . .'

'You're a rather shapeless, shiftless person, aren't you? I don't mean that unkindly. I feel for you. To do your job you must need to feel some sense of belonging to this country, as I do. Yet how can you have that sense of belonging when you have so few allegiances, when you're rootless and alone.'

Jake laughed, nervously, and looked down. 'I don't think that's fair. You hardly know me.'

'I know human beings. I've seen enough of you to believe that I know you to at least some extent. If I don't, I apologize.'

He raised his eyes.

She said, 'The refugees who come through the practice. Terrible stories. The grotesque things they've experienced and witnessed. Yet they bring richness, energy, joy. We should be taking more of them in.'

'I agree.'

'The few women I've met from Raqqa or Aleppo or Mosul or Yemen or Tripoli, they've had an immense struggle to get here. Illegally for the most part, extorted and abused, each one of them. With their children, or some of them, if they're extraordinarily lucky. Their menfolk are usually dead. They have great dignity, and a greater sense of belonging than I see in you.'

'Perhaps they need to belong.'

'And you don't?'

There was no answer to that.

'I've warned you before that you need to be very careful. You're not martyr material. You need to have a plan.'

'I always have a plan, Mrs Masoud.'

'I'd be grateful if you would please not patronize me, Mr Winter.'

There was no answer to that, either. 'Goodbye, Mrs Masoud,' he said with a shy smile.

Leila watched as Rashid entered the street. The street lamps illuminated the scene like spotlights and she was able to track the progress of his distinctive, lanky gait as he walked away from her. The safety signal was that he would wear his hood down. The mechanics of RVs – routes and timings, confidence and duress signals, fallbacks and abort procedures – were second nature to Jake and, no doubt, would be to her as well one day. For now, she felt nervous each time, even after all these months. Jake had said, no, it doesn't go away, and nor should it. This was the first of several relays. She would watch him and, if all was clear, Jake would do a rolling pick-up in the dead ground they'd identified just after the point where Corporation Street suddenly curved, and a tail would suddenly discover it was impossible to make up the distance by taking to the alternates.

No, Rashid wasn't so different from her, she thought again. Parents without money, status or any discernible advantage; taught, however, not to agitate but to improve his lot. And to conform. Aspiration was what the politicians liked to see, and aspiration was what Rashid's parents and her own had had in abundance. Education, education, education: they'd lapped it up.

She knew a little of what this boy, eleven years younger than her, had experienced. She recalled her own years at Manchester High School for Girls, her parents' elation at her exam results and their optimism for her. With her marriage to a non-Muslim, her child and a job they'd initially believed to be a dead end, a glorified clerical post, she'd crushed those illusions. Her rebellion, quite unlike Rashid's excursions into extremism. We all have our ways of disappointing our parents, of betraying them.

But *focus*. Now.

The hood was up and his shoulders were hunched. He moved quickly, hustling his frame along the street. He must believe there was someone with him.

She strained to look at the corner of the street behind him but could see no one. Still no one appeared. Rashid's designated route would take him, via a small passageway on the left, to a back alley where Jake would be waiting in the car. This part of town was full of its little rat runs. Rashid, if he obeyed the drills and continued to suspect a presence, would simply walk past the passageway and wait for the fallback in ninety minutes' time. She hoped he remembered his cover story.

She remained motionless in the car, watching from the back through the gap afforded by the headrest of the driver's seat. They had practised this many times and she knew it was highly unlikely anyone could see her there. Yet she felt conspicuous and a chill of apprehension ran through her. It would be too dangerous to call Jake and alert him. Her mobile phone would cast light.

And there he was. Rashid had been right. A slight figure came round the corner, walking quickly. It was a man, young it would appear, dressed in jeans and a puffa jacket, moving swiftly. Rashid was by this time halfway down the street, out of her sight. The man was gone soon, too, and she reached for her phone.

Rashid picked up his pace. Leila had told him not to alter his behaviour, not until the last possible moment, so he slowed down again. When was the last moment, though? What if he judged it too late? Steady, Leila had said when they were practising for this, keep your breathing even. Use your brains. Don't overreact.

He knew he shouldn't turn around but felt an almost overwhelming need to do so. What was his cover story for why he was in this part of town, out of his normal patch? Momentarily it escaped him. Yes. He was going for chicken at the halal place on Edgeley Road. Yeah, it was a bit of a trek but they did good chicken. Jake had told him to go there one evening so he could describe it accurately and be recognized. And yeah, it was good. Seven o'clock. Believable time. Was the place open on a Friday night? Yes, he'd checked. Hadn't he? Yes; and if he hadn't, Jake and Leila would've.

He didn't sense it any more, that shadow he'd felt more than seen. But that wasn't enough, they'd told him. You have to be certain, we have to be certain. We have your back, don't worry. But if you don't feel right, you abort. Just walk past the alleyway. It's fine. There's always the fallback. Have your cover story ready. If we feel bad about it, the car will just not be there, waiting. Or if we don't have time to clear out, it'll be there with both sun visors down. The alleyway wasn't so far off now.

Leila gathered her thoughts and climbed nimbly out of her car. She peered briefly down the long street and saw both men walking. The follower was gradually catching up with Rashid but not moving quickly. He showed no sign of trying to conceal that he was pursuing Rashid. She turned and began to sprint to the parallel street, trying to calculate the distances, trying to work out her options.

She'd been a good middle-distance runner at school. She remained in good condition, went to the gym regularly. It was not too difficult to accelerate and make ground, calculating which of the snickets she should take through the gaps in the poorly maintained Edwardian terraces in order to emerge approximately where this man and Rashid might be. She was pleased she'd chosen to wear jeans and flat shoes as she ran, heart pounding, the words 'duty of care, duty of care' reverberating in her mind in precise rhythm with the effortful throbbing in her head and the slap of her shoes on the pavement.

There was definitely someone there. He wasn't imagining it. And he was making ground. There was no one else on the street, nowhere to go in this district of blank terraced houses of red brick. Pot luck if he knocked on a door. More likely than not, some red-faced racist would tell him to piss off. He felt the urge to break into a run but resisted it. They'd trained him, somehow they'd look after him.

Movement from his left side now, approaching through one of those narrow paths between the buildings. He turned involuntarily, then forced his gaze back ahead of him.

'Rashid! Rashid, man, hold up.'

He stopped.

'Just not seen you for a while, man. You haven't been to Friday prayers recently.'

He turned. It was the Somali, the thin smiling man who was learning under the imam at the mosque. Tawfiiq was his name. Ultra-faithful, imperturbable, impossible to read. His head was shaved and a wispy beard outlined his jaw. His large brown eyes shone. He smiled at Rashid. 'Hey,' he said, 'how you doing?'

Rashid knew he was glaring at him and tried to soften his gaze. 'Sorry, man,' he said, forcing a sheepish grin on to his face. 'In a world of my own. That's what my mother always says. I've just been busy. You know, work and stuff.'

'Missed seeing you around,' said Tawfiiq. 'You know you shouldn't skip prayers too often,' he added lightly.

Rashid looked into his eyes. He liked Tawfiiq. He looked ageless. 'I know. I'm sorry.'

'No need to apologize, man. Just good to see you. Where you off?'

'Going to stuff my face with fried chicken. The place up on Edgeley Road. You know it? Fancy coming?'

'Nah, don't think so. Love to. Only I got a meeting.'

Leila burst into the street. Rashid was talking to this other man, straight-backed but slight. They were smiling at each other and turned towards her. She was out of breath and ran up to them, at the moment of decision whether to employ force or charm. She put her hand in her pocket.

'Sorry, guys, but can you help, please?' she said.

Rashid looked straight at her. She ignored him.

'Sure,' said the other man. 'What's wrong?'

'I'm just getting a bit freaked, that's all. There's this man following me, I'm sure. It happens. I can deal with it. But there's hardly anyone around, and you guys . . .'

'Look normal?' said the slight man with the hint of a smile. 'What's he like?'

'White guy, balding, quite fat. Fifties? You know the sort.'

'Where is he? Let's find him.'

Rashid was still looking at her uncomprehendingly. Behind the back of the thin man she could see Jake's car pull out on to the road and stop. Its lights flashed briefly.

'There's no need,' she said. 'Just being with you guys will scare him off, I'm sure. I'll be fine. I hope you don't think that I normally behave like a helpless female.'

'Of course not,' said the thin man, with considered gentleness. 'But we can't just leave you here. Where are you going?'

'To be honest, I'm lost. I'm trying to find Bessemer Street.'

'It's back there,' ventured Rashid.

'I'll walk back with you,' said the thin man.

'I'll come with you,' said Rashid.

'No, it's all right,' said the other softly, turning to him. 'You've got your chicken to eat.'

Leila nodded slightly, and Rashid noticed. 'All right then. If you're sure.'

'There's really no need,' said Leila, as Rashid began to move away.

'I'm going that way anyway. My name is Tawfiiq.'

'Leila.'

'You aren't from here?'

'No. I'm visiting. I was looking for a supermarket in Bessemer Street. I wanted to buy some chocolates for my friend. She loves chocolate.'

They started walking.

'You're quite a distance out of your way.'

'I got hopelessly lost. My friend lives in a tall block over there somewhere.' She pointed vaguely with her free hand. 'At least I think so. I'm hopeless. White Rose Court, it's called.' She laughed.

'Ah yes. I know it. It's round the corner from the mosque.'

'That's right,' she said.

'I work at the mosque.'

'You're an imam?'

'Not quite. I'm not yet learned or wise enough. Perhaps one day.'

'Been in the city long?'

'Long enough,' he said. 'I like it here.'

They had completed the small talk and walked a block before he spoke again. 'Where do you live?'

'Birmingham,' she said instantly.

'And your friend, does she attend the mosque? We try to encourage women to come.'

'She's not been here long. And I'm afraid she's not particularly observant.'

'Ah,' said Tawfiiq. They continued to walk in silence.

'Nor am I, if I'm perfectly honest,' she said.

'Ah,' he said again. They had been walking some distance apart; now that gap widened. He moved ahead of her.

'Well, here we are,' he said at length. 'Bessemer Street. There is the supermarket. Goodbye, Leila.'

'Thank you. Goodbye.'

He turned the corner towards the mosque and disappeared. Thirty seconds later Jake's car pulled up alongside her and she climbed in quickly.

'Fallback,' said Jake.

'Fallback,' she said.

'Who is he?' asked Jake almost as soon as they sat down.

'Guy from the mosque,' said Rashid.

'And?' said Leila.

'And what? He's from the mosque. Somali.'

'Carry on.'

Rashid shrugged. 'Just a guy training to be an imam, that's all. Why is it so important?'

Rashid was sitting on the sofa, holding a glass of water, deliberately, it seemed, avoiding Leila and Jake's eyes. Jake knelt on the floor directly in front of him, in his space, and dared him to look away. He didn't.

'You know why it's important,' said Jake. 'He was there when you were on your way to this meeting. It may have been chance, probably was, but it's important because we have to get everything absolutely right. We're intent on looking after you properly and we need to deal with every risk as best we can. All right?'

Rashid's shoulders relaxed and he nodded. 'Yeah. All right.'

'So this Tawfiiq. What do you know about him?'

Leila had already done the homework on the computer. Tawfiiq Mahdi Mohamed, born 25 July 1991, Mogadishu. Legally resident in the UK since 2015. Novice imam, studied at a madrasa in Medina between 2011 and 2014 before returning to Somalia. Fluent Arabic speaker. No adverse mentions, no established connections with others with adverse mentions. Thought to be a religious moderate in line with the mosque's teachings. No foreign travel recorded since his arrival in the UK.

'He's training to be an imam, right? I used to see him down the mosque before I got involved with this lot. He was all right. Then I lost touch after I decided not to go to the mosque.'

'Did he know you'd been overseas?' asked Leila.

'No idea. Wouldn't have thought so. My folks tried to keep it quiet. My mum didn't want anyone at the mosque knowing.'

'He's not tried to contact you at all? Out of the blue?'

'He wouldn't know how. He's not got my mobile number. This is the first I've known of him since, well, I don't know.'

'What about his views?'

'He's one of those sweetness and light preachers, you know? He's not got the hard edge of the older guys. They can be stern. He's not.'

'Did you ever talk to him about jihad?'

'Why would I? I knew exactly where he was coming from. He's a nice guy. Not interested in all that shit. Know what I mean?'

'I do,' said Leila. 'We're going to have to be very careful with regard to him. Tell us if there's any further contact from him. Straight away.'

Rashid shrugged. 'If you say so. But you don't need to worry about Tawfiiq.'

Jake delivered Rashid back while Leila went through his reporting again. He'd said nothing new, but with the microphones they had in place that was to be expected. The map was helpful to visualize and confirm what they'd already pieced together from the recorded dialogue. What was most important was the contact with Rashid as the pressure built, together with the knowledge that he was continuing to report faithfully. He would suspect that the boys were listened to as they planned but he could not know for certain. It was, in addition, reassuring to know that he was keeping his head and not losing his powers of recollection as the day approached.

Jake returned to the room quietly and as they picked inconsequentially at sandwiches they picked at the case.

'This Tawfiiq thing . . .' he began.

'He doesn't seem bothered about it,' she said.

'He wouldn't. It's our job to be bothered for him.'

'We've done all we can. We just need to keep an eye on it.'

'You can never do everything you need to,' he said.

'We can't do everything.'

'Don't I just know it. Where did it turn to crap?'

'Sorry?'

'Abu Omar.'

'You learn from experience.'

'So they say. Or you're doomed to repeat the same mistakes, over and over. I wish I could single out the moment when I got it all wrong. But I can't. I thought I was good at this, but I didn't log all the discrepancies and incongruities. I was swept along. Maybe it was the momentum of it all. But no, it was just me. I could have stopped it, but I didn't.'

She said nothing.

'This must get right up your nose, this soul-searching,' he said.

'It's starting to a bit,' she said. 'If I'm honest.'

'I'm just worried we're missing stuff this time round, too.'

'I don't think so. But, you know . . .'

'Shit happens?'

'That's not what I said. But we just have to do our best.'

'Yeah. Try telling that to the inquiry when it comes round.'

'You felt betrayed?' she asked.

'Of course I was betrayed. The question is, by whom? But that's what we're here for, isn't it? To be betrayed. And in the end we all do the same thing.'

I5

SATURDAY

Up early, to be bussed out to the training facility on the edge of the moors. Big job, this, the full complement had been pulled out. All overtime cancelled for the foreseeable. Met officers to make up the numbers. Mutual aid invoked for West Mids and Lancashire to provide on-call teams in the city. Just in case. Detachment from 22 on standby, just in case too. Barracks opened up, kit bags neatly stacked. They were looking on, the Regiment boys. Hard bastards. He'd been one of them, still was a hard man by any normal measure, knew them for what they were. Shit hot, but still just humans with wives and kids and fears and hang-ups.

Forms to sign. Official Secrets and so forth. Top secret, need to know, you are signing to acknowledge your awareness that you are included on a highly sensitive indoctrination list, you undertake not to divulge details of this operation or its existence to any person you do not know is authorized. Wills carried up in plastic boxes to be gone through and confirmed or redrawn. Long black cars to and fro with the brass. Double guards on the gates and perimeter. Razor wire. All action carefully out of sight of the public. No-fly zone overhead. All discreet and understated. Legal team sitting in one office. Five and Six and GCHQ in another. The Int Cell. And this was just the sideshow. The main ops room was in town.

There was a briefing before they were taken on a walkthrough. Some spook came in to introduce the map jigged up on the big screen. Must be serious if the actual spooks had turned up and were doing the presentations, rather than the CTU civvies.

'This is what the reporting tells us of their plans,' she said, stern and confident, as she clicked. First a series of lines in different colours converged on the stadium, then each colour had its own section, representing one of the suspects.

The gaffer was up there too, and said, 'You'll each be allocated a subject and it'll be your job as a team to know everything about your ground.'

'When we get back to town, can we go on the street to walk it through, boss?' came the inevitable stupid question.

'Of course bloody not,' the gaffer said. 'Operational security. Use today as best you can.'

The woman took them through each of the subjects on the screen. It was neatly colour-coordinated to go with each of the routes. Very slick. 'No need to make notes,' she said. 'There'll be full dossiers in each of the seminar rooms.'

Then the walk-through. The huge area, four or five parade grounds' worth, maybe more, tarmacked over five or six years before so that a street scene could be simulated on it with stage-set buildings. Never before as large as this, though. The joiners and other workmen had done their best. Flimsy building facades cut off just above head height. White tape to represent roads and divide pavements. Makeshift traffic lights with wires dangling from the back. Gaps where side streets should have been but through which you could see the Heath Robinson skeleton backs of other 'buildings' or just trees and grass. It was like they were on a film set, or what Jon imagined one to be like. Still, he thought, they were much like actors, on stage tomorrow and next Wednesday. Except they had weapons that fired live ammunition.

It would be uncharitable to say it was cobbled together. It must have been an extraordinary effort. It'd all been laid on:

the whole of the stadium quarter. Jon Brough and his cohort walked their walk through terraced streets and tried to suspend disbelief. They finally succeeded as they turned a corner on to Stadium Way and saw Stadium Plaza ahead of them and, towering over it all, the representation of the ground itself on a huge screen. It was mind-boggling, like being catapulted into the future, part of some reality show in which they were playing a role. A single role, since they were as one. The muttering and joshing stopped the instant they turned that corner and saw the screen. It was time for lunch.

The power was out and the door had been open when Bilal got there. At least that's what he'd said, waiting at the entrance when Adnan arrived.

'You went in?' asked Adnan.

'Yeah. Just in the hall and switched the light on. At least I tried to. No power.'

Rashid had arrived. 'What's up?'

'Power's out,' said Bilal.

'And apparently the door was open,' said Adnan.

'It was,' said Bilal.

'OK,' said Rashid. 'What do we do now?'

No one said anything. Abdullah turned up and they explained.

'Got no option,' said Adnan. 'Too far advanced to give up on it now. Got to go in.'

Abdullah and Rashid agreed; Bilal wasn't so sure. 'What if it's a set-up?' he said.

'If it is, we're fucked anyway,' said Abdullah, and no one took exception to his language.

'I'll go in,' said Rashid with finality. 'You wait out here. I'll call you in. If I don't come out, clear off. Go home. Behave as if nothing's happened.'

No one stopped him.

He walked through the front door quietly and stood in the hallway, listening, waiting for his eyes to adjust to the gloom. The door at the end of the passage, the door to their room, was open. He didn't allow himself to think, simply covered the distance in delicate steps that he tried to keep silent, and stood before the door. He could see light in the room through the gap. He edged the door open and stepped forward.

'Stop there,' said the familiar calm voice. 'I wondered how long it would take one of you to summon up the courage. Well done. Fetch the others and we'll get down to business.'

Rashid went back to the front door and jerked his head in the direction of the interior. 'Come on. He's here.'

No one needed to ask who.

They filed in and each took a chair in the row lined up just inside the room. He was seated on the floor in his robes, beyond the light that glowed between them and him. Those boots, thought Rashid. Ridiculous for a holy man.

'So,' said the sheikh, smiling. 'Here we are.'

'What's happened with the electric?' said Abdullah.

'You've no need to worry about the electric,' said the man. 'You no longer have any need for this place. This will be our last meeting, my friends, before you meet your destiny. You won't return to this place. You have your plans?'

'Yes,' said Adnan. 'Shall we show you?'

'Are you happy with them?'

'Yes,' said Rashid.

'Then I don't need to see them. You are diligent men.'

'We thought –' began Abdullah.

'Yes?'

'We thought of hiring a van. You know, like –'

'Fine.' He seemed not to be interested. 'If you wish, of course. It's a good idea. And the cars?'

'All worked out,' said Bilal.

'Good. And the rest of your preparations?'

'They're done,' said Rashid.

'Well. Behind the door you will find four rucksacks, for your run-through tomorrow. You will need them next week, too.'

'Is that everything?' asked Rashid.

'Almost. You will meet on Monday and Tuesday to make your final arrangements. Sort that out between you. Be vigilant when you do this. I can trust you to ensure the security forces are not aware. Do not return to this place. It is forbidden. On Wednesday none of you will go to work. Take holiday, fall sick, whatever you need to do. Wait for me to contact you. This is the last time we shall all meet, but I need to see each of you separately on Wednesday, to supply you with what you need to carry out your holy mission. I will contact each of you by the messaging app. After that point you must not meet each other again.'

'But what if our plans are not suited to the weapons?' asked Abdullah.

'Don't fret. They will be. On Wednesday, wait for me to contact you, and be patient. It will be at hand. Be calm. Now go to your homes. Be normal. Enjoy these days. Do your work tomorrow and I will speak to each of you on Wednesday.'

Most of the afternoon they were busy at the laptops provided in one of the windowless rooms, tracking their routes through the streets on the mapping software. Every so often a group covering one of the subjects would gather together in a quiet huddle to discuss tactics, but most of the time it was silent in the room. Jon's team of three had been allocated Romeo, the boy called Rashid. He looked so innocent in the photograph, but then they all did, even down to the assassins in the markets in Kabul. He knew better than to trust a photograph.

At four the coach containing the Five surveillance contingent arrived and then, on the other side of the compound, the other buses with the role-players, some of them designated as innocent bystanders and four of them the lads who would play the boys themselves. Where did they get these people, he wondered, and how did they maintain secrecy? It was time to confab with the Five guys and gals, to map out their dispositions in advance of the first run-through.

By five thirty it was getting dark and they took to the mockup streets. This Romeo was not dissimilar to the real one and they were third up in playing out the scenario. They ran it through, Jon and his two oppos and their driver, their weapons concealed under jackets, in the slipstream of the joint police/ Five surveillance team as it progressed unimpeded to the stadium. Then once more, this time with a hard stop just before they reached Stadium Way. They were called through and the surveillance pointed out the subject. They concluded the stop safely, the three armed officers surrounding Romeo, Jon the lead shot while the other two scanned the vicinity. Simple as. A final run-through with all the subjects in motion towards the stadium, this time with a thinner smattering of pedestrians, and coordinated stops of all four. Then back to the canteen for steaming hot lasagne served out of those long steel trays.

As he ate he thought of it, if it came to it. Shoot-to-kill, to protect the public. A legal execution, in effect. He had no issues with that, provided it was justified. He relied on the system to tell him, and then it was his call in the moment. To kill or not to kill? What is the risk, what is the intent, what are the time tolerances? And then, all these computed, the cold language of the double-tap to the head. It wasn't technically a classic double-tap that they'd exercised; you ran it so that you were close enough not to need to re-aim. Just two rounds pulled off, as quick as. Often, of course, more – and you'd put in six or seven rounds for good measure once the target seemed neutralized. At which point your buddies would be joining in, too. No risks permitted here. The double-tap was to cease brain function instantly and to minimize the possibility of fingers wrapped round initiators actually doing the deed. The brain had to be stopped before the heart.

'No technical,' said Leila to Jake.

'You what?'

'The technical's gone down. There's been a power outage in the block.'

'Surely there must be back-up. Batteries?'

'It seems not. Beside the point now. It's up the spout, that's all we need to know. We're blind as to what they were discussing.'

'Did we get surveillance down there?'

'Some. But there was a big deployment to the training facility. By the time the surveillance got down there, there was no sign of anyone.'

'And the unit?'

'Locked up. As normal.'

'I'd better go collect Rashid.'

'OK, let's be as quick as we can,' said Jake. 'What's new?'

'All right. We met. You'll never believe it. That man was there.'

'What man? The sheikh?'

'That's right. There was no power in the area and the door was open and there he was, large as life. Grinning away. Those stupid boots he wears.'

'No power in the room?'

'No. He had this battery lamp or something.'

'Did you get a better view of him?'

'Not really. Keep your distance, he says. Same old rigmarole.'

'Boots?' said Leila.

'Yeah, these fancy boots. Snakeskin, I reckon. A Flash Harry holy man,' he said with a laugh. 'But the plan's still the same. He's going to contact us on Wednesday, to give us the necessary. We're not to go back there any more. Abdullah's idea about the van, that's a runner. So he'll book that on Monday. Man gave us these bags.' He showed Jake and Leila the rucksack. They checked it carefully. It was a supermarket brand, one of hundreds of thousands. They checked the seams and felt the fabric for hidden compartments. Nothing.

'Mind if we keep hold of this until tomorrow, Rashid?' said Leila.

'Course not. But I do need it then.'

'We'll need to see you tomorrow anyway, before the action starts.'

'All right. It's going to be all right, isn't it?'

'That's why we're talking to you, Rashid. To make sure it is all right.'

'Yeah,' said Rashid.

'We're going to have to trust each other one hundred per cent, Rashid,' said Leila.

'I do,' he replied, looking alarmed. 'Don't you?'

'That's the point,' she said. 'We do, and when it comes to it, that needs to be at the front of our minds. That's what'll get us through. We'll be there with you throughout, though you won't see us, looking after you.'

'Yeah,' said Rashid.

'Right. Until tomorrow.'

'Yeah.'

Stuart Calloway sat in the living room of the Home Secretary's constituency home. The Private Secretary said, 'Weekend surgery over. On their way back, so the protection team says.'

'Weekend surgery? I thought ministers were above that.'

'The Secretary of State is very keen to be seen to be

conducting surgeries when possible. Of course, with such a busy schedule . . . in which case the constituency chair steps in.'

They were interrupted by the sound of the cars drawing up outside. The front door was opened and the Private Secretary went into the hallway, closing the door behind him. The door opened again and the Home Secretary walked in, bringing, so Stuart fancied, a brisk breeze of business.

'Well then, Stuart. Let's have it. Make it quick. I have a family even if you don't.'

The Private Secretary peered round the door. 'Tea, Mr Calloway?'

'No,' said the minister, 'he won't be here long enough. Will you, Stuart?'

Stuart grinned inanely.

'Leave us, will you, Angus? All right, Stuart, let's get to it.'

'The counterterrorist operation I was briefing you on the other day, Home Secretary. You recall?'

'How could I forget?'

'It's nearing the end game. Wednesday, to be precise.'

'End game. I hadn't realized you people actually used that language. Go on.'

'The police, to be blunt, are getting twitchy. Between us.'

'As I understand it, they've a reasonable amount about which to become twitchy.'

'Indeed. You should be aware, however, that we remain rock solid on our assessments and our prognosis. This operation needs to go forward. We cannot afford to miss the boat.'

'And? What are you asking of me?'

'Nothing. Simply consider this. If this were brought to fruition the benefits would be immense all round.'

'Including for government, you mean. And if not?'

'It would be a police decision to intervene prematurely.'

'You're surely not asking me to interpose myself? We've discussed this.'

'Of course not, though a brief encouraging word to the Chief Constable might not go amiss. I was thinking of the inquiry.'

'The inquiry?'

'Its considerations might be heavily influenced by a successful outcome. In fact, its work might well be considered to be of somewhat less general value. It might be considered to be rather . . . marginal.'

'Not to the families.'

'That's true. But matters might become less pressing.'

'I'm rather tired of going round this buoy repeatedly, Stuart. We can't and don't want to influence the inquiry.'

Stuart looked sceptical. 'Of course not. But given the delicate juncture of the inquiry with regard to the US angle, if we could see our way to a short adjournment while the operation plays out?'

The Home Secretary looked at him. 'There may be some legal arguments that could bear airing. They might take up a few days. Wednesday, you say?'

'That's right.'

'If this comes out all right, you'd better have your off-the-record briefings sorted out. Clear blue water between the old ways and the new. Lessons learned. New working practices, comprehensive internal reviews and so forth. Heads have rolled, etcetera.'

'Indeed.'

'If you aren't seen to be cleaning out the sewers, then someone else will have to do it. I have given you fair warning. That it?'

After dinner there were more briefings as they waited for the right hour in the mess room. Intel had been received that the group intended to hire a van. This added a new dimension that would need to be played out on the mock-up. Other kit would need to be brought in. At eight forty-five they filed out into the darkness.

The mock-up town had become more real as darkness fell. It was less easy to spot the makeshift nature of the set, and the street lights that had been built lent the scene a more dramatic quality. In any case, disbelief had been suspended by everyone concerned as they concentrated on their small portions of this whole. This was the one, they were rehearsing for the final denouement and everything had to be spot-on.

Smooth as silk, he thought afterwards. The follow was routine, and he and his colleagues were called through before Romeo hit the main drag to the stadium. There were only two outcomes to be simulated here: the hard arrest and the double-tap. The third option was not to be contemplated. There remained some work to be completed over the next three days on tactics with the van – whether to puncture the tyres, to ram it or to kill the engine technically. But it could be dealt with.

Buoyed, they returned to their barracks. No beers tonight, and early to bed. If tomorrow went well they might afford themselves a modest sherbet, but even then they would be back on the mock-up on the Monday, and the Tuesday, so that they would be ready for the perfect op on Wednesday. There would be little if any sleep had tonight, but in the dorm he prepared for bed and wondered whether everyone, like him, was thinking: what if it all goes off tomorrow? Like last time. They were ready, that was all he knew.

Abdullah

He sat in his flat reciting the texts as he read them. A networked war movie ran in the background.

He had arrived. Truly arrived. These boys were his brothers.

He could weep to think of them: proud Adnan, Bilal with his spectacles, Rashid with that serious frown. In fact he *was* weeping. They had accepted him, the fat white loner everyone took the piss out of, as a fellow warrior. Islam had welcomed him, who repented of his sins and would wash himself of them in the hot blood of the unbelievers. Death was but a warm balm, the accomplishment of a life in submission and acceptance. He would drive that van at speed, slicing through the crowds with a calculated precision, killing as required. At a certain point he would emerge from the driver's seat and continue the killing with whatever weapon was provided, a machine gun perhaps, or even a machete. He would kill without mercy but without ravening lust. Though inwardly exultant, he would need to remain measured and calm if he were to maximize the numbers.

Eventually he would be killed himself. He hoped only for momentary realization, that fleeting chance to anticipate his delicious passing.

Bilal

He spent the evening at home with his parents watching television. This had been the pattern of their lives on a Saturday evening for as long as he could remember, interrupted only by his absence on the battlefield, a subject never mentioned in the household. 'Stay at home for once, Bilal,' his mother had said, 'like we used to.' He'd felt obliged.

His father slouched on the sofa, the mound of his paunch rising and falling as he stared, open-mouthed, at the screen. The bright colours and sharp movements reflected off his spectacles. It came to Bilal that from the other sofa he was mirroring the posture and expression.

'This is crap,' said his sister, only fifteen, and no one picked her up on her language.

His mother dozed next to his father, her laboured breath the beginnings of the inevitable snoring that they all joked about.

'Can we turn over?' said his sister, and when no one said anything she reached for the remote control and changed channels.

Still he watched, dull-eyed, submissive, complicit. Not for long, though. He'd had his doubts about everything. Those people he'd killed out there in the name of Allah. It seemed absurd, obscene and unreal. Now he planned to inflict further suffering and death. But was it any worse than this, an indolent Saturday evening in front of the TV? Perhaps in death he could acquire significance.

Adnan

His last Saturday night on this earth and he did not intend to waste it. To himself, he made no bones about leading a double life, though he kept each element carefully separated from the other. Adnan felt no shame at being two men in this single body. They existed at the same time, in the same breath and thought.

He put on the black trousers and the black silk shirt. Silk socks too, and the shoes that he'd shined before taking a shower. He'd annoyed his flatmates by hogging the bathroom. Never mind, it wouldn't be too long before they didn't need to worry about that. He didn't care about them, anyway. He checked his hair and went out to the waiting taxi.

Once, he'd had a few weeks of pretending to be a Bollywood actor. But the strain of maintaining the accent and explaining how, when he got someone home, a wealthy film actor bummed it in the squalid, poky flat was too much. He found anyway that there was a certain type of white girl who was attracted to the likes of him. Was it the intimation of spice, the dicing with danger? He didn't know, but there was a certain *je ne sais quoi* to him, that was for sure.

He'd booked the hotel. A suite, £658, but the credit-card bill wouldn't arrive until he was dead. He picked up the key at reception, checked the room out, helped himself to a Johnnie Walker from the minibar, and headed for the clubs.

He was well and truly bladdered but in control by the time he hit the Meet Market, which was the way he liked it. He never danced, got impatient doing the chatting-up bit, so it was the ideal place. It did what it said on the tin. Fifty quid to get in, so the riff-raff steered clear. He'd be able to score a line as well, for sure.

She was blonde and to his liking, tall, nice face. Big eyes, snub nose, full cheeks. Tits not too big, like some inflatable doll. Said she was a model, but they all did. It hid a multitude of sins anyway, and by sins he meant sins.

'What do you do?' she said. The music here wasn't too loud, this joint was sophisticated, so they didn't have to shout.

He sipped from his G&T and said, 'Company director.' Not so far from the truth. 'You live locally?'

'Over Leeds Road way.'

'Doesn't mean anything to me,' he lied. 'Just visiting.'

'Business?'

'You could say. I do a bit of football agenting. There's a game tomorrow. Game on for me if I can shift this deal for the end of season. One of my clients . . .' He tapped the side of his nose. She looked impressed. 'State secret. You know,' he said. It seemed she did. Her eyes widened.

'Time to go,' he said, and she didn't disagree.

Later, in the middle of the night, he woke with a start. He'd turfed her out at two – Amy or Emma or whatever her name was – with fifty quid for a taxi back wherever, because he needed the kip. Tomorrow was a big day. He'd told her he had to see his client to talk through the offer of a new contract the next morning. I'll be back here tomorrow night, though. Maybe see you in the lobby, around seven. She'd seen it for what it was, played the game, though. Yeah, sounds good.

Gone straight back to sleep and now here he was. So bloody wide awake it was unbelievable. He could go out right this minute and do the thing, he felt so pumped. Then, just as suddenly, it all went out of him. The fight. He felt as defeated as he'd ever been. It was just as well the end of it all was so near at hand. Touching distance. At bloody City. Would you believe it? A fitting stage for the final act.

Those other boys, brothers they might be but they were different from him. Bilal was a pernickety mummy's boy and Abdullah little more than a fanatical thug. He'd as likely be a member of Britain First as of the caliphate; all he needed was a cause to harness his violent bitterness. In another life Adnan might have liked Rashid, had him as a friend. But this short life, five days remaining, was this life and he hardly knew him.

So tired, but he had to be in a fit state for today's runthrough. This was his calling, after all. He found a miniature of Kahlúa in the minibar – it was just about all that was left – and knocked it back before slumping back on the bed. Four sixteen. He'd sleep in until kicking-out time.

Rashid

Like Bilal, Rashid was at home. While his father listened to the radio and his mother read the Saturday papers he browsed Facebook and Twitter for the latest Trump outrages.

'Want to do the crossword?' his mother asked him.

'Why not?' he said.

They sat next to each other pondering the clues, murmuring to each other as answers or elements of them occurred to them. It had been his father who'd taught him the technique of the cryptic crossword. They'd sat side-by-side when they were away in Whitby for their summer holidays, doing the crossword in the paper his father had bought during his seven o'clock walk. They'd be sitting in the Magpie Cafe with fish and chips, bread and butter and tea, watching the rain. His father loved the seaside, the salty tang reminded him of Karachi, however faintly. Rashid had become completely immersed in this world of anagrams and riddles and wordplay. His mother had previously done the crossword with his father but seemed happy for him to be supplanted by Rashid.

Both sets of grandparents had returned to the subcontinent after retiring, to the heat and the smells and the relative safety of Asia in comparison with this place, with its criminals and fumes and cold. His parents belonged here, and so of course did he.

It would have been six years ago, maybe seven, that it had become so pronounced it could no longer be ignored. Now it was he and his mother who did the crossword together occasionally, while his father whiled away his life in the sometimes distressed and manic, but often happy, oblivion of early-onset Alzheimer's. He was presently largely absent of rage but that might well come, they'd been warned. One of the small consolations of the condition, for Rashid, was that his father had been largely ignorant of his spell abroad and his involvement in the carnage. Now he was back, he and his mother never spoke of it. He knew she was anxious. She asked obliquely where he went in the evenings, to which he replied gruffly, 'Here and there,' but she never probed further. He saw her looking at him, though, all the time. There would, perhaps, come a time when they could talk properly. For the moment they chatted about the crossword or the weather, leaving those many other things unsaid.

Next Wednesday it would be over and a new, cleaner life would begin.

Leila

'How do you think it'll go?' asked Leila.

Jake shrugged. 'Who knows? I'm old enough not to make any predictions. Last time . . .' He struggled for words and, for the first time for a month or more, was close to tears.

'Sorry,' she said. 'I didn't mean –'

'It's all right. We both need to get some sleep. It's going to be a long day tomorrow. We have to keep our heads. The risk calibration's been ratcheted up, one notch closer to complete avoidance. If Rashid does anything untoward, they'll call it there and then.'

'Do you think he will?'

'No idea. I have a better feeling about him than I did with . . . I don't have the same doubts. Anyway, feelings are beside the point. This is where we are, this is where we'd want to be, and this is where we do our job. What time is it?'

'Two fifteen.'

'Bloody hell. I think we've done this to death. Is there anything else?'

'Don't think so,' said Leila.

'You get off, then. You've got your car?'

'Yeah.'

'Straight home, straight in the house, no messing.'

'You're advising me about my security?'

He smiled. 'Text me once you're inside and all's OK. I'll close up here.'

'See you tomorrow, Jake.'

'Yeah.'

They waited patiently through the night. Those covering Adnan had it easiest. They spoke to hotel security and managed to get the next-door room. Two of them took it in turns to walk through the corridor of the fifth floor while the other sat in the room, a stethoscope to the thin dividing wall. The room phone was covered. Down in the hotel's security room others sat monitoring the CCTV of the mainly silent building. The girl was mopped up when she left the room and interviewed under caution by the police. No need to hold her under the Terrorism Act. Poor girl was terrified, and there were no adverse traces. A detective constable drove her home and was deputed to stay with her the whole day. She was so distressed she was glad of the company.

The other crews sat in their cars and vans outside the homes of the other boys, in falling temperatures and driving rain. The pitch would be heavy for the big game tomorrow, one said to another. Correction: today. They would come off shift at nine, handing over to the day crews, but would be required back by early afternoon, in plenty of time for the day's show. All hands on deck. A chance to grab a couple of hours, was all.

16

SUNDAY

Today something would be done about it, and something would be seen to be done. Eventually. Good, whatever that was, could prevail over evil. Or it might, again, fail. Evil might prevail over evil.

Which would be the lesser of the multiple evils? Degrees of differentiation were not pertinent at this moment. He tossed and turned, turned and tossed as he agonized over the *right* thing to do. Right in what sense?

He had set the alarm for five but rose ten minutes before. He switched his mobile phone off and went to the kitchen, filling the kettle and flicking it on, scratching his eyes as if the action would bring some sense into the world. It seemed for a moment that he might have all the time in the world at his disposal, the rest of his life at least, and he shook his head, like a dog flapping its jowls, to wake. He drank a mug of instant coffee, two spoonfuls so the bitterness struck the back of his throat. It tasted of burnt wood.

He put on his running gear and tied his laces carefully in a double bow. He filled his water bottle and placed it in the rucksack he carried on these morning runs, not every day but as often as he could manage. He pulled the pack tight to his back and then removed it to check that he'd packed his keys. He had.

As he left the flat he heard the click of the lock and checked that the snib had engaged and that the door was secure. He was on his way.

The dawn broke tentatively as he ran. It was still dark in the city streets, washed clean by the overnight rain. He ran under the sodium glare and the little boxes with the swivelling basilisk gaze of their cyclops eyes. He did not exert himself, settling into an easy pace. Nice and steady, he thought. His normal route took him down the silent canal towpaths that belonged to a more solid age, with their worts and buttercups and rough grasses peering between the worn paving stones, under bridges whose stone was blackened to a filthy darkness. It could be dangerous down there, people said, with the homeless and the druggies. But they would just shrug amicably at the rich guy in the emerald-green shorts.

Just after the railway station, still boarded up nearly four months on, he dived down the steps to the arches on his way to the towpath via the extensive network of tunnels beneath the modern city, where entrepreneurs of various hues undertook their daily business, often shady: mechanics in grimy workshops fitting reconditioned shocks, vendors of secondhand appliances and industrial machines, buyers and sellers of knock-off IT kit, TVs, audio equipment and whatever electronic gear could command a price. The cafe at the end, selling the full English at less than five quid. None of them open at five forty-five on a Sunday morning. No sign of life.

He diverted substantially from his normal route, tracking back and forth under the arches that extended as far as the suburbs. Eventually he reached the lock-up, where he began his preparations. He released the high-security padlock with one of the two keys but he didn't go in. He bent double and breathed deeply. He loosened his laces. He opened the rucksack and put it on the floor, extracting the items he needed, methodically making his preparations, swallowing his fear.

Finally he took out an ancient pay-as-you-go phone, never used, and switched it on. He knew he would have a faint signal here but not inside the lock-up. He dialled.

'Yeah,' came the sleepy voice.

'We have to meet,' said Jake. 'Urgent.'

'Come on. Give me a break.'

'Afraid I can't. It has to be now. At place D. How long?'

'Maybe ten.'

'Me too. Ten it is, then.'

'What's this about?'

'When we meet.'

Every case had its fallback for a crash meet. In this case it was place D: here, understood between them. He was ready. He had to be. It was in motion. He glanced around for some-where to put his pack. Behind a pillar would do. No one was about to come here for the next few hours at least. He hoped. No, he knew. He was a diligent spook who did his recces.

The padlock secured a chain looped through two crude square holes cut in the battered metal face of the doors. This, too, had been part of his calculation. It was fiddly, though, once inside, to pull the chain tight, lock the padlock and loop it back out so that it could be unlocked from the outside and look as if no one had yet arrived. It took three attempts and some force-ful pushing. There was less give than he'd anticipated. Panic almost set in as he felt the ten minutes expiring and the rasp of the kitchen timer in his head sped towards its final ping. Time up.

Job done, he breathed in the earthy air.

He could not assume but knew, really, that ten minutes was typical bravado. It'd be twenty, more like. It was only a short drive but he'd have to dress and make himself look good. Undoubtedly he'd park under the arches. Meanwhile, Jake just had to wait those inching minutes.

Sure enough, eventually there it was, coming closer and louder, the wheezy clatter of a workhorse diesel, not his normal conveyance. The engine quietened and Jake tried to find a moment of calm so that he could locate the inner tranquillity and physical stillness that would see this done. Much as he liked to know the reasons for everything, there would be no dialogue, no whys and wherefores, no excuses either way. No insincere greetings, the purpose of the meeting tacit and hanging there, dangerous. Pointless to ask why, since neither of them would know. It simply was.

Steps, sounding jaunty, scraping grit on the tarmac, amplified in the silence. Snakeskin boots, no doubt. At least he didn't whistle, though Jake wouldn't have been surprised. There was a metallic fiddling at the door and then the clatter of the length of chain being pulled through the hole, close at hand.

Jake had placed himself in the darkness directly behind the door. In he came, eyeing the length of the lock-up, Jake could see. If he closed the door there would be a messy confrontation at the entrance. Jake had calculated that it'd be left open to await his own arrival, and he was right. He was not thought to have got here yet.

There is something fascinating in watching other people when they believe themselves to be completely alone, unobserved. Simply being, they don't need to be doing anything *of interest* to be of interest. Best if not, in fact: just entirely themselves, neither self-conscious nor aware of anything other than their own selves, the sound of their own breathing, the smell of their own bodies. He was carrying his usual take-out cappuccino casually in his right hand. Jake could smell the coffee. He glanced again down the narrow length of the unit, into the dark space at its distant end where they were supposed to meet.

There, Jake knew, were two chairs and a battery lamp,

switched off. He'd set them up himself this morning. No power and no electricity bills. Just the cash payment every three months to the shyster that owned most of these places. In advance. It was a one-time meeting place not on record at HQ, acquired by his own private enterprise through a series of aliases and cut-outs on the premise of an imaginary business that all participants in the transaction knew did not exist but about which no one asked questions. Off the books altogether and strictly forbidden. One of Jake's insurances: against what? Against contingencies that he hadn't been able to articulate when he'd acquired it eighteen months before but which he'd felt inchoately to be if not necessary then prudent. There was no time to congratulate himself on his unformed prescience.

Zaki Ibrahim would not reach the chairs. Jake moved quickly and economically, conscious of the tiniest rustling noise that his motion caused. This clothing was not designed with stealth in mind. Zaki seemed not to hear him, intent on his destination. Overhead Sunday morning trains rumbled from their platforms. Jake was not complacent. Zaki was at best sly, and at worst a self-satisfied, mediocre epitome of banal evil. Jake could not see his face, and would not. The cold not of icy precision but of sweaty fear ran down his back and he stifled a shudder as he made up the ground. Suddenly, and startlingly, he was upon him.

No words, no acknowledgement, not even an exchanged look to tell him he'd worked it out and was oh-so-clever. Jake wanted to understand but understood, too, that this was a mistake. He never would. The plan was that Zaki would not know anyone was there, let alone Jake, until, possibly, the millisecond of awareness when it was far too late.

Jake raised the weapon and the oversuit creaked audibly and alarmingly. He exhaled through the mask. He placed the barrel of the weapon on Zaki's neck, resting on the top of the vertebra, and pulled the trigger. There was a boom in the arched chamber, this little cathedral, and a recoil. The expulsion of matter through the top of Zaki's head was not visible in the dimness, though Jake could feel a little warm rain. It may have been coffee.

All systems down. No flailing. Power disconnected. Partly for verisimilitude, partly for certainty, Jake gripped Zaki momentarily and fired again, then let him drop.

There was a moment when Jake felt not depression or disgust but a compulsion to raise the weapon to the flesh just beneath his own chin and fire again. It would have offered a kind of symmetry. But he knew he had to think of the rest of the day and Abu Omar.

Rashid, he corrected himself with a start.

He dropped the gun. Acquired from a criminal who'd been on the periphery of a separate investigation and whose details he'd mentally recorded, its serial number had been expertly filed. It had probably been used in other crimes; it wouldn't be used in the future. He'd obtained it in Glasgow two years previously. Another of the insurances against the awful unforeseen eventuality. It hadn't been premonition.

To drop the thing here would serve the fiction of the professional hitman hired by angry heroin traffickers that Jake hoped the police might construct as a working hypothesis to start with. There was no reason, despite his role as a low-level informant, to connect Zaki Ibrahim with terrorism. Until, that is, the police came to search the white Transit van parked outside.

He had maybe a few more minutes of his putative canal run beyond the scope of the city's CCTV before he would be required, for future exculpatory purposes, to reappear for the cameras. He glanced outside the lock-up and all was as it should be. He decided to risk a glance inside the van and went back to Zaki to fish out the keys. Though he already knew, he had to see it to make it real.

The cab was empty. The rear was secured by a large professional padlock with a sign saying: NO TOOLS KEPT IN THIS VEHICLE OVERNIGHT. Inside were four small rucksacks, identical to the one that Rashid had showed him and Leila. He dared not touch them, had no idea whether Zaki had booby-trapped them. It would be just like him to fit an anti-tamper detonating device that he would remove just before they were substituted for the boys' empty bags later in the day. It was foolhardy enough of Jake just to glance in here. He edged open a plastic carrier bag cautiously. It contained four battered mobile phones. Strewn in the dust on the floor were black robes, a checked keffiyeh and – of course – a false luxuriant beard with a tube of theatrical gum. Things must have been catching up with poor old Zaki, Jake thought. He'd have expected him to be fastidious in folding his costume and storing his props securely. Maybe he'd disturbed him this morning in his preparations.

The effect of this get-up would have been almost comical. No wonder he wanted them to keep a distance. No wonder the boys, from some subliminal inkling in their hearts, had laughingly called him the sheikh.

He should have realized earlier. Mrs Masoud had seen it, he was sure. Had seen something, anyway, been too hesitant about her conclusion, or fearful, to give it voice. Zaki must have been laughing all the while.

The game. That's what it would have been for Zaki. Gaming Jake. Gaming the world. Whether he was shifting smack or planning attacks. The buzz of it, having it over the likes of Jake and Dave Philpott, being oh so many steps ahead. Payback for the sins the world had perpetrated on the person of Zaki Ibrahim. But Jake would never really know.

Zaki's network. He must, at least, have had contacts out there from whom he received the details of the boys he would sacrifice. There must have been plans laid. He may have had an infrastructure in this city. But this was beyond Jake, in a place on the distant side of the fog of fatigue he now felt. It would be his colleagues, with their crunching of the data and metadata and their international reach, who would have to unravel all this in due course. He'd reached his limit.

He did not further indulge his curiosity but replaced the keys on Zaki's body before securing the lock-up and going to his own daypack and the carrier bag he'd left beside it. In careful sequence he removed the bright blue overshoes, the plastic bonnet and the mask before stripping off the white non-contamination suit with the texture of coated paper, placing everything carefully in the carrier. He peeled off the latex gloves, turning them inside out, one inside the other, before tying the hand end off in a knot, feeling the air on his hands cooling the sweat. He dropped them into the bag and knotted it. From his rucksack he took another carrier bag and placed the full one inside it, tying this carefully too. Placing the package inside the daypack, he opened his water bottle and took a long drink. He had a day, maybe two, to dispose of the bag. Even when they discovered Zaki's body and searched the Transit it was unlikely that the police would come knocking at his door, but he must be cautious.

He resumed his run, thinking the timing was just about perfect.

He did not know how he could continue with the day. He felt exhausted, contrite, mournful. The temptation to call in sick was all but overwhelming. He might, still, do this. Yet Rashid, and possibly Leila, needed him. Everyone needed him.

As he approached his flat he noticed a large black Volvo around the corner, a driver in the front seat. This was not unusual in this part of town, its affluent executives feeding and feeding from the city economy. But on a Sunday? he thought, mildly curious.

Once inside his flat, he found his mobile on the kitchen counter and switched it on. It immediately emitted a chorus of ringtones and alerts and a flashing light show of notifications. As instructed he rang HQ and was patched through instantly to Stuart Calloway.

'The hell you been?' asked Stuart.

'Out for an early run,' he replied. 'Not much time recently.'

'You're supposed to be on call twenty-four/seven.'

'So sue me, Stuart. I needed the time to think. Leila can cover for me.'

'Today you choose to go offline?'

'For an hour or so.' He sighed, he hoped, with sufficient resignation. 'Sorry, Stuart. What's up?'

'Get your arse down here.'

'Today?'

'Now. You're needed here.'

'What's happened?'

'Nothing's happened. I need you here.'

'But how –?'

'This is for your own good. Your oppo can stand in.'

'She's great. But what if it all kicks off?'

'She can cope. I've told George. I'm telling you to get down here precisely to safeguard the integrity of this op. Now. Get. Your. Arse. Down. Here. There's a car waiting for you.'

'I need to shower.'

'He's ringing the bell . . . now.' Stuart terminated the call, and the entryphone rang.

In his utilitarian flat there were no useful loose floorboards under which he could store the carrier bag, no false-floored cupboards, no unexpected roof voids, no accessible cisterns.

One of his two instant decisions was to take it with him. Having showered and shaved meticulously while Derek, Stuart's driver, sat patiently in the lounge, he packed his overnight bag. He wore a suit but no tie – right, he thought, for the circumstances. As he came into the lounge Derek was consulting his watch. He looked up and scowled.

17

George emerged from the Executive Liaison Group to brief Leila.

'All systems go,' he said.

'Jake,' she said.

'I told you. He's out of it. Stuart's orders.'

'You're joking. He's run this from the start. Without him there would be no operation. No Rashid.'

'I know.'

'He's done nothing wrong. He's been great.'

'I know.'

'This is nuts. Right now, of all times.'

'I know, Leila. There's nothing we can do. We just have to get on with it.'

'It's unfair.'

'Yes. And your point is?'

'Did you have anything to do with the decision?'

'What do you think? Of course not. I've had a blazing row with Stuart over it.'

He would have, but ultimately he'd have conceded. She remembered an earlier conversation with Jake. 'George is great,' he'd said. 'He has integrity. He's a very moral person. He has no sense of deference. But you have to understand that at base he's a company man. This place means more to him than a place of work. It's a belief system. Besides, he's married and has four kids, a Border collie and a mortgage to feed.'

'But Rashid . . .' said Leila.

'Tell me about it,' said George. 'He won't, though. When he

says he'll walk out of the door if Jake isn't involved, he's just posturing. Stuart is right on that.'

'Easy for you to say.'

'True. Have faith in yourself, Leila. You can do it. Rashid believes in you as much as he believes in Jake. Can't you see that Jake has been preparing for this all along? Preparing Rashid for it. It'll be fine.'

'The timing, though.'

'Agreed. But we are where we are. This is what we have to deal with.'

'This is crazy. What do I say to him?'

'Whatever gets you through the night.'

'Can I talk to Jake?'

'No,' he said firmly. 'That's Stuart's instruction. No one to talk to him. Not me, not you. He's incommunicado. Let's just concentrate on what we do now. There's someone you need to meet. Just wait here.'

Jake made to sit in the front seat but it had been moved forward as far as the runners would take it. 'Stuart has long legs,' said Derek, and Jake rather thought that Derek preferred the demarcation of roles and ranks. So he'd climbed in the back, his overnight bag beside him.

He took a call on his office mobile. 'Only got a few minutes,' said George. 'ELG's just finished and there's a load to do. Plus, you're supposed to be in purdah. No one's supposed to speak to you. I've just read the riot act to Leila. Suppose you're on the way down now?'

'Yeah,' said Jake. 'In the car.'

'Right. No need to say anything. Just wanted to say how sorry I was.'

'It's all right.'

'It's not, but Leila will be fine. If she phones, don't pick up.

The ELG went well, by the way. All teed up for today. Everything tickety-boo. Won't go into detail. Listen, Stuart is in a difficult position.'

'I know.'

'He's trying to save the soul of the place, is the way he sees it. With virtually every other bugger trying to destroy it. Ministers are on his case and, in his eyes, the new boss has been shipped in to do a demolition job. Stuart likes himself in the role of messiah. He's very gloomy, though. Just what we need at the moment. A lot on his plate, mind you. A detached boss just waiting for us to trip up so he can clear the stables. Won't involve himself in any decisions in case it makes him complicit. And a Home Sec who says they're all operational decisions. Nothing to do with government.'

'I know.'

'You know how ambitious Stuart is and he's not my cup of tea any more than yours. But he's in an impossible position, trying to keep us in the game. Just don't fly off the handle when you get there. Or do something you might regret.'

Jake chuckled. 'Do you really think I'd do that?'

'No. Again, just wanted to say how sorry I am. Be right as rain by the end of next week. You'll be back in business. Got to go. Over and out.'

Jake sat back and looked out of the window for a while. It looked as if it might be a fine day. Derek was obviously not in the mood for talking, not surprisingly, as he followed the marked police 4x4 ahead flashing its blue lights and slicing through the traffic. Jake delved in his bag for his personal mobile and began browsing. There was a lot of admin that had stacked up.

'Care to use the car's wifi?' asked Derek, looking in the mirror.

'It's all right, thanks,' said Jake. 'Got 4G.'

4G on the M1.

'Please yourself,' said Derek.

It was on. Word came back from the police ops room that the ELG had confirmed all systems go and that they should spend the rest of the morning preparing. They'd come back from the training facility early in the morning. The kit would be cleaned yet again, each would check his or her gear, including the clothing that they'd wear today. They'd had to line up to make sure they weren't all inadvertently wearing the same uniform of jeans, trainers and dark jackets. Bits and pieces had been brought in from stores to ensure that as far as possible they looked like normal members of the public.

He'd had a call from the gaffer, who'd been at the ELG. 'Get yourself over here. Won't take long. Car'll pick you up in a couple of minutes.'

He was shown in by the back entrance and ushered up the stairs to the intel unit behind the secure doors. Jon had been here before, once, but never inside the cell that was inside the cell, protected by a further electronically locked door. Where the spooks lived. The gaffer waited inside a small meeting room along with the SIO and a couple of people he didn't know. The bloke he'd seen once or twice around big meetings. The woman was Asian, tall and young, with an unblinking direct gaze that spoke of a determination he liked.

'This is George,' said the SIO. 'And Leila.' They shook hands pleasantly enough and looked at each other with wary smiles.

The man called George said, 'Hello, very pleased to meet you,' and suggested they should all sit down.

'George?' said the SIO.

'Thanks. You're aware that there's a sensitive intelligence background to this case?'

'Yes,' said Jon.

'Would you be surprised to learn that most of the intelligence we have derives from a covert human intelligence source?'

'I'd kind of worked that out.'

'I want to talk to you about the source. Before I do that I'm going to have to ask you to sign a document acknowledging that you know and that you will deal with this information under the standing instructions. Any issues with that?'

'None at all.'

George handed him a form and he read the rubric carefully before signing. There was nothing that wasn't contained in the criminal law anyway.

'The case officer for the CHIS is Leila,' said George.

She smiled politely, and he returned the smile.

'You're lead shot for one of the subjects of interest in this operation, that's right?' continued George.

'Yes, for Romeo.'

'Well, Romeo is Leila's CHIS.'

Though he'd thought one of the people mixed up in this was an informant, and that suspicion had been heightened when the gaffer had hoicked him out, this was still a surprise. It always would be, he guessed, if Leila's people were doing their job right. He just said, 'Fine.'

'We thought you needed to know and wanted to give you a chance to ask any questions,' said the gaffer.

'Thank you, sir.'

'So?'

'I suppose the only thing is this. I don't know how to ask this politely, but is this going to end up like the previous one? The station attack?'

'Simple answer is I don't know, Jon. We don't think so, but it'll come down to close-run decisions this afternoon and next Wednesday.'

'Why don't we just take them out before this afternoon?'

The SIO interrupted. 'Because as yet we don't have sufficient evidence to charge them, other than for relatively minor offences. We need to collect more.'

'But still.'

'You're right. We'll see come Wednesday when the moment's right to intervene. There'll be another ELG before that. Possibly we'll do the capture earlier in the day, depending on the risks. The ELG today was purely for this afternoon.'

'No thought of disruption?'

'Plenty of thought. Plenty'd like it called here and now. But the ELG has made its decision. Each of the subjects is under twenty-four-hour surveillance, and none possesses any material currently that could pose a risk to the public. To a high degree of confidence, at least. And when the final firearms briefing comes you'll be instructed to use the precautionary principle.'

'Sir.'

'So,' said George. 'Questions. Rather than us all sitting here like a Grand Jury, we thought it might be helpful for you to chat to Leila, to get a feel for Rashid, or rather Romeo.'

'No evidential note-taking,' said the gaffer. 'Background intel. May be admissible in court but no written notes.'

The senior men left the room.

'Well,' said Leila.

'Well,' he said, looking at his hands, which were clasped together on the table in front of him.

'What do you need to know?'

'What's he like, this boy? He is only a boy, isn't he?'

'He looks younger than he is. He's twenty-two. He's a sweet boy –'

'Sorry,' he said. 'I didn't mean that. I don't want to know anything about him as a person, apart from one thing, which we'll come back to at the end. What's he like physically?'

'You'll have seen the surveillance videos and photos, no doubt. They're a good likeness. He's tall and lean and intense. He lopes along but covers the ground quickly. He looks as if he's concentrating on something. If someone surprises him, he can jump. He's quite nervous, quite easily startled. And then he just stares at you as if he's frightened.'

'Is he powerful physically?'

'Not especially, I'd have thought, though I'm not sure. He's quite athletic in an awkward way but I'd back myself in a fight with him.' She smiled again.

'Right-handed or left-handed?'

'Right.'

'Clothes?'

'He doesn't seem bothered. Jeans and a sweatshirt, and that blue jacket on the videos. And you know about the rucksacks.'

'Impulsive? Rash?'

'Definitely not. You should also know that he's been comprehensively briefed on what to do in the event of a police challenge. Keep his hands visible, put them in the air and submit to instructions.'

'Yeah. Final question. We're called through and I'm facing him. Gun's levelled. I shout the challenge. I look at him and he puts his hands up, looking with this innocent startled face at me. I look into his eyes. Do I trust him?'

'I can't answer that,' she said.

'I may have to.'

'I can't predict the circumstances. I don't know what your angle of shot is or how many bystanders there are or what your orders are or whether his stance is aggressive or whether you, in yourself, can interpret the expression on his face and trust it.'

'Do you believe him?'

'I can quote you all kinds of crap about never believing,

retaining an open mind and staying sceptical. All of which are true. It's by no means conclusive, even in my head, but I wouldn't be here if fundamentally I didn't believe him. And will he obey instructions? On balance I think he will. He's not an idiot.'

'But don't blame you if he blows me and a hundred others to oblivion.' He smiled to lessen the harshness. Or possibly to increase it.

'That's about the sum of it,' she said. No smile from her to soften it.

Before they drew in at the main entrance the police car peeled away and headed for its next task. The car was checked before they slid slowly down the ramp and into Stuart's parking space below the building. Derek opened the door for him.

Jake shouldered his bag and said, 'Just going to say hi to Norman. That is, if he's still chief car washer.'

Derek tutted and raised his eyebrows.

Norman was a sad-eyed widower in his sixties, once a military policeman, then a surveillance officer, and latterly a driver for the brass, now in charge of the wash area for the important cars. When Jake had had a posting in facilities management for a year, to 'round' his career – it hadn't worked – he'd got to know Norman. He had nothing to do without his wife and always put himself on the roster for Sundays. 'Good time to get the office shipshape. Sort out all the stuff that's stacked up during the week. All those emails. Invoices,' he'd say. Both knew it was to bury the emptiness.

He was in the tiny windowless office. 'How're you doing, son?' he said when Jake looked round the door. 'Cuppa?'

'No thanks, Norm. In a hurry. Not often I get down to the smoke so thought I'd pop my head in and say hello. Got to see Stuart. You around later?'

'Should be until five,' said Norman.

'Maybe catch you later, then,' said Jake. 'Got somewhere I can chuck this?' He waved the carrier bag in the air. 'Had my breakfast on the way down.'

'Dumpster's where it always was,' said Norman, and Jake waved his goodbye. Before he turned the corner into the parking area he slid back the metal lid and tossed the bag in. The dumpster was for the rubbish from the garage – oil filters, filthy rags and lengths of dirtied blue cleaning paper, and containers for oil, screen wash, shampoos and waxes – and was cleared early each Monday morning, for landfill.

Derek was waiting impatiently by the entrance into the building, holding the door open. 'Lift's held,' he said curtly. Stuart's Private Secretary was waiting in the lift; he smiled at Jake but said nothing.

'Jake,' said Stuart. 'So glad you could make it. Tea? Coffee?'

'No thanks.'

'All righty. Greg, don't think we need you for this. Close the door behind you, would you, please?'

Stuart sat in the armchair, leaving Jake to perch on the sofa.

'I can understand why you're not happy.'

'Hmm,' said Jake.

'How will Leila cope?'

'She'll do fine.'

'I was right after all. This is in your interests as much as anyone else's, you know. No one wishes to place you in the way of harm. You're better off out of it.'

'What shall I do now I'm here?'

'Do what you want. Catch up with your expenses. Write some think-piece on the future of the covert human intelligence source if you want. No contact with anyone up there, though.'

'Leila's in the firing line now?'

'Comes with the territory. I understand it was you and George who pushed her virtues so hard. So we'll see.'

They looked at each other.

'You need to see the bigger picture, Jake. There is a context.'

There's always a context, thought Jake.

'What with the inquiry, we're struggling for credibility. It's important we get this op right. People wouldn't be impressed if we fouled up and the officer at the centre of it all was in fact the person in charge of Abu Omar. I'm being blunt, you understand, for brevity. Busy day.'

'Why didn't you move me earlier, then? It's not the greatest timing.'

'I've been saying for some time. George was resistant. Recent developments –'

'The disclosures at the inquiry? The Americans?'

'Amongst other things, yes. We've had to re-calibrate. You're much better out of it . . .'

There was more. There usually was with Stuart.

'I've been wondering,' he said. 'There may be a way out of this pickle. The inquiry and all that.' He waved his hand vaguely.

Jake waited. Stuart looked at him, steepling his fingers.

'This inquiry,' he said, 'is more than inconvenient. It's becoming damaging, especially since the American thing. There are those agitating for it to be troublesome whom we'd normally expect to be on our side. I can't expect it's much fun for you either.'

'Not exactly.'

'I've been chatting to the lawyers. They wondered whether it might be in your best interests to refuse to give further evidence.'

'On what basis?'

'On two grounds. First and foremost because it could prejudice any future legal proceedings that may take place. If, for instance, you were to be prosecuted, God forbid, the case could be put out of court because of statements you made under duress in the inquiry. The second reason would be because of that very badgering. You could claim, with justification, that the questioning to which you've been submitted amounts to harassment of a witness and that it has placed you under mental stress. This way, you see, we can turn the so-called latitude the Chair's extended to our advantage.'

'How do you think that would play with the public?'

'We'd just have to play it by ear. Take it on the chin. Better than the alternative.'

'What about government?'

'Government's rather hoist by its own petard. Made it a judicial matter, so has to play by the rules the judiciary set. Just duck out of the inquiry for the next couple of days. Claim illness, stress, whatever. Get your lawyer to talk to them. We'll help.'

'You asked me to find my own legal advice because the Service's interests might diverge from mine.'

'You know very well that was no more than a legal nicety. We've always stood shoulder to shoulder. Look, it's a racing certainty that after next Wednesday the inquiry will be ancient history. Kicked into the long grass. Government loves to associate itself with success.'

'And dissociate itself from ignominious failure.'

'Don't speak like that. It's all going to be fine. HMG will want the inquiry out of its hair. Some way will be found.'

'And the possible charges against me that the inquiry's raised in people's minds? Murder? Manslaughter? Misfeasance in public office?'

'I was coming to that. I think we can massage that. The legal process is a tortuous thing. But I think that if we apply enough leverage the CPS may well come to a judgement that if they bring charges at all it will be for lesser offences.'

'But no guarantees?'

'You've run enough assets, Jake, to know that you can't give guarantees. You've spoken the words enough times, you probably helped write the script.'

'Yes. And the point is, surely, that you actually can't influence the CPS. Other than with genuine legal arguments. They don't take kindly to leverage.'

'Well, ye-e-s. But I'd like to think that, in exceptional cases, for reasons of national importance –'

'One bound and we're all free. Except for me of course. I was forgetting that. The fact that you'd like to think that doesn't exactly sound like any kind of assurance, Stuart. But I'll give it due consideration.' He looked, expressionless, into Stuart's eyes.

'Your brief knows how to contact our legal team.'

'Yes. So I do whatever I want today?'

'Stick around London. Don't go back. Pop up to the ops room about half five. Things should be starting up in earnest then. I'll be there.'

'Think I might catch up with some personal correspondence.'

'Good,' said Stuart, ushering him to the door.

'Don't have any writing paper or envelopes, though.'

'Shirley,' said Stuart to his secretary, irascibly, 'get some of that nice notepaper for Jake here, will you? Not the headed stuff. And envelopes.'

'Got any stamps, Shirley?' said Jake.

He found a quiet room away from the hurly-burly where he could concentrate. He did not consider himself an impulsive person. The plan had been there all along, never to be implemented. Just another little insurance policy. We all needed insurance; it was just prudent.

Until now. It had been from Stuart's call that morning that

the idea had suddenly sprung, and then the resolve: do it now. His second instant decision.

He had a number of tasks. First, he composed a long letter to his lawyer asking him to confer with the Service's legal team and with the counsel to the inquiry. At all events, he would be unable to attend the inquiry the following day owing to his indisposition through unspecified ill health. For his lawyer's information only, he indicated that he felt so distressed by the events of the past months and the inquiry that he could not bring himself to give further testimony at this stage. His lawyer had told him earlier that, should he begin to feel under undue stress, a doctor could be found who'd swiftly sign the necessary paperwork. Jake was beyond caring.

He wrote to George, briefly, to apologize. He wasn't strong enough, he wrote, and it was an effort to keep self-pity from his tone. He wrote to his parents, asking for their understanding and hoping to see them soon.

In his letter to Leila he wrote: 'Be better at coping than I was. I couldn't square all the circles. I was betrayed, and in the end I too betrayed. You'll be better at this than me. You have stronger principles. You're made of sterner stuff.' Platitudes and clichés rolled on to the page. They were all he had.

He thought again and added a postscript: 'I'm hoping that by the time you read this you'll have had a joyous reunion with our friend (I'm not being facetious or sarcastic, by the way) who's emerged safe and sound from the day's events. If so, please pass him my best wishes, together with my apologies; to be woven in, of course, with whatever fiction you've had to concoct to explain my absence. I'll think of him often. I hope that, however this unravels, our friend – and you of course, of course – come through with no damage direct or collateral sustained.'

He paused and looked up before resuming his tasks. He

recalled those evenings at the training centre, when the old and not-so-bold retired officers were invited to give the new inductees the benefit of their experience in a last hurrah as they sipped their post-dinner drinks. A different world, these old men – for they were all old and all men – inhabited where, in their imaginations at least, their derring-do exploits were conducted with smooth urbanity at cocktail parties or in business-class lounges, words and tradecraft flowing like sweet water. Yet even in this down-in-the-dirt, life-and-death world the job, he had to admit, was much the same. More fear, more heart-in-the-mouth decisions, but still managing the actualities and the choreography to accomplish that magic: the bond. Still, where he was destined he wouldn't be offered the option of coming back to deliver his august insights in the form of fireside stories.

There was little time for such daydreaming. Mind you, at the moment everything felt like a daydream.

'With love,' he wrote, and sealed the letter.

He put his office credit card in an envelope together with a note to Finance Section asking for it to be cancelled. He wound an elastic band around his official mobile phone together with its charger and a note explaining that he would no longer need it, and placed both in the internal mail. They would be on their way on Monday. He looked at his watch: twelve thirty and time to go.

As he left the building he handed his pass to the security guard, saying, 'Would you mind looking after this for me, please? Won't be needing it for the foreseeable.' A puzzled look, nothing more.

On the Heathrow Express he switched on the mobile, the new mobile, the one that had been waiting in its packaging for almost a year until today, the one whose rental had been paid on the dot by direct debit from the bank account he'd had in

Auckland for six years now, against this possibility. He'd used it for the first time in anger this morning on the way down, to make all his bookings.

He'd always been taught when abroad to have an escape passport, hidden safely, just in case. He'd never thought he'd need an escape passport in England, cached at home in the little safe secured to the bedroom floor inside his wardrobe. Until, that is, one morning it had occurred to him, not in response to an incident, almost simply because he could. Another identity was a resource against the unknown. It was, he supposed, a natural compulsion for someone in the business, and perhaps he'd always known he'd have to run away one day.

It was more than an escape passport, it was an escape persona, a fully formed being that in fact was him. Had been him, anyway, at a time almost beyond recall, growing up in the Bay of Plenty, going barefoot each day to school in the sun. The New Zealand passport was in his Maori name, with his father's surname and his original given name – the ones that his parents had thought would expose him to ridicule at school when they'd relocated to the UK – as was the account at the National Bank, the credit card and the mobile phone account, all registered at his uncle's address just outside Tauranga. From the age of six he'd been someone else entirely, Jacob Winter, adopting his mother's maiden name as his own last name, and he doubted that records here showed that earlier being at all.

The orthodoxy with escape passports was: always have as much cash as you can cobble together, and always travel first class if you can. But only as long as you're fully documented and backed up: you'll not want to be confused with a drug dealer. It won't help you with the police or border authorities, but anyone else you meet will always incline in your favour, whatever their training. They'll think twice, three times, before challenging a wealthy, resourceful, influential traveller. Be bold.

Regrets? Too many to itemize. Hordes of them, clamouring for attention, crying to be recognized as the decisive one. Had he let everyone down? Of course he had. George and Leila would be disappointed in him, to use a mild expression. It would pass, though; like all of us he was ephemeral. He was not the noble soul even he'd believed himself to be. Integrity was an unaffordable luxury item, not even an optional extra.

He'd lost sight of the path, any path, and subsided into sense-lessness, the latest example of which was Zaki's murder. This escape was a kind of suicide. He was killing Jake Winter.

A thought for Zaki? The thought was more for himself. His regret was not so much that he had killed him, but that he had concealed the fact, possibly beyond discovery. Sure, murder was wrong, an easy thing to say flippantly. It was absolutely wrong. But there were no right choices. Among the multiple-choice tick-boxes there was no correct one. There was no box labelled 'none of the above', with the added rubric 'not on your flaming nelly'. He could not bring himself to be contrite about the act itself, only about his cowardice afterwards.

It had been an evil committed on behalf of his fellow-citizens, without their knowledge or approval. He had not taken their sins upon himself; they belonged resolutely to that wholly unholy alliance of state, institution and every individual. He'd been simply an emissary, prepared to confront the contradictions. Someone had to.

Until now it had always been possible to manage the apparent dissonances: between audacity and keeping people safe, between the partial truths told by sources and the whole truth of what actually happened, between fragments of conflicting information and the necessary precision of judgements, between hope and hard fact. There had always been a course to be navigated, somehow preserving integrity and getting stuff done. Abu Omar had broken that, and Jake had discovered the breach was irreparable. There was no finessed solution here other than the bludgeoning violence he'd delivered. He'd lost the power of ambiguity and lost control. What was left was self-preservation.

Mrs Masoud, of course, had been right, on all counts. Perhaps she'd known, perhaps she'd simply sensed. Just possibly, she hadn't known it was Zaki. Although Jake had registered some of the incongruities about the sheikh – the notion that it was a role-play rather than a reality, the artifice of the get-up, those fancy boots – he'd failed to piece it together into a suspicion. She'd seen more clearly, in that intersection between intellect and instinct that had been absent in him. She'd seen something more than a petty crook.

He checked in at the desk, taking his overnight bag as a carry-on, and headed for the first-class lounge, where he would sit behind a newspaper with a soft drink until his flight was called.

18

They were permitted to lie in this morning, so they'd be fresh. There was a wide choice of breakfasts in the canteen: the full English, smoked salmon, steak and eggs if required. Someone would inevitably crack the warped joke about the condemned man and the hearty breakfast. Jon Brough had got up early, as usual, and eaten his normal muesli, yoghurt and fruit. Routine helped.

Like any other: that's how you began a day when you might, quite deliberately, kill another human being on a perfectly lawful basis. It had somehow to feel normal, though it never would. He'd killed before, of course he had. While his military training had conferred a certain call-and-response automaticity, a number of processes clicking in beyond instinct in reply to a set of closely defined circumstances until that moment when the trigger was pulled and – tap-tap – it was over, it presented an emotional gap, especially afterwards. It was quite unlike killing as a grunt alongside your brothers-in-arms, in the heat and the noise and the smell and the fog of war. Passion was not required in his line; cool efficiency won the day. Team oppos were present of course, and you had to work together, but each faded to being another objective variable, together with the enemy, as you navigated towards an outcome. Just another set of angles and trajectories to be calculated instantly. It was afterwards that your mind had to work overtime to do its settling of accounts and reconciliation of the balances. Even at that stage, in the military life, the same as in this one, you didn't submit to emotion. Counsellors would take you to one side, to encourage you to open up and unpack all your troubles from your old kit bag, but who in their right mind would do that? Once PTSD was mentioned in your presence you were doomed. Might as well get your coat.

He stopped looking out of the window and returned to his book. It looked a good day for it out there.

Adnan was hungover. Situation normal for a Sunday morning. He could shake it off easy-peasy, as he usually did for a game down the parks.

He wished he could go to the game today. The Liverpool fans would be making their way along the M62 over the Pennines, up the long haul to the tops at Saddleworth and across the moors, bleak and cold, slanting rain that would cease as if by magic once they were this side. Past the little white farmhouse hunched between the carriageways. Past the normal bottleneck at the Bradford and Leeds exits, and further east along the M62, not, however as far as the North Sea coast at the end of the motorway. Sun was out here. Nice day for it. Never mind, he'd record it on the box and watch it on fast-forward, or maybe just see it on *MOTD*. Impossible not to know the score, though, given where he was going.

Leila shivered in her quilted jacket as she waited in the back of the van. Far too early, she knew, but it posed no security risk, this nondescript van parked unobtrusively and perfectly legally. She felt she owed it to Rashid to be certain of being there, ready when he needed her. The team that was watching him reported that he was still at home. This was as it should be. A quick calculation showed that he wouldn't need to leave for another two hours. She was ready.

Jake had been right. Right, that is, when he'd said he'd got it all wrong. However much she liked him, however much she'd looked up to him, he'd made a horrendous mistake, a series of them, that she was determined not to repeat.

When she'd first been selected as joint case officer for Rashid, she'd vented. 'Don't think you can use my faith as some kind of tool. Don't imagine I'll be stepping in as the token Muslim to work magic with this person. I won't allow my beliefs to be used in that way. I'm not going to start debating doctrine. I'm not about to try to map out his path to spiritual salvation.'

He'd waited for her to finish before saying, 'That's not it at all. I wanted you to be involved because of you. The fact that you're a Muslim means nothing. For the purposes of the case it's immaterial whether you're a Muslim or, for that matter, a woman. You're the right person, you're good at the job – better than me, probably – and that's what we need. I trust your judgement and your skill, that's all there is to it. I'm fresh out of vision. We need yours.'

Before the Abu Omar case reached its horrific denouement, they'd been in the office doing their own separate write-ups.

'It's all technocratic twaddle,' he'd said suddenly.

'What?'

'People seem to think this can be reduced to systems. Pro formas before you meet someone, checklists, risk assessments, psychological profiles, pro formas after meetings, casework reviews . . .'

'Yes, well –'

'Strategic analyses, coverage mapping, covert human intelligence source policies, liaison groups, operational strategy meetings, wellness diagnoses. The business is actually quite simple. Two or more people come together, one tells the other some secrets, and the other converts what is said into something that's valuable and useable without jeopardizing the first person.'

'Up to a point.'

'Sorry?' He hadn't been accustomed to being challenged. Not by her.

'It can't be that subjective. Not any more. There has to be some rigour.'

'Quite. All this flannel doesn't help. Just adds to the verbiage. We need to cut through the crap.'

She understood now that his petulance had been displacement for what was really worrying him: Abu Omar and the case's doomed trajectory.

Once, Jake had been her role model. He'd shown her how to do this stuff. Though he, with the modesty he wore on his sleeve, would no doubt say there were no such things as role models. He'd been the one with the wise words, the one who'd impressed with his demeanour and results. The one who'd handled Rashid with such gentle facility.

But he'd worn her to the bone, no matter the pain and injustice he'd suffered. Whatever George had said about cutting him some slack. She could see that he'd failed, that he'd lacked courage. At root, she could not say that Stuart was wrong to hook him from the case, even at such a late stage. She was now left to pick up the pieces.

She thought of everything she'd learned. Find something to like in them, however difficult. Most of them think of themselves as outsiders; but remember, they're generally no more outsiders than any of us. They're just needy – but you have to meet that need. It's not about being clever, it's about being right. These are just ordinary human relationships in extraordinary circumstances. Don't exploit them, find the common ground. It's not the flash tradecraft that matters, it's the bond.

It maddened her. He'd been so wrong – inexcusably so, whatever allowances she tried to make. He'd been wrong about the Abu Omar case. He'd probably been wrong about everything, with his little homilies about personal integrity and authenticity. Sound bites, the lot of it. He'd probably never believed them himself in the first place. He'd said he'd let her down, and he had. When they next met in the office, she'd have it out with him. She wouldn't make the same mistakes. For now, though, she needed to concentrate and rehearse once more what she would say to Rashid.

Stuart Calloway picked up the phone and told Shirley he needed to speak to the Chief Constable. He held the line while she called his staff officer.

She reported back to Stuart. 'He's not available. He's in a meeting.'

'Well, tell his staff officer to bloody well get him out of his meeting pronto. Meanwhile get me Julian.'

Julian was the senior legal adviser, young and fresh from Treasury Solicitors, so a whizz-kid. Trusted by government, not so much by Stuart, he was a tall, willowy, quite beautiful creature with a casual, vague manner that disguised a dangerous skewering intellect.

'What can we hang on Jake Winter, then?'

'Hang on him?'

'For a swift departure.'

'W-e-e-ll, I suppose . . .'

'Yes?'

'We could float the idea of exploiting his approach to the possibilities of the Americans using inhumane treatment with Abu Omar.'

'Torture? Do you think he'd be tolerant of that?'

'Not for one moment. All his contemporaneous notes, all his interview recordings, they all point to a very assiduous good little soldier. And I can't imagine anyone who's been in this place after the Iraq fiasco could fail to understand their obligations.'

'But?'

'His responses under oath. He's much more equivocal about what the Americans may or may not have done.'

'And might they have mistreated the asset?'

'Who can know? I'd hardly have thought so. They know the minefields as well as we do. I speak to counsel over there all the time. They say they're just as rigorous in theatre. I know, they would say that, wouldn't they? There's a new wind blowing there, too. That's not the issue, though. If you wanted to stretch a point you could pick out the discrepancies between Winter's statements on file and on tape, when he knows he's speaking for the record, and what he's said in the hothouse of the inquiry room. The discrepancies could be argued to be suggestive of a tacit acceptance that bad things happen which he's happy to ignore. And tacit acceptance isn't acceptable. It's a breach of all of our codes.'

'I don't like it. Though it would be satisfying to hang such a self-righteous prig as Jake on his lack of ethics.'

'Well, it's risky and untested but it may be a legally acceptable route. You might even get the odd plaudit from the liberties lobby if you played your cards right.'

'I doubt that very much. Not much kudos for them in that. But could you get someone to work up some options? Today? I'd like to give it some thought before the fun and games start this afternoon.'

'Sure thing.'

At last he was there. The surveillance team reported his approach and, sure enough, there was that tentative rap on the door. The surveillance team leader said into her earpiece, 'Good to go. He's clear.' Surveillance and the lurking firearms team would be in the vicinity, disposing themselves ready to pick up quickly for the next stage of this journey. They would alert her to any problems.

She opened the door and he stepped past her quickly.

'Where's Jake?' he said immediately.

'I'm sorry, Rashid,' she said. 'His –'

'No,' he said. 'You're not doing this to me. You get Jake here.'

'I can't do that. He's at the hospital. His little girl was knocked over by a car.' Where was her moral compass now?

Rashid looked at her questioningly. 'I didn't know he had kids.'

She knew Jake had neither children nor partner. She'd researched her selected mendacity in the case files and was confident Jake hadn't mentioned his circumstances to Rashid. It wouldn't have been his way. She thought fleetingly of her own family, Anoushka and Robbie, but could not afford to dwell there more than a moment.

'Well, you do now,' she said. 'Normally they take second place. But now . . .'

He gave this consideration. 'Fair enough. It's off, then. I'm on my bike, man. This is all going to shit.'

'This couldn't be helped.'

'I know. But right now, it's a bad moment. Terrible.'

'I know. So what do we do?'

'I walk away.'

'And where will that get you? You know as well as I do how those people would regard that. You don't walk away from something like this.'

'You sort it. You take care of me, just like you promised. There's no choice, the way I see it.'

'No. We just carry on as planned. Do you not trust me?'

'Yeah, of course I do. It's . . .'

'What? I know this as thoroughly as Jake did. We came up with everything together, the three of us.'

'This is too much to take in, dropping this on me now. It's easier to call it off. Think of some excuse.'

'There are no excuses. It isn't easier. We'd do our best to look after you of course, but these boys would still be on the loose to do what they want. We carry on, nothing changes, apart from Jake not being around.'

'I don't like it. This is fucking shit.'

'No one's asking you to like it. I don't like it. But nothing changes. It's as safe as it ever was. We haven't got the time to think. The moment's now. We are where we are. We've little choice. Unless you have no faith in me, we should stick to the plan. No hesitation. Now's the moment. This very second.'

'No, no, no,' he said, but even as he raised his eyes to look at her she knew she had won.

'All right then,' she said after a pause. 'No contact with anyone?'

'None,' he replied.

'You've prepared as you were instructed?'

'Yeah.'

'The others?'

'Just said, not spoken to them. Far as I know, they're just doing their own thing.'

'Here's your bag' she said, and handed Rashid his rucksack, which he slung over his shoulder.

Rashid looked at her, full of doubt. 'I don't like this.'

'No one does. This is where we keep our nerve. Most likely it'll all be fine. You'll do your bit, we'll meet up at the agreed place half an hour after, and we'll plan for next week. But we have to be on our game.'

'Right,' he said, questions still in his eyes.

She was tempted to utter some worthless phrase like 'You're very brave' or 'I'll be with you every step of the way' to smooth the goodbyes with sentimentality. Never do that, Jake had said, never mask the reality. He was right on that. These moments need to be lived in their full intensity, on both sides.

'Will she be OK?' he asked.

She coughed. Jake's notional daughter. 'I don't know. Let's hope so. Nothing you or I can do about it. We just have to focus on this. You'd better be going. Everything clear in your mind?'

'I suppose so.'

'Could you take off your coat, please?'

'What?'

'You know we have to, Rashid.'

He gave her his coat and it felt warm from his body. She went through it slowly, methodically, calmly, feeling the seams and the padding as well as searching the pockets. Nothing. She called in one of the team waiting outside. He and Rashid avoided looking at each other and they exchanged no words as he frisked Rashid. He left without saying anything.

'All right, said Leila. 'You know, no diversions. Not for anything. Straight through, as we've talked about. That route. No other. Take it steady. Normal pace. Ready?'

'Ready as I will be.'

They looked at each other and smiled. Before she knew it he was gone and the door clicked quietly to.

'Bob. How's life?'

'Hello, Stuart. Social call, is it?'

'Not exactly. Thought it might be a good moment to touch base. How are things going?'

'Everything seems to be under control. So far as it can be.' The Chief Constable chuckled. 'Having kittens down in London, are we?'

'Of course not,' said Stuart affably. 'Bob, let me get to the point. I need to speak to you. Something new has come up. Intelligence from a super-sensitive source. Under no circumstances for evidential use. Of impeccable pedigree, thought to be right on the money.'

'Yes?'

Stuart stood and began pacing behind his desk. 'I can't stress the sensitivity enough. This source is in a potentially highly exposed position. Upstream. I've briefed the Home Sec and the Commissioner is aware in general terms. I've suggested that each deny all knowledge of this information if questioned and I'd ask the same of you. I myself will refuse to be pressed on the matter. My own staff on the ground have no inkling of the source or the intelligence.'

'Where is this leading, Stuart?'

'The information has just been passed to us. It cannot under any circumstances enter the evidential chain. I will deny its existence. It's of direct relevance to your op. According to the report I have in my hand what they are terming a run-through is in fact anything but a dry run. These people are equipped to murder. What we may have on our hands is a reprise of the station incident. Given the numbers of people involved, it could be worse. Each of the four conspirators is equipped with an explosive device.' He held an office circular in his hand as if it offered his patter greater plausibility.

'Including your primary source?'

'Including him, yes. Of course he may be operating in entirely good faith.'

'I won't indulge in an "I told you so". But I told you so. You realize the implications of this?'

'I do. Far be it from me to suggest what you do with this. But you may judge that your op should be brought to a conclusion before these people get anywhere near the football stadium. A hard stop.'

'And the information is reliable?'

'Its derivation is highly sound. Can I guarantee it's accurate? Of course not. It's in the nature of intelligence . . .'

'You understand the difficulties? My officers have trained

for a hard stop scenario, of course, but a lot depends on a compliant response from the subject. My officers have been briefed to deploy with extreme caution with regard to public safety.'

'Indeed. I wish we weren't in this position. But weighing public safety –'

'I don't need you to tell me my responsibilities on that score,' said the Chief Constable sharply. 'My predecessor's experience provided us all with a reminder about that, if ever we needed one.'

'Of course. I know you won't be keen to be in the same boat.'

'I won't be keen, Stuart, to endanger the lives of people in this city. This information changes everything. You knew that, of course, with all your "far be it from me" nonsense. It leaves us in a right pickle as far as the policy log is concerned. And if the hard stop gets messy, my officers won't be able to rely on your intelligence to defend themselves.'

'I'm sorry about that, but we must afford the source of this new information maximum protection.'

'And if we deploy with lethality unnecessarily, you'll wash your hands of it? I'm on my own?'

'It's not easy, Bob. Wish it was. Goes with the territory.'

'I'll speak to the SIO. Goodbye.'

'Good to speak, Bob. I trust your judgement implicitly.'

'I don't care what you think of my judgement, Stuart. You'd best be concerned with your own.'

'Good luck.' But the line had already gone dead. A bit prickly, Stuart thought, but neatly finessed.

The yips, golfers called it. Last-minute staggers and stutters, possibly from fear of completion. Or, more charitably, conscience: that thing he thought he'd lost years ago in the icy furnace that is Whitehall. Unusually, he'd had a sleepless night. That the blameless sleep the undisturbed sleep of the innocent is the opposite of the truth. He was glad to see those old friends, fear and uncertainty, pulling him back from the brink, loom again. He was alive once more.

This was it. Rashid walked purposefully towards the stadium, not too fast, not too slow. Important not to be self-conscious, though it was difficult to avoid it with the eyes of the secret world on him. How many guns were pointing at him at this moment? Keep your nerve and, like she said, it would all be over before too long. He reckoned he was maybe twenty minutes from the ground, so probably in half an hour he'd be on his way, bumping shoulders with the crowd leaving the ground on his way to the next RV with Leila.

It was cold but the day had been bright. Ambling along the street of terraced houses, he squinted as he looked to the sky. He was grateful for the coat. Abdullah would be approaching from beyond the opposite end of the ground, Bilal and Adnan from the two other quarters.

This was what it'd feel like on Wednesday – much darker then, though. It occurred to him that he wouldn't need to do this walk ever again. He'd have to discuss with Leila, or Jake if he was back by then, whether he could bunk off out of it after the last meeting with the other boys, once they were launched on their own separate trajectories. It would be all up then, anyway. No way would he be able to go back to anything once the thing was wrapped up. So what would the point be? It'd only be dangerous. He hoped they'd be able to net the other boys safely and without any fuss. He wasn't exactly fond of them but they were people too, whatever anyone else thought. Jake had said they'd take care. He liked Jake. He was the man. Poor guy, with his daughter. No time to think of that, though. Sodding awful timing.

He liked Leila too. She was all right for a Manc. He was

slightly afraid of her. Not of old Jake, though. He could've run rings round him, he reckoned, so trusting. Such an open book. But he'd chosen not to.

Apart, that is, from not telling him what he'd really got up to out there.

They were people too, those he'd killed. He'd been instructed that they were enemies and he'd believed it, to begin with. Old and young, men and women, kids sometimes, all weeping and pleading in that moany way that was so grating you yearned to do it quickly and get it over and done with. You knew that if you saved them you'd have their awful, keening gratitude. Then someone else would do them. And then you too. All you could do was harden your heart, deploy a glassy stare and do it. Until the point you couldn't any more and the dams burst inside you. You could never show it, though.

These were the thoughts you had on a cold Sunday afternoon when the sun had vanished from the sky, leaving the darkening blue of night, and the street lights set the city alight.

On the move again, thankfully. The three of them in the deployment car with the driver, keyed up. You couldn't avoid being keyed up. If they were needed, Jon would lead them as they were called through the cordon. He hoped they wouldn't be.

They could hear the comms as the clandestine convoy, Romeo its unwitting leader, made its way along the planned route towards the ground. What could the hold-up have been? mumbled the two other shots. No idea, he said, though he thought he did know.

A message came through: Romeo is not, repeat not, believed to be carrying. The driver turned the ignition key and took them to the next stopping point so that they remained within spitting distance of the retinue.

*

235

Did she have time to pick up a coffee from the machine on her way up the stairs to the ops room? No, she decided, though she could do with one. She was much too on edge to divert en route. Maybe one of the others would be making a brew before it all began in earnest.

She used her access card to open the door, and one or two people turned to look at her. Most, though, were concentrating on the action. It was hushed in here and the lamps were dimmed. The large room had several distinct areas. The head of the firearms team sat with headphones on at a table, his people around him. The surveillance was managed close by, coordinators keeping an eye on the overall picture. The Int Cell, where she was heading, was in another corner, staffed by police and her own colleagues, taking what feeds there were from technical and from the chatter on the airwaves and passing them to the command team at the centre of proceedings, on a slightly raised podium, presided over by the SIO in his expensive suit. The Int Cell seemed to have little to do; their work might well already be complete, bringing everyone to this moment. Rashid had been condensed to intelligence. There were small clusters of people at the fringes of the room, busy with tasks about which Leila knew nothing. There were rooms leading from the main ops room, where mysterious subsidiary activities were taking place, some, she knew, occupied by people with whom she worked.

Most people watched the screens that were suspended from the ceiling and gave a confusing account of what was happening. There were further screens at desk level offering greater granularity, which juniors observed intensely, searching for anything out of place.

She stopped for a moment to make sense of it. Gradually the moving mosaic of pictures started to come together. Each screen was labelled: Alpha (which was Adnan), Zulu (Abdullah),

Bravo (Bilal) and Romeo (Rashid). A fifth screen showed the concourse in front of the stadium and on the sixth was a moving map on which dots representing the boys edged inexorably towards a common centre. The boys were making their way towards this point in their own ways. Bilal shuffled with a swing of his shoulders, Abdullah looked intently in front of him, Adnan strolled casually, his hands in his pockets, while Rashid's gangly lope and nervous expression called out to her. The steady burble of the comms was calming.

She saw George at the Int Cell table and waved to him. He nodded grimly back and she walked in his direction. Not long to go.

In London, Stuart decided to pop up to the ops room for a while. Show one's face, rally the troops, could do no harm. It must be about time.

He crept in quietly. This was no command centre, he knew. No orders were issued here. This was now entirely in others' hands, and he had no influence. The intelligence had been fed and the cards dealt. All that was to be done was to wait. He felt the tension in the murmuring. It would be surprising if there hadn't been that additional frisson, given what had happened the last time.

He walked to where he could get a better view. People turned, and he nodded beneficently. Someone offered him her seat, which he refused with a smile. He said nothing; and nor did anyone else.

He was mildly surprised Jake Winter wasn't there. He'd invested so much in the enterprise, nurtured his case, spent uncomfortable nights nudging the thing along, counselled his man. This had been Jake's baby and Stuart had suggested he be here. It could be pique, Stuart concluded. It couldn't have been pleasant for Jake to have been pulled from the action so late in the day. Jake hadn't seemed the sort of person to store rancour, but one lived and learned. His absence wasn't so great a loss.

There was a bustle in the room as the Chief Constable, fully uniformed and wearing his cap, entered. He gave an easy, breezy smile and said amicably, 'You've better things to do than to watch me,' before strolling over to the central podium where Silver Control, the command team headed by the SIO, sat. There were quiet words and the SIO stood. Placing his hand on the man's shoulder, the chief smiled as if he'd heard a good joke, and they walked slowly together towards the glass-walled conference room at the rear of the ops room. Time was creeping in the story told by the screens, the small figures converging on the centre of the moving map. Others Leila did not recognize arrived at the same time and scurried into the conference room. The chief's staff officer went to the firearms group and whispered to the team leader. He stood and went into the conference room, too. The staff officer came over to the Int Cell table, approaching George. 'The Gold team is just convening for a few minutes, sir. The chief wondered whether you might like to attend, as an observer.' George stood, put on his jacket and shrugged at Leila.

Leila stopped watching the screens. The men in the room were, it seemed, having a convivial conversation. They were smiling and there were occasional bouts of laughter to be heard. Then they became serious, leaning earnestly forward as the chief spoke. There were nods, and the men left in turn, hurrying back to their desks.

'What's going on?' asked Leila.

'They're pulling the plug,' said George. 'The arrest team's going in now.'

She glanced at the screens and then her watch. The boys were at least five minutes away from the stadium. 'Why?'

'No idea,' he said.

'But –'

'No time, Leila. I have to speak to London.' He already had the phone in his hand.

Rashid felt calmer now. It was going to plan. He couldn't see the followers he knew were there but their invisible presence was soothing. They're there to protect me, at least partly, he thought. A few minutes more, that was all.

19

Jon

The message to the car, and they were out on foot instantly. The car pulled away, the blue lights behind the front grille flashing. No siren. The surveillance team leader came to them, his baseball cap already on. They'd put theirs on too. Before they moved off, Jon spoke into his mouthpiece. 'Confirming we're going for a hard stop.'

'Confirmed,' said the voice of his ops room supervisor. 'Take up a standby position and await further orders.'

He signalled to his team that they should not yet take out their weapons. The surveillance team leader led them past her own people. As she did so she pointed them out silently. There was no one else in sight. They stopped suddenly and she pointed. From an angle they could see Romeo about fifty yards ahead. They waited for a moment and Jon told them to take out their weapons. All safetys were removed and they nodded to each other. Romeo was moving forward, and still the final order hadn't been given. They had to move. The road dog-legged at the point where Romeo was now walking and he swerved to the left at the same pace, moving out of view. Jon knew the topography. There was an alternate, via a footpath that ran parallel and came out on to the next street.

'Come on, come on, give the order,' he muttered as he and his team sprinted in their rubber-soled boots. He signalled to one of his men to follow Romeo from the back while he and the third member of the team ran up the alleyway and turned sharp left into another, skirting the large plastic recycling bins. It was close to completely dark now. They stopped in the shadows near the end of the alleyway and took up position, listening to the running commentary of Romeo's approach in their earpieces. 'Come on, come *on*,' thought Jon, or whispered it.

'Handover of control to you,' came the dry message from the ops room. All this would be recorded on hard disk for the audit afterwards. Force Internal Standards. Firearms Team Performance Review. IOPC, if it came to it. 'Go.'

He spoke to his team quietly: 'Go, go, go.'

Leila

'Why?' she wondered aloud as she watched the deployment, transfixed. George just looked at her. The images showed Rashid approaching the point where the officers waited. She couldn't see them but knew they were there. Another officer was coming up fast behind him but he was oblivious, it seemed. She could see the automatic weapon the officer held. It would be a matter of seconds now. On the other screens similar flurries of action could be seen but she was interested only in Rashid.

She hoped. All she had now was hope that throbbed like a muscle, pulsing in her brain, pounding in her chest. It was pared down to this: bare, sinewy, desperate hope. The alternative was panic. She hoped she'd see Rashid again shortly and knew she'd somehow have to control her emotion when – if – she did. She hoped Rashid would do all he'd been told, that he wouldn't forget something in the heat of the moment. She hoped the officers wouldn't be precipitate. She hoped she'd been clear enough with the officer she'd spoken to – his name had been Jon – to convey the right sense of Rashid. She hoped that Rashid was, in the end, not one of the bad guys.

Abdullah

Across the city, like the other three converging on the stadium, Abdullah trudged intently. He muttered to himself as he walked, knew he was muttering, did not even try to stop himself. He stared ahead at the ground as he gathered pace. Almost there. His head was bursting with ecstatic terror.

He heard a noise directly in front of him and raised his eyes to the world, as if he were newborn and had only just discovered its existence. The sky was a luminous deep blue, punctuated with the glitter of the lights. He could hear the roar of the football crowd. In front of him stood a man wearing a cap with POLICE emblazoned on it, shouting at him, holding a gun with a flashlight attached to it, dazzling him.

The realization was a slow burn with a sudden, abrupt arrival. A smile seeped on to his face and he reached inside his jacket. This was his moment. It'd been forbidden, he knew, but he'd had to. The knife had been his grandfather's, a trophy from the war: a dagger as keen as the day it had been manufactured, its point lethally sharp, protected in its metal scabbard, a gunmetal grey swastika crafted on its hilt. He would have blood, even as this man screamed. Then, just as he felt the metal of the handle and before he'd begun to withdraw the knife, he felt an impact above his left eye and slumped.

Bilal

He heard the pops nearby. His path to the stadium took him within fifty yards of Abdullah's and he understood immediately what was happening. It was not something he'd rehearsed, even in his head, even in his worst imaginings.

He looked at the man who had appeared almost magically

in front of him, shouting in English, which now seemed a language he could not understand. No doubt he showed his confusion. He sensed rather than comprehended what the man wanted and raised his hands before noticing the weapon pointing at him. He turned and began to run and felt a pain in the back of his head. But nothing more.

Adnan

He was trying to work out what the score was from the noise of the crowd but it was an impossible task. The sheer sound gave him that thrill, but he'd have to wait until he mingled with the departing crowd to find out what had gone on. Pity: there was nothing better than a game under the floodlights. The all-red Liverpool kit and the all-blue of City's, on the bright green of the turf, all lit up. Cold night sky on which your breath formed clouds. Sparkle. Tension. Excitement. He dug his hands deeper into the pockets of the expensive leather jacket he always wore to matches.

He'd have liked to be able to claim that he saw it coming. But he didn't. Must have been Abdullah who sold them, was his first thought as the police officer faced him, tensed and ready, the weapon aimed at his head. He could sense there were two others, at least, dancing round him and probably more.

'Take your hands out of your pockets,' the man screamed.

Now was as good a time as ever. It'd been a shit life, anyway. He shrugged, smirked and kept his hands where they were.

Leila

In the ops room she maintained outward composure, with difficulty. Calls would already be being made to the Independent

243

Office for Police Conduct so that their investigations into three fatal shootings by police could commence. Would it be four? The SIO was furiously dictating his policy log into a voice recorder. The Chief Constable looked broken but would have to rouse himself for media conferences.

George touched her arm. She turned to him, barely recognizing him.

This was the end of it. This was the opposite of success. Three boys were dead and Rashid would be too, in a few moments. This was for sure: no one could risk letting him run now. Last time's fuck-up was already in all their minds. So it had been supplanted by another fuck-up, just one that was more amenable to media spinning. Her certainty that Rashid was carrying neither explosive nor weapon, her faith in him, counted for nothing. What had happened? Had the police suddenly become twitchy for no good reason? Had one of the boys done something that raised the temperature beyond tolerable limits? Had new information, contradicting Rashid's, been received? Was Rashid, after all, way beyond her belief, bad?

They would now never discover the man orchestrating this, the sheikh. They would be no closer to him. Sooner or later this drama, on a different stage, would be repeated.

Jon

This was the moment. Jon led as they ran towards the subject and everything from here was on automatic pilot. They knew each other's movements so well. They circled the subject and kept moving. Jon was directly in front of him and gave the challenge and instructions.

This was Romeo. Rashid was his name. Christ, he was young in the flesh. He looked terrified, but who wouldn't? Jon adjusted his position backwards ever so slightly while the other two danced on their toes, keeping mobile, alert, their focus on Romeo. 'Look into my eyes,' he said, and the boy tried to. The flashlight mounted on his weapon bore into the boy's face, but he looked into Romeo's eyes, to try to divine what was there. This harmless-looking boy. What was it Leila had said? The words from the briefings and manuals scrolled through his mind with supreme irrelevance: lethality, court proceedings, ethics, public safety, self-defence, justified homicide, double-tap, unreasonable force, preservation of human life, collateral damage. The instructions had been clear: the precautionary principle. We won't let any of you be hung out to dry. We know how fine the balances are. We've lived it. We'll back you all the way. That's what the senior officers always said. For all he knew they might actually mean it.

He fell back on training and instinct: the instinct that was trained and the instinct he felt for this fellow human being. He, Jon Brough the person, not Jon Brough the police officer and former SAS trooper accustomed to dispatching the enemy on the battlefield.

Less than half a second could pass between the first challenge and the decision that had to be made, while the shock reflex took time to form in Romeo that would dissolve into his response. Yield or fight. Surrender or press an initiator. Jon Brough did not need half a second to decide.

Rashid

It happened so quickly he couldn't piece it together. He didn't see them until they were there, three of them, circling like crows. They weren't in uniform but they wore caps with POLICE across the front. They were carrying guns and a light shone into his eyes.

'Armed police,' shouted one. 'Hands away from your body, in the air. Look into my eyes. Keep looking into my eyes.'

He raised his hands but he couldn't look into the man's eyes. The light was too bright. This was not how it was supposed to end.

Author's note

Anyone who has ever had a book published will know that it's a long process. I completed my first draft of the first chapter of *A Fatal Game* in May 2017, just before the London Bridge attack. The ideas were in my head long before that. I have no knowledge, beyond what I have read in the media, of the London Bridge attack itself; but I can't argue that it, along with the many others of which I've been aware at close hand or more distantly, did not inform the narrative. I can say unequivocally, though, that it didn't provide a singular stimulus for the book. The inquest arising from the deaths in the London Bridge/Borough Market terror attack of 3 June 2017 began in early May 2019 and at time of writing is due to finish at the end of July.

A Fatal Game is not *about* any specific event or its aftermath. None of its characters represent any individual of whom I'm aware. What drove me to write this novel was the desire to imagine and portray the dilemmas facing those caught up in such events – whether terrorists, victims, survivors or those in law enforcement or the secret world – and how they deal with them. I was struck by the degree to which in such circumstances we all crave a certainty that is elusive if not illusory, but I wasn't trying to make a point of any kind. Instead, I was trying to place myself in the position of each of the individual actors in this narrative and to see whether any answers – to anything at all – emerged. Not surprisingly, none did: just more and more questions and apparent paradoxes. Sometimes, though, questions begin to explain things, just a bit.

My feelings for those who suffer as a result of such attacks are deep and heartfelt, and stem from a long career trying to prevent these things. *A Fatal Game* isn't intended to make any statement other, perhaps, than to show sympathy for all of those involved: the victims, the survivors, the police, the spooks and yes, though it is painful to say so, the terrorists too.

NS
May 2019

He just wanted a decent book to read ...

Not too much to ask, is it? It was in 1935 when Allen Lane, Managing Director of Bodley Head Publishers, stood on a platform at Exeter railway station looking for something good to read on his journey back to London. His choice was limited to popular magazines and poor-quality paperbacks – the same choice faced every day by the vast majority of readers, few of whom could afford hardbacks. Lane's disappointment and subsequent anger at the range of books generally available led him to found a company – and change the world.

'We believed in the existence in this country of a vast reading public for intelligent books at a low price, and staked everything on it'
Sir Allen Lane, 1902–1970, founder of Penguin Books

The quality paperback had arrived – and not just in bookshops. Lane was adamant that his Penguins should appear in chain stores and tobacconists, and should cost no more than a packet of cigarettes.

Reading habits (and cigarette prices) have changed since 1935, but Penguin still believes in publishing the best books for everybody to enjoy. We still believe that good design costs no more than bad design, and we still believe that quality books published passionately and responsibly make the world a better place.

So wherever you see the little bird – whether it's on a piece of prize-winning literary fiction or a celebrity autobiography, political tour de force or historical masterpiece, a serial-killer thriller, reference book, world classic or a piece of pure escapism – you can bet that it represents the very best that the genre has to offer.

Whatever you like to read – trust Penguin.